Be mine, the v[...] *everything you've e*[...] ...[...] desire Remy felt was intoxicating. It dug into the deepest recesses of her heart and turned her inside out. She couldn't have walked away from it even if she wanted to.

It showed her a dozen children scattered among the buildings, laughing as they bantered in front of their easels. The smell of turpentine paint was on the wind. Remy watched herself weave through the students, gently coaxing the masterpieces flowing from their brushes.

An art school. For all the talented kids who needed to escape their small towns and see the world. She would foster a new generation of creativity. The image was so clear she rubbed her eyes to make sure it wasn't real yet. This village held the answers that she had been desperately searching for, a way to find her purpose. It seemed to know just what to show her to hit all the right chords.

And underneath the pull she felt, Remy sensed a terrible loneliness coming from the property. It wanted to be loved and would promise anything it could not to be alone anymore. "We are two of a kind, aren't we?" Remy whispered.

Praise for Taylor Hobbs

"I'm reading [*CLOAKED*] and have fallen in love with the world and characters she has created. It's an adventure from the very first page!"

~ Mary Morgan - Award-winning
Celtic Paranormal Romance Author

Sonder Village

by

Taylor Hobbs

This is a work of fiction. Names, characters, places, and incidents are either the product of the author's imagination or are used fictitiously, and any resemblance to actual persons living or dead, business establishments, events, or locales, is entirely coincidental.

Sonder Village

COPYRIGHT © 2019 by Taylor Hobbs

All rights reserved. No part of this book may be used or reproduced in any manner whatsoever without written permission of the author or The Wild Rose Press, Inc. except in the case of brief quotations embodied in critical articles or reviews.
Contact Information: info@thewildrosepress.com

Cover Art by *Debbie Taylor*

The Wild Rose Press, Inc.
PO Box 708
Adams Basin, NY 14410-0708
Visit us at www.thewildrosepress.com

Publishing History
First Mainstream Fantasy Edition, 2019
Print ISBN 978-1-5092-2569-9
Digital ISBN 978-1-5092-2570-5

Published in the United States of America

Dedication

For Westley, my own little miracle

Chapter One

Sonder *(n.)*: the realization that each random passerby is living a life as vivid and complex as your own

"I bought a village. In Spain."

"*You bought a Spanish villa?*" Anita's voice shrieked through the phone, and Remy pulled it away from her ear.

"No," Remy said, willing her best friend to focus. "I said I bought a—"

"You little bitch! I knew you were up to something with your impromptu Europe trip. Okay, tell me where it is, and I'll meet you there. I'm literally packing right now. I can't believe you kept this from me! You are so going to pay for this, in alcohol, of course—"

"Anita!" The babbling stopped, and Remy felt safe enough to continue. "I bought a *village*. Not a villa."

"What are you talking about? You can't just buy a village."

"It's an abandoned property in Ortigueira. It's made up of seven buildings that are basically falling down, but now it's all mine." Remy couldn't help the hint of pride that crept into her voice when she described her own little spot of paradise. Abandoned for over one hundred years, the village was the exact opposite of a sound real estate investment.

"I'm confused. You bought a pile of bricks for your mid-life crisis instead of a vacation home we can actually use?"

"You should see it, Anita. There's a mill, and what used to be a bakery, and a barn, and these amazing houses that I can fix up…"

"Oh God. You're like that stupid family who bought a zoo!"

Remy pinched the bridge of her nose and tried to stave off the coming headache. "The Spanish government put all of these old properties up for sale after their economy crashed a few years ago. The village I bought was only two hundred and fifty thousand dollars."

"But what are you going to *do* with it?"

"I'm going to live there." Stunned silence met Remy's declaration, and for the first time since hiring Anita almost a decade ago, her agent was speechless. "Are you still there?" Remy asked.

"You want to leave New York? Permanently?"

"There's nothing left for me there, Anita. And I'm not talking about Jack. I'm talking about my career. You've been patient with me, but I know you're anxious for my next exhibition. I'll be honest, I've gotten nothing done. My process in New York isn't working anymore. You saw the sales from the last auction. Even my fans can tell my paintings lack the essence they used to have."

"Remy, I know it has been a hellish past year for you, but I really don't think running away is the answer here." Anita's tone lost all sense of her earlier comedic outrage and had been replaced by genuine concern.

"Anita, I don't need to *be* in New York to paint.

2

Whenever I finish a piece, I can send it back to you to put up for auction."

"I'm not talking about your career. I'm talking about *you*, Remy. What is going on with you?"

"Christ, everyone knows the tragic story—you best of all. Headline news in the art world—*Fairy Tale Romance Dead, Auction House Owner and Painter Split.*"

"Don't talk to me like I'm an idiot, Remy. This isn't just about that. You haven't been completely honest with me, and it hurts. I can't support you if I don't understand you."

Anita was absolutely right. Remy hadn't been one hundred percent honest with her friend, but she could hardly acknowledge to herself what she had done. Putting the truth into words would have made it too real, so instead she let it fester inside of her, keeping it from burdening others.

Anita, lacking imagination, probably thought it was an affair that made Remy suddenly decide to divorce Jack, her husband of fifteen years. Her friend was waiting for a confession that would never pass her lips, though, because Remy still loved Jack. The real problem was that Remy didn't love the person she had become.

Poor Jack had been blindsided by Remy's decision, and begged her to work things out. "Why now?" he kept asking. "What did I do?"

"Nothing," Remy repeated. "You did nothing wrong."

She let him keep the penthouse and moved into a studio apartment uptown. Gossip about their split, the "Golden Couple" of the New York art world, spread like wildfire through their circle. Whispers based on speculation and hearsay revolved around them for weeks, and Remy's last gallery show provided the theatre for the showdown.

Jack had put off signing the divorce papers until the last possible minute, determined he could convince Remy to change her mind. He had shown up to the trendy warehouse without orchids, his usual gesture of good luck before a show. The phantom scent of love gone by seemed to fill the air between Remy's paintings. Jack stood before her empty-handed, as if saying, "This is me. Am I not enough?" A lone fragment of real life that didn't fit in among the two-dimensional worlds that Remy created on canvas.

Remy hadn't trusted her voice, so she wordlessly handed him the manila envelope and a pen. She watched the last bit of hope die out of his eyes. They held such acute pain that the artist in Remy wished she could capture it, if only to share the tragic beauty with the world. If she could paint it, then maybe it would help her heal, too.

But she held no brush, and before she could mentally capture his expression, it was replaced with a fiery rage. Remy instinctively stepped back, and the sound of heels on hard wood echoed through the room. It broke the moment of silence that paid tribute to the end of their marriage.

It shook Jack back to his senses, and he looked down at the paperwork in his hands. Remy risked a quick glance at the clock. Her guests would be arriving soon. She held her breath and prayed that they wouldn't be interrupted. Jack had to go through with it this time. He couldn't keep putting it off forever. This was as good a time as any to say goodbye—their last public appearance as husband and wife.

He signed them, a hastily scribbled signature that nearly missed the line entirely. Remy exhaled, part relief and part sob. He shoved the envelope back into Remy's hands and walked away. Before she could process what was happening, or even go after him for one last hug, the gallery doors opened, and impeccably dressed men and women of all ages poured inside. She didn't have time to mourn and plastered on her public face. She greeted everyone with a fake smile that fooled nobody.

Remy assumed Jack had left, so she had to do a double-take two hours later when a rumpled figure wove his way through the displays toward her. She had been explaining her inspiration for a particularly dark piece to an interested reporter, who wasn't buying into her vague, generic answers and kept pressing her for more details. The interruption was almost welcome.

A glass of whiskey sloshed in Jack's hand as he glared at her with red-rimmed eyes. "*You*," he slurred, and an entire room full of people in tuxedos and ball gowns fell silent. This was the showdown they had all been waiting for, the real reason attendance was more than double what it had been the previous year. Everyone wanted a front-row seat to watch the drama unfold.

Remy stood tall amid the unwanted attention. Jack stopped in front of her, took a deep breath, and looked ready to let her have it. She regarded him for just a moment, less than a foot of space between them, and calmly turned and walked out of her own art show.

"Hey! I'm not done," Jack shouted behind her.

But I am, Remy thought. She kept on going. The sea of people parted in front of her, their faces all a blur. *If I stay, it will destroy him.* For her sake and his, she needed to leave. Divorce was not enough to put distance between them. Jack would always try to come back. She feared that, eventually, she would let him.

Once outside, she hailed a taxi and ordered the driver back to her apartment so she could pick up her passport and credit cards. There was nothing else she wanted to pack. It all reminded her of a life she wanted to leave behind. Remy turned off the lights and left the door unlocked, the burden of material possessions lifting as she mentally let them go.

She hadn't bothered to change, and still wore her floor-length red dress when she arrived at the airport.

The attendant jumped when Remy slammed her card down on the counter. He looked up, an annoyed expression on his face until he saw the desperation etched in the woman's features.

"Get me as far away from here as you can," Remy said.

Tens of thousands of travelers had come through his line over the years, but he could remember the faces of the few who were truly running away. All were the tragic heroes of their own stories, ones with endings he would never know. He held up a finger while he typed on his computer. "We have a plane leaving for Madrid in an hour."

"Perfect."

****

Escaping. That was what Remy had always done. Escaping from Louisiana, and then New York. First from her family, then her marriage, and now her career.

Remy always pushed forward, on to the next without looking back.

That screaming feeling of "get out now" finally stopped the minute she stepped foot onto that Madrid plaza. She was quiet inside, and she wondered how long it would last before the compulsion to run pulled her onward again.

The Spanish sun beat down on her head where she stood, wobbling a little in her high heels. An unexpected feeling of familiarity surprised her as she looked around. Why would a Louisiana girl feel at home in Spain? She didn't even speak Spanish, for Christ's sake. Nope, fate had not played a hand in deciding her trip. She knew that with absolute certainty. The first available flight had been the first available flight, nothing more. She hadn't made a wish, she was certain of that.

Trial and error had taught her a harsh lesson growing up. She learned never to make a selfish wish for herself, and how to clamp down hard on any personal desires that snuck their way into her brain. There were always unintended consequences and factors that Remy couldn't control whenever she uttered those forbidden words—*I wish...*

Her nana had understood. The only person who believed the barefoot, dirty, tear-stained girl who came running up the road spinning a wild tale of the family dog's recovered health while her brother was taken to the hospital. Nana saw the truth only a life spent on the Bayou could rationalize, and helped explain it to a frightened six-year-old.

"Remington, this is a curse. Inside your blood. Meddlin' with life and affectin' the give and take.

You're messin' with the balance of things. It's unnatural, it's what it is. Promise me, girl, you won't tell nobody 'bout this, what you think you did. Nana will protect ya. Folks 'round here migh' think you got the devil inside of ya. Best keep yer mouth shut about it, but you can't do it again."

Who was Remy to question it? Any explanation was better than no explanation at all, and her nana's reasoning at least gave her some small measure of control. And she didn't do it again. Or at least, she tried, but sometimes the words just slipped out.

Remy tried to fit into her small town, and even though the rest of the populace didn't know about her curse, they still found her to be "other." Too strange, too proper, too curious for her own good. Wanting to know about music instead of fishing, reading instead of watching football.

Life was spent staying out of the way while her father drank and her mother took care of Jameson in between shifts at the diner. Remy's brother never fully recovered from his time at the hospital, and doctors said that the fever had addled his brain. He walked slow and talked slow, even by the town's standard. Remy tried to help her mother and her brother, but it was like Jameson knew that his sister was to blame for his condition. He screamed and swung at Remy when she got too close, and so there was nothing for her to do but find a creative way to escape. She spent hours locked away in her room, scribbling away with whatever nub of crayon she had pocketed from school or splintered pencil she had found on the ground. While she sketched, she dreamed of all the places she could run away to, but oddly enough, Spain had never captured her imagination. Until now.

****

Remy spotted a cafe that looked open, despite it being the siesta hour. With a purposeful stride, she crossed the square and sat down at an outdoor table. As she waited for a waitress to come by so she could order a much-needed glass of wine, another shop front caught her eye.

BIENES RAÍCES, the sign read. *I wonder what that means,* she thought.

"¿Puedo ayudarle?" A voice next to Remy startled her back to her location.

"Um, English? Do you speak English?"

"Sí. You are American?"

"Yes, I just arrived an hour ago." The waitress eyed Remy's clothing and lack of luggage but said nothing. "Can I have a glass of wine? Red, please. Whatever you have is fine."

"Of course. Anything else?"

"Actually, yes. Can you tell me what 'beenes races' means?"

The waitress looked like she was trying not to laugh. *"¿Perdón?* What?" Red-faced, Remy pointed at the sign across from where she was sitting. *"Oh.* I think it is, how you say, estate? Real estate? Houses, no?"

"Okay, thank you. Sorry for the confusion."

As Remy sipped her wine and stared at what had to be the closed sign on the door of a real estate office, she thought about how excited she and Jack had been when they rented their first apartment together. They had budgeted and planned, deciding which room to dedicate as her paint studio and which room would be a nursery.

It had been everything Remy thought she wanted,

until she started to feel like a stranger in her own home. That's when she insisted that they move. *Forward, always running forward.* Jack put up with her insane desire to uproot many more times over the years, and they moved five more times until they ended up in the penthouse. He put his foot down after that. Remy still left.

To shake herself free from delving too far into difficult memories, Remy left her almost-empty glass on the table along with a few bills and started toward the office.

The inside of the window was plastered with single-page flyers. They each tried to crowd to the front, saying "Pick me! Buy me! Rent me!" The desperation of a collapsed housing market stood out clearly amid the chaos. Remy's eyes flitted from photo to photo in the enormous collage. She wondered where the families that used to occupy these homes had gone. From apartments to farmhouses, family legacies had been abandoned all over the country as people left their small towns in search of work and opportunity.

Most listings were average-sized, though a little smaller than the typical middle-class American home. The photos had a richness, though, a sense of history and culture that the high rises back in New York would never possess. They were *cheap*, too, if Remy interpreted the numbers at the bottoms of the flyers correctly. They were either prices or phone numbers. Either way, almost everything would be less expensive than her studio back in the city.

Back in the city. Not "back home." It wasn't home. But here, in the country where she felt at peace for the first time since she could remember, maybe this could be home. What would it smell like? Could she hear her neighbors? Walk to the market? Would she have enough space for her canvases? But none of them felt like the right fit as her imagination wandered through the listings.

Still lost in the flyers, the jingle of keys to her left alerted Remy to the arrival of the shopkeeper.

"Please, come in. I can help you find what you are looking for," the owner said in a crisp English accent. With ash gray hair and ruddy pink cheeks, she moved with precision that made her look years younger than she must be. Remy felt like she already knew the woman's story—a second chance at a life far away from her rainy homeland. A woman who refused to surrender to arthritis and the sedentary stability of retirement.

"You looked lost staring at the window. I knew you must be a foreigner. Not sure where to begin? Have a seat, and we'll get you sorted."

Remy passed into air-conditioned comfort and sank into the guest chair across from a cluttered desk. She could already feel the blisters forming on her feet after almost twenty-four hours in her eight-hundred-dollar shoes. Why had she paid eight hundred dollars for shoes that she always regretted the next day? Why did she continue to wear them if they hurt her so badly?

"American looking for a holiday home here?"

A lump formed in Remy's throat, and she didn't trust herself to speak. She shook her head and tried to swallow.

Understanding dawned on the owner's face, and she reached across the desk to grip Remy's left hand, encompassing the ring tan line that refused to fade.

"You can tell a lot about a person by their hands, you know," the older woman said. "You have strong hands; you will be okay."

Remy looked down at her nails, bitten off to the quick to avoid getting paint stuck underneath them. That was the excuse she always gave Jack. The real reason was that she used to stuff her fingers in her mouth as a child to stop herself from accidentally saying the words Nana told her never to say. *I wish*...Old habits were hard to break.

"I'm Maggie, by the way."

"Remy," she whispered. Then she cleared her throat and pulled her hands into her lap. Sitting up tall, she said, "I'm looking for something a bit more permanent than a vacation home, I think."

"Did you see anything in the window that struck your fancy?"

"I'm not really sure..."

Maggie peered at her for a long time, and Remy shifted in her seat.

"None of these are for you," Maggie declared, gesturing to the window. "You want something more, am I right? You are an old soul. I can see that." Maggie rummaged through her stacks of loose papers and stuffed folders. The digital age was about two decades late in here. Remy thought she even saw a Macintosh computer in the corner.

Maggie spun around, holding a manila envelope. "How about something unexpected?"

"What do you mean?" Remy asked, confused by the question.

"Would you like to buy a village?"

****

The next day, Maggie and Remy drove six hours northwest to Galicia. Fortified with new, sensible clothes and a good night's sleep, Remy felt ready to tackle her next journey. *Forward. Always forward. Don't look back.* She had left her red dress in a silken heap on the hotel floor. The shoes she had thrown off the balcony.

"I have yet to see this property myself," Maggie told her as they started their road trip. If it was considered weird to road trip with your real estate agent, Remy didn't care. Being with Maggie felt a little like having her nana back. She was brutally honest, intuitive, and knew when not to talk.

"How did you find out about it, then?" Remy asked.

"A friend of mine is a real estate agent in the province of Coruña. He's had this listing for months and been unable to find anyone interested. He thought I might have better luck in Madrid. There are not a lot of people in these smaller provinces anymore. It is hard to find buyers outside of a big city." Maggie let another car whiz by them on the highway, content to take her time. "Everyone is in such a bloody rush these days," she muttered, then continued. "You're the first person I've shown it to, matter of fact. I just knew that the right person would come along for it."

Maggie's words gave Remy pause, and she wondered if she was just another dumb tourist about to be suckered into a bad deal. Maggie seemed so genuine, though, that Remy felt guilty for doubting her.

"Any Spanish ancestors, Remy?" Maggie asked, distracting Remy from her negative thoughts.

"I don't know," she confessed. "My heritage is

kind of messed up. My momma's side is Irish, and my daddy's is German, or so he claims. But I don't think it applies to me anyway."

"You can't find out?"

Remy sighed. "I don't think my dad is really my dad. Though my momma will swear that he is until the day she dies."

"I just thought with your coloring"—she gestured to Remy's dark hair and dark eyes—"that there might be some in your blood."

"Maybe," Remy answered. It all came back to the blood. Curses and wishes in stifling nights when the air hung so thick that each breath felt like drowning…Remy unrolled the window and inhaled. The fresh scents calmed her, and her heartbeat slowed. *I'm not in Louisiana. I'm in Spain.* Desperate to change the subject from her past, Remy asked, "Where are we meeting your friend?"

"We will pick him up in Ortigueira. It's the nearest town to your village. It's small, less than ten thousand people live there. He will show us the way to the property. It is up near the Port of Espasante."

Remy was pretty sure there were more than ten thousand people crammed into her *block* in New York. *If I buy the place, I'll be the outsider again.* Then she laughed to herself. If she became the crazy old American who lived in the hills and painted on everything, then so be it. It didn't matter what people thought of her anymore.

"We're almost there," Maggie said, and she exited the main highway. They both remained silent until they reached the town and picked up Sebastian. From then on, there was not a moment of quiet in the car.

Maggie's friend turned out to be the most enthusiastic person Remy had ever met, and she'd spent fifteen years reining in Anita. His boundless energy was only held in check by Maggie's serene confidence, and Remy was more than happy to move to the back seat while the two of them caught up.

Maggie navigated the narrow, winding streets while carrying on a conversation in rapid Spanish. Tuning them out, Remy focused on the scenery whizzing by her window.

Ortigueira was adorable, there was no other way to put it. Restaurants and bars lined cobbled streets, and most everyone was on foot. It had a small-town charm to it, but it was a mix of old and new. Repurposed historical buildings were now banks, offices, and courthouses. Among the whitewashed buildings and sparse palm trees, Remy also saw evidence of gastropubs and trendy cafes among the traditional architecture. As soon as she blinked, though, they were through the town. *Already?* Remy thought, disappointed. *Maggie wasn't kidding when she said it was small.*

Her disappointment soon turned to excitement when Maggie turned up a dirt road. They bounced up a drive that was almost three miles long. Just when Remy started to get carsick, Sebastian turned around to look at her with a huge smile.

"Close your eyes, close your eyes!" Sebastian demanded. To humor him, Remy pretended to do so, but squinted through the windshield anyway.

"Okay, okay! Get ready, *Señorita.*" Sebastian slammed his door shut and opened Remy's with a flourish. "This—" He paused dramatically. "—is your new home!"

Remy opened her eyes fully, slid out of her seat, and nearly fell back into it again. Maggie, misunderstanding Remy's astounded reaction, was quick to jump in.

"Many of the buildings will need to be fixed up to become structurally sound. But the grounds are extensive, and you have your own well—"

The last time Remy had cried was three years ago in the doctor's office. She hadn't even shed a tear when she told Jack she wanted a divorce. But seeing the village for the first time unlocked a flood gate.

Tears streamed down her face as she took in the entirety of what would become hers. In that moment, she saw it all, restored to a new glory. *Be mine,* the village whispered. *I can give you everything you've ever wanted.* The desire Remy felt was intoxicating. It dug into the deepest recesses of her heart and turned her inside out. She couldn't have walked away from it even if she wanted to.

It showed her a dozen children scattered among the buildings, laughing as they bantered in front of their easels. The smell of turpentine paint was on the wind. Remy watched herself weave through the students, gently coaxing the masterpieces flowing from their brushes.

An art school. For all the talented kids who needed to escape their small towns and see the world. She would foster a new generation of creativity. The image was so clear she rubbed her eyes to make sure it wasn't real yet. This village held the answers that she had been desperately searching for, a way to find her purpose. It seemed to know just what to show her to hit all the right chords.

And underneath the pull she felt, Remy sensed a terrible loneliness coming from the property. It wanted to be loved and would promise anything it could not to be alone any more. "We are two of a kind, aren't we?" Remy whispered.

"*Mi amor,* why do you cry?" Sebastian wrung his hands together and shared a glance with Maggie.

Remy smiled through her ruined makeup. "I want to see the rest."

Chapter Two

"You know," Sebastian said as they hiked over to the barn, "I think that you must be a miracle of *el Camino de Santiago*."

"The hiking trail?" Remy asked, confused.

Sebastian let out a gasp and put his hand over his heart. "*Mi amor,* it is so much more than that! You know nothing of the history of northern España?"

Fearing she might have gravely offended him, Remy tried to backtrack. "I think I've heard of the Camino. It started out as a pilgrimage, right?"

He sighed. "*El Camino de Santiago* begins in many places throughout Europe. A pilgrim may start in France, Portugal, even Germany or Italy. But all routes lead to the Santiago de Compostela, within Galicia. It is the church where Saint James is buried, for it was he who brought Christianity to the Iberian Peninsula."

"And have you walked the Camino?" Remy asked.

"When I was a young man, searching for life's answers, I walked one summer."

"Did you find what you were looking for?"

Sebastian stopped, and got a faraway look in his eye. Then he spoke words that were not his own, reciting melodious words from memory. "The pilgrim route is for those who are good—it is the lack of vices, the thwarting of the body, the increase of virtues, pardon for sins, sorrow for the penitent, the road of the righteous, love of the saints, faith in the resurrection, and the reward of the blessed, a separation from hell, the protection of the heavens."

Remy squirmed, suddenly realizing that she had asked Sebastian a very personal question, and he had been right not to respond to her directly. "I'm sorry, Sebastian. That was rude of me. That passage was beautiful. Where is it from?"

He gave a little bow of his head. "The Codex Calixtinus. A guide for those embarking on the Way of Saint James. You are not walking the Camino, but are on a pilgrimage just the same.

"The Kingdom of Galicia has had a long history of miracles, and not just on the Camino de Santiago. There are a few that took place in this very village. We have no proof now, though, other than the stories handed down. The Catholic Church refused to document them. But I can still feel it here, and that is all the proof I need. Can you feel this is a place for miracles?"

"If it was so great, then why was it left to rot?"

Sebastian must not have heard her as he flung the barn doors open. The smell of ancient hay and dust lingered, and Remy sneezed uncontrollably until Sebastian handed her a handkerchief and dragged her back outside.

"Have you ever thought about keeping horses?" he asked, bouncing on his toes.

****

Maggie begged Remy not to spend the night out at the village. "The paperwork will take a while to go through," the Englishwoman said. "Why not stay in town until the sale is finalized?"

"Maggie, I'll be fine. Sebastian said he would loan

me his son's camping gear for as long as I need it."

"You will be out here all alone! What if something happens?"

Remy tried not to laugh. Just because she had eschewed much of her bayou upbringing didn't mean she hadn't picked up a few skills in her youth. Sleeping under the stars was one of the few fond memories she had from back then, on the nights when being inside her house was unbearable. Nothing but a velvet sky and her thoughts, listening to the crickets chirp.

She needed to find that clarity now, after such a whirlwind of a day. Part of her reluctance was because she was afraid to leave the village. If she went to a bed and breakfast in Ortigueira, she could talk some sense into herself and walk away from the deal.

No, if she was going to jump right into such a crazy decision, then she needed to jump in with both feet. That included showing the village that she belonged to it as much as it belonged to her. Building that trust would have to start tonight.

Sebastian had left the women at the village to go pick up Remy's supplies and returned to find them having the same conversation as an hour before.

"At least sleep in the main house," Maggie pleaded. "There is no need for this tent nonsense."

"No, it has to be here," Remy said, and shook out the tent canvas. The trio stood in the middle of the village, where Remy imagined that the town square would have been. A crossroads through the village, just as she was at a crossroads in her life. Though it was a bit superstitious and maybe a little bit silly, the artist in Remy appreciated the symbolism.

"Well, I'll be here first thing in the morning to

check on you," Maggie said. "I won't drive back to Madrid until I know you are okay."

Remy leaned in to give her a hug. "Thank you, Maggie. For bringing me here. For everything."

Maggie snorted. "Don't make me regret it! I would never forgive myself if something happened to you. I'm beginning to think this wasn't a good idea—"

"It was the best idea! You were right all along. The village and I are a match."

Maggie shivered in the evening breeze. "I'm glad you feel that way. I can say, after being here all day, I am not sure that I feel the same way about this place as you do. It has potential, but the longer I stay, the more I get this feeling…Oh, never mind. I'm just a doddering old lady. You have more courage than I, sweet girl."

"She will be safe," Sebastian insisted. "The village will look after her." He leaned in and kissed both of Remy's cheeks. "*Buenas noches,* brave American!"

As Remy watched Maggie and Sebastian drive away, Remy hoped her new friends wouldn't lose sleep over her tonight. Her stomach growled, reminding her that the supper Sebastian had dropped off along with the camping gear remained untouched. Too tired to build a fire, Remy dug into the cold fish stew. Sitting on her sleeping bag, she ate slowly, savoring each bite and trying to remember the last time she had enjoyed food so much.

In their early days of dating, Jack liked to take Remy to Michelin-starred restaurants and exclusive wineries. Starry-eyed in her first real relationship, Remy was too touched by his efforts to tell him that she felt more comfortable staying in and ordering Chinese food in sweatpants. But gradually, as she was accepted into his world—the art world—her tastes had changed. Or, at least, she thought they had.

In their past few years together, food and dates had merely become a distraction. *Look how lucky we are,* Jack seemed to say, whenever he whisked her away to try and break her out of a depressive spiral. *We can go wherever we want, whenever we want. Nothing holds us back.* Expensive food, drinks, wine, booze—it all blurred together. For the life of her, Remy couldn't taste a single flavor.

But this, a supper of cold fish stew with only herself for company, tasted like life. Or maybe her taste buds were coming alive again with the rest of her. With an empty bowl and a full stomach, Remy settled in for the night.

Voices woke her around midnight; the sound of a boisterous celebration echoed through the village streets. Remy rubbed her eyes and tried to figure out where the noise was coming from. *A wedding, maybe? Drunken party-goers who got lost and ended up in my village?*

Remy had brushed off Maggie's concerns earlier, but in the middle of the night, they seemed less foolish. She tensed, waiting for more clues before she made her presence known. She listened harder, and suddenly realized she could understand what they were saying. *Are they speaking English?* she wondered. *No, I don't think so.* It was more like a switch had flipped in her brain, and the essence of their words untangled themselves in Remy's mind. It was as frustrating as trying to read in a dream, because the second she thought too hard about it, the voices stopped making sense.

Remy forced herself to relax. They, whoever *they* were, sounded like a mix of men and women joking and teasing each other. They were making fun of one of them for being in love with someone named María. Then one of them, a boy, suggested that they go back to the party. The voices suddenly stopped, leaving an eerie quiet.

Grabbing her flashlight, Remy braved a few steps past her campsite. "Hello?" she whispered. *There is no way they disappeared so quickly.* "Hello?" she said, louder this time. The wind picked up and whistled through the empty buildings.

I've lost my mind. While hanging between the magical limbo of sleep and wake, the half-conscious state had played tricks on her. Reality told her that she was alone. She had spent the day dreaming about restoring the village to life again, so it was no wonder her mind had created a celebration in the town square.

Sleep took a long time to find Remy again, and when the dawn rays hit her face, the details of the night before were hazy. Then the urgent cry of her bladder superseded all other thoughts, and Remy hurried over to a nearby tree. Crouching low, she let out a sigh and a stream simultaneously. The sigh turned into a giggle when Remy realized another reason why Maggie was so concerned for her welfare last night—the complete lack of plumbing—but she had been too proper to say so!

I should make her super uncomfortable and talk up the view from my "bathroom" today. I should insist that she give it a go. Truth be told, Remy had never peed in a more glorious place before. The golden sunrise illuminated the surrounding wilderness, skimming off the roof of the barn tucked away farther down the hill. Remy straightened up and turned around to look at the crumbling buildings of the village. It felt like it was smiling at her. Everything was bathed in a safe and cheerful light, and her tense night became a faded memory. There was nothing for her to worry about here.

A glimmer to her right caught her eye as Remy walked back to the campsite. She reached down and grabbed the long, slim glass bottle resting on the dirt. "A wine bottle!" She shook it and heard a slight sloshing at the bottom. There was no label, and the cork in the neck looked strong. Could there still be wine in it, after a hundred years? Remy uncorked it with a pop, bracing herself for a sour stench to invade her nostrils, or at the very least, to be disappointed with rainwater and mud inside.

Instead, it smelled sweet; sweeter than any wine that Remy had ever tasted before. She put her eye to the opening and peered inside. Nothing suspicious, or gross looking. It just looked like regular red wine. So, like a baby with an oral fixation, Remy decided that her other senses weren't enough. She had to put it in her mouth.

She would just swish and spit, the way Jack had taught her at wine tasting events. That way she wouldn't get a nineteenth century rare disease. It would be her own little disgusting secret. Hell, she had already peed out in the open today. *Well, Jack, if only you could see me now. Cheers!* Remy lifted the bottle to her lips and poured a little of the alcohol onto her tongue.

Flavor exploded in her mouth, and Remy forgot to spit as she savored it. *I need to save some for Jack!*

Remy snapped back to herself and lowered the

bottle. She no longer shared anything in her life with Jack, a fact that still took some getting used to. Remy corked it while keeping her eyes peeled on the surrounding area for more bottles. No such luck. *Well, there goes a solid plan for getting drunk before eight a.m.* She made a mental note to ask Sebastian if there were any cellars hidden on the property.

The wine had awakened her hunger, and Remy meandered past the mill, where the orchard trees grew untamed, to find breakfast. She plucked a swollen pear and bit into the sun-warmed fruit. Juice rolled down her hands, and in a few bites, it was gone. Remy reached for another as she continued down the overgrown path. Feeling like Hansel and Gretel, she dropped pear cores behind her to mark her way back.

Sebastian had told her that the village property stretched all the way to the Bay of Biscay. She couldn't remember exactly how far that was. He had told her in kilometers, and Remy had always been bad with numbers.

The gently sloping trail seemed to have no end as it meandered exactly as it pleased. Trying to get her bearings, Remy turned around to look for the roof of the main house, set at the highest point in the village, but it had been swallowed up by the trees around it. The only way to go was forward, and the trail had to end eventually.

Remy was starting to sweat by the time she heard the faint roar of the water. Her mouth was sticky from the fruit, and the wine bottle remained clutched in her hand. *Why did I bring this with me?* Wading through the brush, she bent to scratch an itch burning on her leg.

The distant cry of a gull kept her from turning

around. The end was close enough to smell now, and it gave her motivation to push through her discomfort. The trees thinned out, and then she was surrounded by blue.

Up on a cliff, Remy gazed out at an endless expanse. Out past the steep drop off in front of her, fishing boats dotted the horizon. The culture and history of Galicia swirled in the cold depths of the bay, colors so rich they could never be replicated on a palette.

With baby steps, Remy inched closer to the edge. The ground looked sturdy enough, but it was herself she didn't trust. It had happened more than once, that urge to jump. She wasn't suicidal, she never really had been. Depressed, yes, but never suicidal. But the feeling that accompanied standing on the edge of a tall building or bridge, of letting go just to see what would happen, had always called to her. The call of the void.

For safety's sake, she put her butt in the dirt and scooted forward as far as she dared. There was a long, thin stretch of sand directly below the cliff that curved its way north along the coastline. The gentle waves lapped up against the shore, and she longingly wondered if there was any way to get down there.

How long had it been since she'd walked in the sand? Sat motionless and listened to the waves? She ached for the ocean to cleanse her, to be the baptism into her new life. Maybe if she washed herself free of her past, she would be able to paint again.

Remy crossed her legs and closed her eyes. She tried to clear her mind. The trick was to empty all her thoughts until a flash of inspiration struck for her next project. It usually happened all at once—the colors, the movement, and the message behind the canvas. It came to life in her mind, and her hands would simply copy it down. Having never been formally trained, Remy never jumped to technique or strategy when painting. She just *did it*, purely on instinct.

Until she couldn't anymore. Her mind's eye remained empty, just as it had been for months. Remy's concentration switched focus onto her heart pounding in frustration. The rhythmic beat drowned out the soothing sound of the waves, and blood rushed in her ears.

"Arrghhh!" Remy's eyes snapped open, and she grabbed the first thing she saw, a sun-bleached scallop shell, and threw it off the cliff.

This is my punishment. The universe had to keep the balance, and even though Remy had tried to punish herself by divorcing Jack, she knew deep down that it wasn't enough. She didn't get to pick her own penance. It never worked that way.

Maybe it was time for her to let this aspect of herself go, anyway. It had been time for her to move on from her marriage and her dreams of a family, so why not her art? *There is more than one way to live and be happy.*

Holding onto a more positive attitude, Remy adjusted her butt and attempted to meditate again. This time, though, she didn't even try to summon an image for her art. She just simply sat and felt the breeze on her face. Her chest rose up and down as she inhaled, each breath feeling like its own eternity until it transitioned into the next. Seconds felt like hours, and her anger eased.

She would have sat there on the edge of the world indefinitely, but the feeling of someone staring at her pulled her back. Remy wrenched her eyes open and looked around. She was still alone on her ledge, but a figure down on the beach had appeared.

The person was too far away to get a good look, but Remy felt sure that it was a man. He walked barefoot, leaving tracks in the sand. He put up a hand to acknowledge her, and then clasped his hands behind his back to continue walking. He bowed his head, as though searching for something. He stopped, bent down, and pocketed an item he'd scooped up.

Remy took her eyes off him for a moment to rise to her feet, and once she stood up all the way, she couldn't find him again. Squinting, she peered down to where he'd last been. There was nothing there, and the waves washed the footprints away.

Damn. She wanted to ask the stranger how he had accessed the beach. If he was a local, then maybe he would know how to get down the cliff. While shaking her legs to get the blood flowing, Remy gave the water a last, wistful glance.

Oh, can't forget the wine bottle, she reminded herself, before she started back up the path. The cool shade of the overgrown trail embraced her. Remy felt her cheeks with the back of her hand and pulled away at their heat. She wondered how long she had been sitting in the sun. Without her phone, she had no idea what time it was.

She was almost back to the village when she heard voices calling her name. "Remy! Remy! Where are you?"

Thoughts of her midnight visitors flashed through her mind before Remy realized it was Sebastian and Maggie yelling for her. "Here! I'm here!" she called back, emerging from the orchard.

"Oh, thank God. Sebastian! I see her," Maggie sounded weak with relief, and Remy felt a stab of guilt for making her friend worry.

"Where have you been? We've been searching for you for an hour! I was sure something happened to you last night!" Maggie, sweaty and red-faced, collapsed onto a rock, fanning herself.

"Maggie, you shouldn't be out here in this heat! Come on, I have water bottles back at the tent."

"You didn't answer my question," Maggie said, giving Remy a stern glare.

"I was up early this morning and decided to explore a bit more. I found the trail that leads to the bay and followed it down. I stayed longer than I meant to."

"You shouldn't do that to an old woman. I was up half the night fretting about you, and then I dragged Sebastian up here early only to find what? An empty tent? And no sign of you!"

More than ever, Remy felt like a ten-year-old girl being scolded by her nana. It had been a long time since anyone had outright scolded her. Most people had tiptoed around her the past few years, worried that anything they said or criticized might upset her. It was so refreshing that Remy had to hide a smile.

"What can I do to make it up to you, Maggie?" Remy asked, appearing appropriately contrite.

Maggie sniffed. "I wouldn't say no to a spot of breakfast before I hit the road. There is a superb restaurant in town I keep hearing about."

The old woman seemed determined to make sure that Remy left the village at least once before the real estate paperwork was finalized. Remy half-expected

Maggie to have made arrangements at the B&B for her and forbid the "camping nonsense" once they got to town. Laughing, Remy said, "All right, you win. Let's go into town. I suppose I should get the lay of the land sooner or later."

Sebastian was waiting for them at the car, looking thoroughly disgruntled and less like the Christmas elf hopped up on sugar that Remy remembered from yesterday.

"I told you, Maggie, no reason to worry. She is fine. Now, I need some coffee."

"But Sebastian," Remy said, "I have something that's way better." She taunted him by dangling the bottle of wine in his face. "I found it on the property, and it is amazing. I want to know where I can get more, and I figured you would be the person to tell me where it's from."

His sleepy eyes lit up as he grabbed the bottle from Remy. "No label?"

"Nope. But it is the sweetest thing I've ever tasted. Pure magic."

Regaining some of his trademark excitement, he yanked the cork off and sniffed the contents inside. Frowning, he tipped the bottle and poured the contents on the ground. The liquid that ran out was not the deep red Remy expected. Brown sludge splattered onto the dirt.

Seeing Remy's stunned expression, he started to laugh. "Oh! That was, how you say, a practical joke? A prank?" Sebastian clapped her on the shoulder. "All right. You tricked me. I truly believed you! You have the acting gift."

"But it wasn't supposed to be…" Remy took the

bottle back and eyed it with confusion. The wine had been just fine a few hours ago. There was no way she would mistake red wine for dirty sludge water, and it couldn't have gotten contaminated during her short excursion to the bay. She hadn't dreamed that, too, right? Maybe this was why she couldn't paint anything anymore—her basic senses were starting to go haywire.

"You must have known I was coming here with bad news and wanted to punish me," Sebastian said, still chuckling. The outright panic on Remy's face made him rush to reassure her. "Nothing that bad. Just that we have much to do to sort your paperwork. You will have to apply for a residence visa in Spain for investors or self-employed, and a work permit, eventually..." Sebastian continued his technical chatter during their drive into town.

It seemed that Remy was in for a rather large headache dealing with all the legalities that being an expatriate entailed. Their arrival at the restaurant finally interrupted him just as Remy's migraine was starting to set in. With a sigh of relief, Remy exited the car out onto a flagstone path that fronted the marina docks.

Wooden sailboats bobbed alongside sleek, expensive yachts. Old and new merged to create a view that enchanted every passerby, especially their trio. "Makes you wonder what this place looked like way back when, doesn't it?" Maggie said, shading her eyes with her hand.

"It was probably a lot more rustic," Remy guessed.

"When you go up to *el Porto de Espasante*, it is like stepping back in time, right, Sebastian?"

"Why is that?" Remy asked.

"It is still a fishing port, mostly commercial. Less

than five hundred people live there year-round. Plenty of trading through there, though. Be careful up there alone," Sebastian said, with uncharacteristic seriousness.

"I doubt I'll spend much time outside of the village. I'll have so much to do over the next few months."

Maggie turned her gaze to Remy. "Don't spend too much time alone. Being too isolated can do strange things to people."

"It will give you all the more reason to come visit me!"

Maggie pretended to give a little shudder. "Not until you have a working toilet, that I can promise!"

****

Proper plumbing ended up being the least of Remy's problems over the next few weeks.

Word spread about Remy's purchase, and soon Ortigueira knew all about the crazy American who bought the village. A grudging respect also emerged at her insistence to do much of the work herself. If a foreigner was to own such a special piece of their country, at least she seemed to be of the right character and mindset to do so.

As Remy grew to be recognized around town, the citizens would gossip and nod in approval to each other as she passed. "Look at her," they whispered. "She must be Galician."

"You know, she looks like my aunt's cousin's paternal grandmother's side. It is all in the chin."

"Oh yes. And her eyes. Purely Galician."

"The village called one of its own back home."

"It was right that she bought it."

And thus, Remy was accepted into a small and tight-knit community, though she didn't realize it at the time. She spent most of her time in a fog, caught up in her vision for the village.

The village was to be Remy's greatest work of art. She saw the final product in her mind's eye just as she used to see her finished painting on a blank canvas. It was a way to flex her creative muscles again, even though her brushes were still blocked. Losing herself in a project again felt amazing, and the blood, sweat, and tears that accompanied her art were more than metaphorical this time. Well, maybe not the tears. The tears were always the same. She forgot all about New York, Anita, her career, the divorce, Jack…and when her body fell into her sleeping bag each night, she slept a dreamless sleep until morning.

The village hummed with a happy energy now that it was being restored. Remy didn't hear any more weird noises and didn't stumble across any mysterious wine bottles on the property. Even the orchard and the bay stayed off her radar while she focused on her rehabilitation plans for the houses.

One morning while picking up supplies, she finally slowed down enough to charge her phone while at a café in town. Real life hit her like a slap in the face.

Fifty missed calls? Afraid to even check her email, Remy just decided to trash them all directly from her inbox. *If it's really important, someone will send it again.* Sighing, she steeled herself to listen to her voicemails.

Most were from Jack. He sounded drunk in all of them. Remy deleted those as soon as she heard his slur.

A couple were from her lawyer. Those she needed

to listen to like a responsible adult, but not while she was in public.

There were about ten from Anita, ranging from concerned to pissed off to "over it," as her best friend described. All of them ended with a graphic threat of what would happen if Remy didn't call her back. Most notably, Anita threatened to track her down and punch her in the boob.

Recognizing that she couldn't put it off any longer, Remy stepped outside to call Anita. Her agent answered on the first ring.

"You're alive!"

The sheer pitch of her voice was enough to make Remy want to hang up the phone. But if she did, Anita would probably think Remy had a *Taken* situation going on and would report it to INTERPOL. So, Remy took a deep breath and told her. "I bought a village."

Chapter Three

"*Señora,* there is someone looking for you." The cashier who rang up Remy's groceries every week gave the store entrance a meaningful look. "A man was in here earlier, asking if anyone knew you."

Remy swallowed. "Who was he? What did he want?"

"He was very rude. Demanding to know about the artist who moved here; where he could find the American painter. I told him I knew no painter."

She tried to breathe. "Was he very tall? With silver hair? Probably wearing a suit?"

Her friend nodded.

"Jack." *Damn, Anita.* Why couldn't she just keep her big mouth shut? Odds were that Anita had let something slip to the public in order to garner mystery around Remy in anticipation of her next collection. What could be more exotic than a runaway artist? Anita's job was to put Remy's work at the forefront of everyone's minds and maintain the buzz. The line between best friend and agent was blurred sometimes, and Remy often wanted to strangle Anita for always assuming she knew best.

Of course, Jack had found her. All he was waiting for was a little crumb of information, enough for his detectives or whoever he hired to get started on the trail. He couldn't be here for money or hope that they could reconcile. It was over. Their divorce had gone through; Remy's lawyers had informed her of that. It had been a simple split—Remy had let Jack keep almost everything.

An image came to mind—Jack's rumpled hair as he gallantly brought her breakfast in bed. But his face— it took more than a moment to remember his smile. Remy jolted in surprise when she realized it had been weeks since she tried to picture his face. How could she forget someone she saw every day for fifteen years? It frightened her how quickly something that meant the world to her could disappear.

But now that his deep green eyes burned their way back into the forefront of her mind, Remy couldn't focus on anything else. She missed him like a punch to the gut, almost doubling her over as she left the market. The temptation urged her to give in.

Just one more night. Just one more time. He would be a familiar and comforting presence in the upheaval of her new start. Remy realized just then how bone tired she was from being stretched outside of her comfort zone for so long. It was terrifying trying to get her feet underneath her, but she hadn't let herself realize it until now. She wanted, no, *needed* his arms around her, to hug her and let her be something less than strong and independent for just a few moments.

All that awaited her back at the village was another long, hot afternoon of clearing out rubble from inside the ruins of the bakery, and she simply couldn't face it today. Picking up her pace, Remy put her groceries on her moped and roared off in search of a man who would stick out like a sore thumb in her town.

He wasn't hard to find. Remy found him arguing

with a food-cart vendor and gesturing wildly. The vendor pretended not to understand Jack and turned his back to him. As Remy parked, she saw Jack approach a pair of old ladies, obviously asking an urgent question. They just shook their heads at him.

Remy felt touched by everyone's protectiveness, even if it wasn't necessary. There wasn't a soul in Ortigueira who would give Jack directions to Remy's village. Maybe she was doing better here than she thought. Feeling stronger than she had a few minutes ago, Remy approached.

"Jack."

He whirled around, sweat dripping from his brow and staining his too-tight collar. His eyes were wild, but clear. *He hasn't been drinking. Good.*

"Remy!" Jack moved forward as if to hug her, but Remy took a step back.

One of the old women, a widow who still dressed in black in memory of a husband decades dead, reached out and touched Remy's arm in concern. "*¿Bien?*" she asked. *Are you okay?* The widow looked like she wanted to take Remy with her as she continued her walk past the church, but Remy nodded that she would be fine. Unable to convey further concerns, the widow gave Jack one last glare as a warning and hobbled away with her friend.

"I'm so sorry," Jack said. "I had to come all the way here to apologize for everything. All those phone calls, harassing you…It wasn't me. You know that isn't me. I've just been so lost without you and—"

An audience had quickly gathered around the couple, and none of their expressions were friendly toward Jack. Remy held up a hand. "Let's go someplace private and talk, okay?"

"I see you've made loyal friends here." Jack chuckled nervously and unbuttoned his suit.

"And you heard I bought a village. From Anita, I'm assuming." Remy led him over to her parked moped.

"At first, I thought she was making it up to cover for you, but that was the same story I heard over and over from everyone. A village. Wow."

He actually sounds impressed. In a sudden burst of pride and generosity, Remy asked, "Do you want to see it?" *After all, he's come a long way...*

"You want to show it to me? Because according to everyone I talked to in Ortigueira, this mystery village doesn't even exist."

Remy straddled her baby blue moped. "Hop on the back, and hold tight." Jack opened his mouth to protest at the indignity, but apparently thought better of it and snapped his jaw shut.

Weaving up the narrow roads, Remy could hardly keep her attention on what was in front of her. With the familiar strength of Jack's arms hugged tight behind her, his scent, his heat, and the feel of his heartbeat was enough to send her into a trance. This was her safe place for so many years.

However, the moment she entered her village, she snapped out of it. When she crossed over the property line, flashes of the last year of their marriage broke the spell, and she almost lost control of the handlebars. The moped skidded to a stop, and Remy flung herself off it. Disgust with herself and her behavior welled up, and she couldn't look at Jack.

Selfish, selfish, selfish, a voice in her mind taunted.

What was I thinking, bringing Jack here? The village was her sacred space. He didn't *fit* here. He was a reminder of everything she wanted to forget. *Well, maybe not forget. I don't deserve to forget. But at least move on from.* And she would never move on if Jack kept showing up in her life.

"Why did you come here?"

Jack raised his eyebrows at her abrupt attitude change. "I came to convince you to come back to New York."

That wasn't what Remy was expecting. "Why?" she asked, bewildered.

"I know that our marriage is over, Remy. But at least when you lived in the city, there was still the chance we would run into each other. I could see you at auctions. We could talk sometimes. I know it was hard, but it was better than nothing. The possibility of seeing you got me out of bed each day."

"Jack, you know that isn't healthy—"

"Yes, I've lost my wife," he said, tears gathering in his eyes. "But no one ever talks about how you also lose your best friend at the same time. I know you're going to say it's a bad idea, but do you think we could get to that point, one day? Friends? I need you in my life. And I would hate to think you ran away from your old life back in New York because of me. You deserve to be there, too. It is just too hard to go through this without each other, Remy."

The anguish in Jack's voice twisted her heart, but what he said only solidified her reasoning behind moving to Spain. Jack deserved better. He didn't know that she had betrayed his trust as a wife and a friend, and telling him now would only destroy him further.

Maybe if Remy had stayed in Louisiana, having a baby would have been easy. After all, it was never something that people planned for; it always just happened to girls when they hit their teen years. There was something in the water that led to kids having kids in her backwater town. Accidents were embraced as "God's plan," weddings were thrown together at the last minute, and one by one they all dropped out of high school.

But not Remy. By the time everyone else was on their third or fourth child, Remy was living the starving artist's life in the big city. Even though she was surviving on ramen and hope, she still pitied everyone who never made it out like she did. But maybe leaving had been the cost of having a healthy baby.

It was hard to think about all the things she had done right in life when her empty arms ached to hold the little ones that she lost. Why were babies a natural course in life for some, while for others it was like climbing a mountain? Each inch of ascent a herculean effort, only to fall before the summit?

Doctors blamed it on a number of factors. Remy just blamed herself. For waiting too long, for assuming she could have it all, for letting the baby fever consume her and her marriage. She hated herself for hurting Jack each time she bled, for failing those little innocent beings that her body created and then killed.

When they finally started trying for a baby five years into their marriage, Remy and Jack were pretty smug that they conceived during the first month. They had a loving marriage, a stable home, and more money than they knew what to do with. Obviously, a baby was the logical next step.

Glowing with pride, Remy had let Jack announce the good news to their closest friends. It never occurred to her that something could go wrong, until it did.

"It's just a fluke," a doctor told them. "One in three pregnancies ends in a miscarriage. Most women go on to have a successful pregnancy right after. There was nothing you did wrong. You're still young enough, and you have time."

Trying to conceive after a miscarriage was a special kind of hell. It seemed like everywhere Remy looked, she saw pregnant women and children. Her first pregnancy had awoken something in her that would not be quieted until she brought her own child into this world. The hopes and dreams that had appeared when she first got pregnant had nowhere to go once the baby was gone.

Sex became a chore as they tried each month with no success. One year later, Remy came out of the bathroom waving a stick with two pink lines. This was it, she was sure of it. There was no way she would lose two babies in a row.

But she did. And then a third right after, and a fourth another six months later. At that point Jack called for a time out. At the time, Remy had resented him, but they both needed a break to heal. Remy's art was suffering, and Jack didn't recognize himself in the mirror anymore. *Who are these people?* they asked each other. *These once-vibrant adventurers determined to take on the world?*

For Remy's thirty-fourth birthday present, Jack gifted her a round of IVF as a last-ditch effort. "This is the last time, Remy," he said, as they arrived at the clinic. "I can't do it anymore. After this, I'm done. I have you. That's all I need in this life to be happy." The emotional toll of four losses in a row was something that neither of them were willing to go through again, but IVF was the glimmer of hope they needed. Remy was eager to agree to any of Jack's terms if it meant they got to try one more time.

Even in the face of all past evidence to the contrary, Remy convinced herself that this time it would work. She didn't feel the pain of the needles, the invasive exams, or the roller coaster of hormones the doctors put her on. Jack, however, kept reminding his wife that nothing was guaranteed, and that they needed to be okay with whatever the outcome was.

It didn't take.

With that negative test result, a strange sense of peace came over Remy. It was a relief not to obsess anymore and decide that their nightmare was over. They had reached the end of the line, and for that, Remy grateful. She was just so tired of hurting.

"It kills me that I can't give you what you want," Jack told her. "But I think we need to close this chapter and move on." Remy wholeheartedly agreed with him, and they were able to get their relationship back on track. The experience left them a little older, a lot wiser, and with deep lines in their skin.

But Remy was proud of the marks left on her body. It proved that she had been through an ordeal and made it out stronger than she was before. Scars and stretch marks proved that her babies had existed, and nothing could ever take that evidence away. She told herself she was still a mother and hid the hurt every Mother's Day when Jack never thought to get her a card.

Therapy helped make her whole again. However,

the year of progress she made disappeared in an instant when she got a phone call from Anita. It yanked her off the path to wellness and sent her into the worst spiral of her life.

"I did a stupid thing. Nobody else can know. Please, Remy, I need your help."

It took all of Remy's willpower not to simultaneously laugh and sob into the phone. Did the universe really hate her that much? *Just give the baby to me.* She bit her tongue bloody to keep from saying the words. What kind of a person would say that to their best friend? That would ask them to go through the trauma of pregnancy, birth, and giving up a child?

Anita had been there for Remy through every pregnancy loss, though she was staunchly child-free in her beliefs. Remy had leaned on Anita for years, and all Anita asked was for her to be in the waiting room. One afternoon while Anita undid a mistake that would have affected her whole life. Anita's baby was not Remy's baby. Remy could get through a few short hours. She just had to keep reminding herself that before she could go home and numb the pain with a bottle of vodka.

Before Anita was led into the patient room, she gave Remy a tearful hug and said, "I wish we could switch bodies." Remy squeezed her tightly, and rage seared through her. It wasn't rational to be angry with Anita, but the hate and resentment consumed her for a split second. And so she let out the words that she had sworn to her nana never to say. "I wish I could have a baby. I'd give anything for it…"

Anita pulled away and gave Remy a guilt-ridden look. Remy stared back, horrified, though for a different reason. Once the words had escaped her mouth, there was no going back. *I wish...*

The entire time Remy dealt with infertility, she had resisted making a wish for herself. There was always a cost to the words, and she could never control the consequences. She couldn't put others in her life at risk, and nothing, not even a healthy child, would be worth the cost of a lifetime of guilt. Jameson's fate still haunted her.

As she sat alone in the clinic waiting room while Anita went through with her procedure, satisfaction crept over Remy. Why shouldn't she wish for something good for herself? What was wrong with wanting something so basic and instinctual? Why did she have to be the morality police and decide what was worth the consequences and what wasn't?

She had exhausted all her other options already. Jack's drug arrests in his early twenties hadn't seemed like such a big deal until the adoption talks started and then immediately stopped. Remy had paid her dues. It wasn't her fault there was no other way for her to have the family she so desperately wanted.

She went home and seduced Jack that very night. He had no idea what she had wished for, that she was ovulating, or what he had unknowingly consented to. Remy pulled him into her twisted plan without warning, though he had made it perfectly clear that he could not handle another loss.

But it won't be a loss this time, she told herself as an excuse. Jack would be so happy when it all worked out. He wouldn't consider the fact that his wife had used his body to trap him into another pregnancy. The end would justify the means.

For the first three months, Remy was a ghost. She

could hardly look Jack in the eye, fearing she would reveal her secret. She couldn't tell anybody until she knew that the baby would stick. So she hid. Citing a new project as the reason for her absence, Remy painted with a bucket right beside her to throw up in when morning sickness gripped her.

Anita assumed Remy was avoiding her because of the abortion. Jack thought his wife was going through another bout of depression and urged her to open up to her therapist. Remy just locked the door to her studio and painted canvas after canvas as a distraction.

That series of paintings were not the hopeful, vibrant paintings one would expect from a woman creating the miracle of life. They were dark—more disturbing than any collection Remy had created before. Nothing happy would flow from her brush, but she couldn't paint anything else. Her mind's eye controlled her hands, and she was left at the mercy of her subconscious.

It all became clear to Remy at her twenty-week appointment. Her baby—a boy, as she would later find out—had a heart condition incompatible with life. Doctors told her that if she carried to term, her child would survive a few days at most outside of her womb.

"But I said it!" she wailed, eyes glued to the ultrasound screen. "I wished for it! I said the words! I should have a baby—" She shook uncontrollably, threw up all over herself, and then blacked out.

He would have had your nose, Remy wanted to tell Jack, as they stood in the village square. *They showed me his profile on the ultrasound. He would have looked just like you.* But Jack would never know of their son's existence. The single baby that could have been born if

Remy had allowed it. To protect both her boys' suffering, Remy shouldered the burden. She cleared her throat and looked away.

"So, how long are you staying in town?" she asked.

"Until you agree to come back to the States with me," Jack said, brushing the tears from his face and pretending they never happened. He had poured his heart out to his ex-wife, and all Remy had given him back was a polite question. They both felt the awkwardness between them, a distance that couldn't be closed.

"Jack, I'm building a life here. I'm not going back. Honestly, I think it would be better for both of us if you left sooner rather than later."

"You bought a *village*," he said, getting angrier. "And you live here *alone*. Nobody needs that much space. It's just you, surrounded by houses that are falling down. You need to be in a place that's living! This is the past. Everyone else has moved on from here, and for good reason. I can't stand the thought of you being here by yourself. It's dangerous and stupid, Remy. Come back to the real world."

"Thank you for your concern," Remy said stiffly, feeling protective of her village as it was assaulted by Jack's insults. "But I'm getting by here just fine. Plus, I won't be here alone forever."

"Are you telling me there is someone else?" Jack's voice was deadly calm.

"Don't be dramatic. No. I'm restoring it for..." she hesitated, not wanting to reveal her long-term plan. "I'm exactly where I need to be right now. The rest is really none of your business. I don't need to explain myself to you."

"You're right, you don't. But you're going to have to start explaining yourself at some point, because sooner or later everyone in your life is going to get pretty fed up with the response that you just get to do whatever you want, whenever you want. We aren't asking for much, simply to be let in instead of locked out of your life."

"I'm staying here."

"Fine. Then I'll be staying at the hotel in town."

"For how long?"

"As long as it takes."

"I won't be seeing you around," Remy warned. "This isn't healthy for either of us. Please reconsider and go back home. Don't come up here again."

"I'm trying to do what is best for you, Remy. I'm trying to help. Let me help."

She deflected his patronizing remark and changed the subject. Anything to just get him to leave. "Do you need a ride back into town?"

"No," he said. "I'll walk." He spun on his heel and stalked off. Clearly their interaction hadn't gone how he had envisioned it.

Remy watched him disappear down the dusty road, feeling a mixture of relief and more than a little bit of regret. *He'll forgive me for this someday.* He had a right to be angry and frustrated with her right now.

She searched through her grocery bags, leaving them where they sat on the moped, except for the wine. From her purse she pulled out her trusty bottle opener and went to find a shady spot. The rest of the work today could wait. Emotional exhaustion had melted her bones, and her brain needed a break.

This was a new tradition—every three days Remy

would buy a different bottle of red wine in her never-ending search to find the magical bottle again. So far, she hadn't had any luck, but it wasn't for lack of trying. Even though the first sip always disappointed, the rest of the bottle went down smoothly. Over the past few weeks she'd had the opportunity to try some truly spectacular vintages.

I so deserve this, she told herself, and popped the cork. Taking swigs from the bottle, she watched the shadows lengthen and the pain in her heart began to ease. The afternoon heat lulled her into a meditative calm as she tried to forget. Her thoughts turned to the village, and while she wondered if Jack had made some good points after all, the view in front of her gradually began to shift.

The crumbling wall at her back grew smooth and hard, and the uneven pokes into her spine disappeared. Dirt under her butt turned into soft grass. Deep ruts from wagon wheels drew the route through the village, highlighting the roads most traveled. The main house directly across from her transformed. Shutters were thrown open and sheets fluttered in the soft breeze. The front door was painted a shocking bright red.

Remy stood up and swayed, clutching her head. *How much have I had to drink?*

She stumbled farther, and rounded the corner to see the mill, astonished that the windmill was turning. The wind wafted the scent of freshly baked bread from the bakery.

It's like a movie set. Perfectly charming, but totally empty. A ghost town that lacked anything real. Open-mouthed, Remy took it all in, amazed to see her dream for the village come to life. Her vision had been a bit more modern, but some of the details, down to the red door on the main house, were pulled from her mind's eye. At the same time, it felt wrong. The cold quaintness of it all chilled her. She felt a shiver run down her spine.

Look at how beautiful I can be, the village seemed to say to her. *Stay with me. Be with me. Fix me.*

All thoughts of Jack and her inner turmoil disappeared as Remy wandered like an almighty being through her creation. Was this the village in its former glory? Had she created this, or was the village telling her how it wanted to be?

Feeling more than a little spooked, Remy picked up her pace and headed for the orchard. *I'm just drunk. None of this is real.* A walk and some fresh air would do her good, and by the time she came back, the village would look the same as it had through sober eyes.

Her feet remembered the path's twists and turns to the cliff, and soon she was running. Resisting the urge to look back at the village to see if it had returned to its dilapidated state, she kept her eyes straight ahead. Part of her didn't believe her feet would stop in time, and the other half of her urged her to go faster anyway.

Weaving through the orchard and the underbrush, Remy blazed her trail like a wild animal. Her heart threatened to break out of her chest. An athlete, Remy was not. She swallowed back the urge to vomit as she pushed her body as far as it would go in its current state. *I'm never drinking again,* she promised.

A shadowed figure stepped in front of her, and though Remy tried to put on the brakes, her momentum carried her directly into them. She slammed into a warm body at full force, and it knocked her backward.

She tried to say "Ow!" but all the air had escaped her lungs.

Dazed, she stared up through the trees at the late afternoon sunlight dappled through the leaves. Everything was spinning. She closed her eyes against the brightness, and her last thought was wishing that she could have kept running forever.

Chapter Four

When Remy opened her eyes again, she didn't recognize where she was, but the headache was familiar—wine hangover. There was nothing else like it.

Shit. What was I thinking? Remy remembered being confused and upset while drunk, and somehow she'd had the bright idea to go jogging to sober up. "I guess it worked," she groaned, and sat up. It had probably been the combination of her exercise and her impromptu nap. *But how exactly did I end up sleeping in the dirt?*

The outline of a man stepped into view. "Damn it, Jack, I told you to *go away,*" Remy said. Obviously, her ex-husband had gotten turned around on the singular path that led to town and ended up walking in circles around her property. The man could organize a stock portfolio in mere hours, but God forbid anyone give him a map or directions.

"I swear to God, Jack, I'm done having this conversation."

"*Buenas tardes, Señora,*" the man said.

Okay, not Jack. Just a strange man on my property. Don't panic. "Who the hell are you?" Remy said. She refused to be afraid, even though the sun was about to go down, this man had knocked her out, and there was nobody else around for miles. She struggled to her knees, hoping it would make her look and feel less vulnerable than being slumped on the ground.

The man bent down and extended a polite hand. "*Lo siento,*" he said. *I'm sorry.* The words translated themselves in Remy's consciousness without a pause. *Huh, maybe my complete Spanish immersion is starting to work.* That thought gave her some comfort as she eyed his hand warily.

It was strong and tanned, though the remnants of old cuts had left a chaotic pattern of white scars. A laborer's hand. Her gaze followed up his arm, where he was wearing a somewhat billowy white shirt, open in a V at the chest, and a plain vest. His hair was a riot of dark curls, surrounding a lean, sun-weathered face. When Remy's eyes finally saw his, she relaxed just a bit. His warm brown eyes held nothing but concern as they looked at her.

"What are you doing on my property?" she asked, but took his proffered hand, and he hauled her to her feet. She swayed a bit, feeling the effects of her drunken afternoon more heavily than usual. When she felt steady enough, she let go.

"You must have hit your head hard," he answered. "Are you lost? Is that why you were running?" Again, Remy understood him perfectly, even though she was pretty sure he wasn't speaking English.

"I apologize for the collision," he said, giving her a little bow of his head. "I was on my way up from my beach walk. It was my fault; my head was lost in the clouds."

Did he just say beach walk? "Can you show me how to get down there?"

He tilted his head. "Simply follow the path. It is

steep, but take care and you will be safe. I can escort you, if you wish."

"I looked and looked last time I was here, but never found a way down."

"Then I will show you myself," he said. "Forgive my rudeness, I have yet to introduce myself. My name is Bieito."

"Nice to meet you, Bieito. I'm Remy." She held out her hand, and Bieito seemed surprised. He took it gently in his own, but Remy gave it two firm shakes. His eyebrows shot up.

"You are not Galician," he said.

"No, I'm American. I just moved here. You haven't heard about me in town? You must be the only person who hasn't. Apparently, I've been the hot gossip around here, though I can't understand why. I'm really not that interesting, and mostly keep to myself—"

"You speak very strangely." Then, realizing what he had said out loud, Bieito blushed. "Pardon me. I have never met an American before. Your Spanish is very good, especially for a foreigner."

Remy laughed. "Okay, buddy. You don't have to suck up that much. I don't care that you're trespassing. I was just surprised to see you."

He looked confused, and Remy got the distinct impression that they weren't on the same page, much less the same book. Her unexpected guest was too polite to try to clarify their conversation, so he gestured to the end of the trail where the trees thinned. "Come, this way. I shall walk you down to the beach. A lady like yourself should not be unaccompanied so close to sundown anyway."

Once the pair stood side by side on the cliff, Remy

inhaled the salty smell of the bay and sighed with contentment. The breeze washed away the last of her nightmare from earlier, and the hangover loosened its grip.

Bieito had been watching Remy's face transform into pure joy. "I spend all day on the water, yet I still come down here to think. It is a good place to be alone," he said.

"You won't mind sharing your beach with a stranger?"

Bieito gave her a shy smile. "If it has been calling to you this much, then you belong down there as much as I do."

"That's exactly how I felt when I arrived at my village! It called to me, and I couldn't say no. It was the oddest feeling."

"Galicia is the place for miracles. Ask and you shall receive."

"That's what I am most afraid of," Remy muttered. "Now, where is this secret way down?"

Much to Remy's shock, Bieito pointed to a path carved into the cliff. It was hidden behind a boulder and began a few feet down from the edge. *How did I miss that before?* she wondered, peering at the treacherous descent. Driftwood poles poked up every few feet, strung with thick rope to serve as a flimsy guardrail.

Bieito jumped down, light as a cat, and turned to look up at Remy. "I will catch you," he said.

"Here it goes," she said, and stepped off the ledge. Just as he had promised, Bieito caught her waist securely and set her down, releasing her immediately when both her feet were planted. "That wasn't so bad," she said, smoothing her hair down and trying to appear nonchalant. Getting back up would be another story, and Remy suspected that it would include a lot of awkward scrambling.

"Your American style—it is much easier to move around in men's clothing, no?" Bieito observed.

"I'm a jeans and t-shirt kind of girl," Remy said, thinking it a bit odd that he would comment on her clothing. She knew she wasn't as dressed up or fancy as a lot of the Spanish women she had seen out in Ortigueira. Still, her outfits didn't stand out *that* much in town. There were plenty of other women who wore shorts and tennis shoes. Remy looked down at her stained work shirt and ripped jeans. Her original plan for the day had involved a lot more work with a wheelbarrow and a lot less work with her ex-husband, a wine bottle, and an unexpected 5k run. No wonder Bieito thought she was lost and most likely deranged.

"Follow me, and watch your step," he instructed, and started down the slope. Remy trailed after him, grateful that he kept looking back over his shoulder to check on her. He gave her a reassuring smile.

Bieito looked like someone who spent the majority of his time outdoors, but it was difficult to discern his age. Remy suspected he had to be around her own, though. He didn't seem like a cocky twenty-something, nor a middle-aged man who fought aches and pains as a normal part of life. There was a timeless quality about Bieito, a grace in the way he held himself. He was confident without the swagger, and seemingly polite to a fault. He didn't seem to mind that Remy had overthrown his plans for the rest of the day. He was, in fact, eager to help her out.

To fill the silence on their way down, Remy asked,

"Do you live nearby?"

"Yes, in the village up the hill, but I work out of the port."

"*Porto de Espasante*?" The place that Maggie had warned Remy about—rough fisherman in an industrial community. She couldn't picture Bieito there.

"Yes, my father, brother, and I." He seemed strangely reluctant to talk about his work, so Remy decided to change the subject.

"I'm an artist," she volunteered. "Or, was. Kind of. It's up in the air right now."

"An artist! Why are you not in Barcelona? Or even Madrid? Ortigueira is a strange place for one such as yourself."

"But it's the place for miracles, right? And I need a miracle."

They finally stepped into the narrow strip of sand, their feet disappearing as they sank into the softness. Bieito offered her his arm. "I got it," she assured him. Laughing, she kicked off her shoes and ran toward the water.

Icy, clear waves ran over her tired feet, soothing them up to her ankles. New energy flowed through her, and Remy wanted to immerse herself completely in the water. She longed to let it float her away on its whims and be controlled only by the tides. But she would have to be satisfied with a foot baptism instead, as her toes soon grew too numb to stand it any longer. She regretfully exited the water, but as a slightly new and improved version of herself. Bieito still stood on the shore, watching Remy splash back to him. He was clutching something around his neck.

When Remy reached him, she asked, "What's

that?"

"Pardon?"

"Around your neck. A cross?"

Bieito unclenched is fingers and held a necklace out for Remy to see. It was a pure white scallop shell on a leather thong. "This is the token of the travelers on the Way of Saint James. Surely you must have seen it before?"

That shell did look familiar, but Remy hadn't seen it on a necklace. "All Camino travelers wear it?"

"Most do. It shows that all roads lead to Saint James, no matter where you start. It represents the paths we choose to walk because we all have many ways of getting to the same destination. The important thing is to pick a path and see it through to the end."

"Where did you get yours? On the trail?"

He smiled at her. "I picked mine up on this very beach. It called out to me."

Leaving Remy to contemplate his words, Bieito walked up to where the waves crashed onto the sand and picked up a floating stick. Absentmindedly, he began to sketch something on the ground. Before Remy could see what it was, saltwater erased it.

"Do you draw, too?" Remy asked.

Bieito shrugged. "For my own amusement, sometimes," he confessed. He shoved the stick in Remy's direction. "You are the artist," he said. "Draw a picture for the sea."

Remy stared down at the tool in her hand, so similar to the thousands of sketch pencils she had held over the years, but it felt more foreign than it had any right to be. It was like she had suddenly lost the ability to walk.

She tried to empty her mind to conjure up her picture, to let her hands move freely as they brought an image to life, but she still saw nothing. There was a deep emptiness inside of her, a void that she could neither bridge nor fill. "I can't," she said, and dropped the stick onto the ground. Turning away from Bieito so he wouldn't see the tears in her eyes, Remy took a few deep breaths.

I'm acting like a child. Worse, she realized, *because a child can poke a stick into the sand. It shouldn't be such a big deal!* But it was a big deal, and only getting worse as the paralysis took hold of Remy more frequently. *Pretty soon I will be afraid to write my name.*

"I did not mean to upset you." Bieito's hand came to rest on her shoulder. "It was for fun. I apologize if I put pressure—"

Remy let out a harsh laugh. "No more than I put on myself, Bieito." She turned to look at him, not caring that her face was now red and blotchy.

"I will draw something to cheer you up," he declared. "I will make you smile again!" He bowed to her gallantly and picked up the stick. "Behold, the masterpiece," he said, and got to work. With a few quick strokes, it soon became apparent that Bieito was drawing some kind of animal. A little snout and a curly tail—

"A pig!" It was cute, almost cartoonish.

"I must not be as terrible as I feared if you can recognize it." As soon as Bieito said that, his drawing was washed away. "The sea gives me many chances to practice."

Remy thought about what it would be like to have

her paintings just disappear. To work for days or weeks, perfecting the color and brushstroke, only to be left with nothing at the end. What would she create if she knew it wouldn't hang upon a wall forever? An exercise in skill without reward. Each painting would stand alone and only exist for a brief amount of time. Wouldn't that make each piece all the more precious?

Where would my canvases go when they disappeared? Pictures in the sand returned to the sea. Maybe her creations on canvas would dissipate back into the universe, their energy dispersed into the cosmos, like her babies had been. She liked to imagine that her paintings would join her babies somewhere.

"I'll try your way," Remy finally said, hand outstretched for the stick. She stood on the waterline, ensuring that her picture would be short-lived. Closing her eyes, she searched for a good memory. She settled on her first morning after deciding to buy the village.

With hesitant strokes, Remy sketched a small figure, what a person might look like from far away. Then with ever-increasing confidence, her strokes created a cliff-side, adding depth and dimension with broader movements. Before Remy could decide whether or not the figure in her picture was about to jump, the cold salt water hit the back of her legs, and the picture was gone.

Remy felt a flash of irritation, and then immense joy. She looked up at Bieito with a big grin on her face. For a few successful minutes, she had lost herself in her picture. "You're right—this is fun."

"Did you draw what was in your heart?"

"I think I did." Triumphant with her tiny breakthrough, Remy threw the stick back into the bay.

That was enough for now. She also realized that this was the first time in years she had allowed anyone to see her draw. Usually she was only able to create behind closed doors. Bieito had allowed her to work in peace but was still an encouraging presence all the same.

"I am envious that you found your purpose in life," Bieito said. "You do what makes you happy."

"And you don't? You don't like fishing?"

He gave Remy a wry smile. "I try to find happiness. Sometimes little glimpses are enough. I am drawn to the sea, but for reasons other than fishing. Still, a man must support his family any way he can."

His unexpected statement jolted Remy. "You're married?" she asked, internally chastising herself for being so surprised. He was handsome and kind and sweet—of course he would be married.

"No, I'm not. But I help my family in any way that I can."

"And you help me." Remy meant for her statement to be a lighthearted joke, but it sounded more like a whispered confession. The romantic sunset splashed their faces with soft pink light, illuminating their serious expressions. Bieito stared at her, but neither one of them moved any closer. Remy broke first, looking away and clearing her throat. That snapped Bieito out of his trance and he shielded his eyes with his hand.

"The sun will be down soon. I should escort you back to your home."

"Oh, that isn't necessary. It is a long walk from the cliff, and you should get back before dark too."

"What kind of a man would I be if I let you walk home alone?"

Remy could see that there was no dissuading him, so after one last, longing glance at the stunning backdrop, she started her hike. Bieito followed behind her this time. Remy was sweating by the time she finally reached the top and prepared herself to scramble over the last few vertical feet. She felt Bieito's hands grip her waist and give her a boost.

Stepping back to allow Bieito space to climb up, she watched as he basically leaped hands-free onto solid ground.

"Which way to your lodging?" he asked. "Or, you can always accompany me to supper at my village," he offered shyly.

Remy shook her head. "I'd better be getting back. Raincheck? Maybe next time." She hesitated, wondering if she should ask her next question. "When can I see you again?" Time with Bieito would keep her mind off Jack.

"Sunday. Where can I find you?"

"Why don't you just give me your number?" Remy said, reaching down to pull out her phone. Looking down, she quickly typed in her passcode. When she looked up, Bieito was no longer in front of her.

What the hell? "Bieito? Bieito! This isn't funny." Remy searched her surroundings to see where he could have disappeared to. The only footprints up on the bluff were her own. *Maybe he went back down to the beach before saying goodbye.* She ran to the edge and skidded to a stop. There was nothing underneath her. The path was no longer there.

Pulse racing from her near miss, Remy rubbed her eyes to clear her vision. The sun had almost set, casting odd shadows that tricked her mind. It would be dark soon, and Remy had no desire to stumble back to the village without a flashlight.

Not in the mood to humiliate herself even further, Remy decided to preserve what was left of her dignity and walk away. *He probably didn't really want to meet up with me later. He was just being polite until he could slip away.* She wasn't about to go running after some man who couldn't be bothered to say a proper goodbye.

Did I give off a needy vibe? Remy wondered. It had been so nice to talk about art and life with someone her own age, who knew nothing about her past. And what had she done? Started crying because she couldn't draw in the dirt with a stick.

Squaring her shoulders, Remy turned her back and marched home. The rooftops of the village were the first to greet her, and she was relieved to find that they were back to the same almost-collapsed state she had grown to love. Passing the barn, she was thankful to see that there were no wagon ruts though the dirt. The bakery no longer smelled like fresh bread and had her wheelbarrow parked out front. There were no sheets hanging from the windows of the main house, but the next sight made her stop in her tracks. The confidence that Remy felt at regaining her sanity vanished.

The door to the main house was painted bright red.

****

Remy thought she was still hallucinating the next morning when she saw a familiar face come up the road. She had been sitting at her campsite drinking coffee and looking at the surrounding houses, pondering which structure would be least-likely to collapse on her if she decided to move into one of them. The main house had a lot of questionable beams holding up the second floor, so that was out. It needed additional help from a professional contractor. The smallest house, a cottage, really, near the bakery seemed like the most likely bet.

It was just big enough for one person, maybe two, to live comfortably. She pictured a front porch to incorporate some indoor-outdoor living space for the simple home. *Put a comfortable chair and a little side table for my coffee...Who am I kidding—the table will be for my wine. All that and a good book. It will be nice to have a roof over my head again.*

It wasn't that she didn't enjoy camping. She really had loved sleeping outside for the last few weeks, but she was living in canvas walls while surrounded by buildings that she already owned. The mid-day heat was beginning to drive her crazy, and stone walls would be cooler. *And an indoor shower—God what a luxury that would be!*

This morning it was finally decided—Remy would tackle the little cottage as her next big project instead of trying to spread her efforts around the village. She ignored the voice in her head that pointed out that she was just too chicken to go near the main house or the bakery after her "break from reality," to put it tactfully. It wasn't necessarily what she saw that scared her, but the fact that she had hallucinated something so *real.* The power of her mind frightened her in the way that it had completely taken over her senses, and she felt like she couldn't trust herself anymore. It was a completely different feeling than getting lost in a painting. Her hallucinations felt like a hostile takeover of her own being.

And speaking of hostile takeovers, one was coming

up the road right then. "That's far enough, Jack," Remy called out to him. "I told you not to come back."

"I came to help." Jack's deep timbre reverberated through the empty streets and reached Remy as loudly as if he had been standing right next to her.

Remy felt her blood begin to boil. What *was* it with Jack that he refused to take no for an answer? While it had been charming when they had been dating, albeit less so when they were married, his stubbornness had apparently reached new heights while divorced. He pretended to listen, nodded along, said all the right things, but when it came down to it, Jack did what Jack wanted to do.

And now he was here again, stomping all over her sanctuary. The last thing she wanted was memories of him imbedded in the construction of her fresh start. Yes, she had had a moment of weakness the day before in bringing him here, and yes, part of her still wanted him. But he had officially gone too far.

When Jack got close enough for Remy to see what he was wearing, she burst out laughing. He'd had the audacity to go out and buy brand-new work clothes and shown up looking like an overgrown Bob the Builder. His construction worker's costume even consisted of a mostly-empty tool belt with a sole hammer sitting jauntily on his hip. His jeans were pressed, and his boots didn't have a speck of dirt on them. He carried a hard hat in the crook of his arm, preventing any chance of hat hair.

When Remy finally regained control of her giggles, Jack stood right in front of her, with a frown on his face and hands on his hips.

"Jack. I just have one question—Can you fix it?

No. You. Can't."

"Remy..." Of course, he didn't get the joke.

She sighed. "Leave."

"Now just listen." Jack held up his hands as if to touch her, but wisely ran them through his hair instead. "I thought a lot about what you said yesterday."

I'll bet you did, Remy thought. *That's exactly why you're here this morning after I told you not to come back. You thought about it and did exactly what you wanted.* What Jack wanted was to swoop in and be the hero, the way he had dazzled a small-town girl so many years ago. But Remy was the villain in his story, not the damsel in distress; he just didn't know it. She sure as hell didn't need any saving from him.

"This village is important to you." *No shit.* "I should be more supportive. So here's the plan—we fix it up together."

"'No' is a complete sentence, Jack."

"Hey, I'm not trying to get you to move back to New York anymore, am I?"

"What do you want, a cookie?"

"I want you to take the help of a *friend.*" His emphasis on the word was the last straw for Remy. She didn't know whether to be furious or insulted that he thought so little of her intelligence. She was a master manipulator, something she wasn't proud of most days, but this effort was just pathetic.

If Jack wouldn't have an adult conversation with her, then maybe her actions would be enough to get the point across. Remy fixed him with an icy stare and turned her back on him.

"Where are you going?"

"By the time I get back, I want you off my

property." Remy straddled her moped, parked in the same place she'd almost crashed it yesterday. She jammed the helmet onto her head and started the engine, wishing it was a motorcycle or something that sounded the least bit intimidating. The whine of three horsepower would have to do the trick.

Leaving a dumbfounded ex-husband in her cloud of dust, Remy yelled over her shoulder, "Don't touch anything!" She was halfway to town when she looked down at the full basket of groceries perched on her handlebars. *Damn it.* She'd forgotten to unload everything last night after her encounter with Bieito. Due to the fact that she also still wore the sweats she slept in, hadn't brushed her teeth, and wasn't wearing a bra, Remy decided to avoid the most populated parts of Ortigueira.

Skirting down side streets with no real destination in mind, Remy tried her best to forget about Jack. *How long should I stay out?* she wondered. It depended on how long it would take Jack to give up his efforts at the village. *So, probably not long.*

As she whizzed past the northern part of town, a light purple building caught her eye. The parking lot was empty, as it was still very early. Remy pulled into a space and killed her engine. A sign read '*Biblioteca*'. *That's book store, right? Or library?* Either way, it would be a good place for her to kill some time. She could disappear among the stacks and read all day, and no one would bother her.

Remy started to get excited at such an unexpected but relaxing way to spend the day and bounded up the few steps to the entrance. She pulled hard on the handle. Locked. The hours of operation weren't listed, probably because everyone in the small town had them memorized. Remy would just have to be patient.

Stomach growling, Remy returned to her moped and dug through the basket. Moving aside wilted lettuce and an avocado that had become overly ripe in the sun yesterday, Remy found a couple of gorgeously plump oranges. Reclining on the steps, she dug into the peel, and the fresh scent of citrus erupted around her. For a moment, the fruity spray on her face felt like the spray of saltwater.

In all her confusion about Bieito's disappearing act, followed by Jack's unwelcome presence, Remy forgot to marvel at the fact that she had sketched. Somehow, talking with Bieito had loosened something inside of her that no one else had been able to. Even though he had left so rudely, Remy knew that they weren't finished with each other. She still needed him. He could be the key to pushing past her artistic block altogether.

Should I go to the port and try to find him? No, too stalkery. Maybe she could ask around town instead. She didn't know his last name, but Bieito didn't sound like a common name. Plus, she knew where he worked. That would narrow it down a bit.

As her strategizing kicked in, Remy felt ashamed at her selfish motives. *Be my friend because I need your help.* Yeah, that was a sure way to convince Bieito that she was a good person. Remy knew that ultimately he would become another casualty in her path of destruction. Perhaps he could sense that she was a ticking time bomb, and ran away yesterday before he was drawn in so deep he couldn't escape.

A little old man on a bicycle broke Remy out of her

negative thoughts. He gave her a small nod as he dismounted and chained up his bike. He started speaking to her in rapid Spanish, and Remy didn't understand a word of it. *So much for thinking I've immersed myself.* It turned out that her communication with Bieito must have been a fluke, or the result of hitting her head. Whatever the cause, she reverted to a wide-eyed freshman in Spanish 101 with this gentleman.

"*Hola!*" she said, stopping the man mid-sentence. His eyes grew wide as he realized she had missed the entire conversation. He gestured to the door of the building, pointing at her, and then back at the door.

"Yes, please!" Remy said, nodding and smiling.

The man's wrinkled face didn't crack a smile as he shuffled up the worn stone steps. He pulled a key out of a deep vest pocket, unlocking the door before gesturing to Remy rather impatiently. *Well, come on then!* he seemed to say. *It must be an emergency if you've been waiting for me all morning.*

The cool, dark interior smelled of musty paper. The man disappeared to turn on the lights, and in the flood of illumination Remy easily determined that she was inside the town library. He returned to see what she needed so urgently.

Remy cleared her throat. "Ah, sorry," she said. "Just want to look around." She pointed around all the stacks and threw her hands up in the air like, "I don't know!" If old men were in the habit of rolling their eyes, Remy was certain that's what he would have done. Instead, he shrugged and left her alone.

She meandered through the shelves until she found a very small section with English titles. Most were travel guides, though the entire collection of Harry Potter also took up some room among other world-famous titles. There was nothing that Remy hadn't read before, and she felt a little disappointed. She was hoping to pick up some DIY books on construction or gardening, and this little library didn't carry anything like that. At least, nothing in English. *Maybe I can find some in Spanish and follow the pictures. Like Ikea furniture.*

After walking over to what looked like the non-fiction section, she began pulling out hardback books at random and flipping through them. "Yes!" she exclaimed, then remembered she was in a library. The book she held in her hand looked like a cross between a history book and an architecture guide, a perfect reference for restoring old buildings. Tucking it under her arm, she continued her search.

Getting deeper into the history section, Remy knew she wasn't going to find any modern guides, but the hauntingly beautiful pictures drew her in. That same feeling of elegant melancholy compelled her to purchase the village. As she worked her way further back, there were even photos of the 1800s, gritty black and white snapshots of hard faces with laborious day-to-day lives.

These might be people who lived in my village! Remy thought, excited. The next book she picked up seemed more like a scrapbook. It was filled with yellowed papers covered in elegant script and long-faded newspaper clippings. This book was older than the rest. She carefully turned each page until two were stuck together in the middle.

Remy set the book down on a table, and inch by

inch peeled the pages apart. Between them lay a small sketch of a woman in profile. *Why, we could be sisters,* Remy thought, shocked. The artist had not signed their name. The picture was simply titled *La Americana.*

Sparked by a sudden desire to know more, Remy started pulling books off the shelves and looking for more clues. Anything that looked at all relevant to her, whether it was in reference to the village or the Galician people, she stacked on a table.

Remy was so absorbed in her task that she didn't notice the librarian standing in front of her until the old man cleared his throat. He held up four fingers. That appeared to be the maximum amount that Remy could check out at any given time.

Overwhelmed, Remy considered her teetering stack of over fifteen books. *Okay, the architecture one, the scrapbook, this one that looks like a history textbook, and one about the Camino.* That would be enough to get her started. In an epic version of Jenga, Remy extracted her choices. When the librarian glared from her to the leftover books, Remy got the hint and put them back to the best of her ability.

The old man's judgmental stare made her uncomfortable, so Remy decided to change her plan to be inside the library all day. Internet translations were only going to get her so far with these books anyway, and a Spanish friend was likely a better option. Seeing as the librarian was not going to be that friend, Remy wondered if she could get Sebastian to help her. *Or maybe Maggie!*

It would be the perfect excuse to get out of town while Jack insisted on staying in Ortigueira. She could also really use the older woman's advice about the situation, as well as what to do about Bieito. A longing for female bonding hit her, and Remy realized, startled, that she hadn't talked to Anita in weeks. Due to her best friend's blabbermouthing, Remy couldn't trust their conversations anymore.

Deep down, the person that Remy most wanted to talk to was her nana. With Nana, Remy could have told her everything, even the more confusing details of the past few weeks, and wouldn't have to worry if she sounded crazy. Her grandmother would have come up with a pretty good explanation for what was happening. And this explanation, though in no way scientific, would seem like the most obvious thing in the world.

Nana's advice had worked to protect Remy and others all those years ago, except for the occasional slip up when Remy let her mouth speak while disconnected from her brain. There was no cure for Remy's curse, but without Nana to guide her through it, Remy shuddered to think of the damage she could have unwittingly caused.

Nana would say that the village was cursed, too. Me and the village, quite the pair. It might be cursed, but it didn't feel evil, much like how Remy felt about herself. But now that Remy was supposedly older and wiser, she would have to come up with an explanation for the strange occurrences herself.

But on the subject of men, particularly handsome disappearing fishermen and ex-husbands, Remy felt that Maggie would be a good substitute for grandmotherly advice. She could go to Madrid by bus and spend much-needed time getting men out of her head with copious amounts of wine and sightseeing. Maggie would also have great ideas on how to restore some of the buildings, particularly advice on how to design her cottage.

Excitement bubbled within Remy as she darted outside to her moped. *I'll run home, pack a few things, not tell Jack where I'm going, and by the time I get back, I'll have a plan for my cottage, my books translated, and my head put on straight again.*

"Bye, Ortigueira!" she shouted as she whizzed up the road back to the village. However, as if by speaking the words aloud, she jinxed it.

Chapter Five

When Remy pulled up and didn't see Jack among the buildings, she breathed a sigh of relief. He hadn't lasted long, just as she'd predicted. Jack was stubborn, but also hated being uncomfortable, and the mid-day heat was anything but mild. Assuming that her ex had gone back to his hotel room for a siesta and air-conditioned comfort, Remy cheerfully made her way over to her campsite to pack in peace.

Shoving a few meager outfits into a backpack, Remy was done in no time. Life was so much easier when she didn't care what other people thought of her appearance. If she ended up needing nicer clothes, Maggie would be more than happy to loan her some for a night out.

Remy couldn't leave just yet, though. While she had accumulated a great deal more of her own camping gear over the past few weeks, the fancier items—like her water purifier and solar charger—were still on loan from Sebastian. It wouldn't do to ruin the stuff he had so graciously let her borrow, so Remy broke down her campsite and decided to stash her supplies in a building while she was away.

As she made her way down to the little cottage, Remy noticed that the wheelbarrow usually parked in front of the bakery was missing. *Damn it, Jack, I told you not to touch anything!*

After a brief scan of the square, she saw it parked in front of the main house, halfway filled with new debris. Her irritation started to morph into real concern when she saw Jack's helmet hanging from one of the handles. Of course, he wouldn't have actually put it on; it was just for show. But Jack also wouldn't have left it behind if he really did go back to the hotel.

"Jack? Jack?" Remy shouted at the house. She waited for him to swing the red door open so she could give him a piece of her mind.

There wasn't even the creak of a floorboard to indicate his presence. She inhaled through her nose, trying to stay calm rather than jumping to conclusions. The air was dead quiet, and Remy only heard the sound of her breathing.

She approached the house as she would a wild animal—with slow, even steps and her hand stretched out in front. Her palm touched the door, and when she pushed it inward it squealed in protest.

"Jack?" she whispered, feeling the need not to frighten the house any further. Remy rounded the corner and saw a thick layer of new dust had settled over the floor, barely covering size twelve footprints. Then she saw the actual boots themselves, poking out from underneath a two-hundred-year-old wooden beam.

Remy ran to him, coughing as she stirred up the air. *Please be alive,* she thought. A thick support beam had fallen from the second story and appeared to have knocked Jack sideways across the dining room. It lay across his thighs, pinning him to the floor, but that was the least of Remy's concerns.

The back of Jack's head rested on the fireplace stones, blood pooling underneath matted hair. *What do I do?* Remy squeezed her eyes shut to try and make sense of what had happened. She felt like she was moving in slow motion or watching a scene from a movie. It was all a dream—Jack wasn't really here. He was safe and at home, back in New York. He never came here, never saw Remy, and she never left him alone in the village.

He was pale as a sheet, and not moving. Needing to touch him but terrified of hurting him at the same time, Remy brushed her fingers across his cheeks. The jolt of his still-warm skin, with just the smallest hint of stubble, broke through her denial and ricocheted Remy from spectator to participant in a split second. It was enough to spur her into action.

"Can you hear me? Jack?" Her hands wandered to his chest, where its slight rise and fall indicated that he still lived. "Oh, thank God," she murmured. *But you have to wake up.* Breathing wasn't worth much of anything if he was brain dead.

A soft groan escaped his lips and gave Remy enough reassurance that he might regain consciousness while she dialed one-one-two. With surprisingly steady explanations, she conveyed—in English—to the emergency operator exactly what had happened. It was only at the end, when they assured her that an ambulance was on its way, did she start to break down.

"*Gracias,*" she whispered, and stayed on the line. Jack didn't make any other movements, but now Remy prayed that he would stay unconscious and protected from pain until the medical personnel arrived. Remy had no idea what to do if he woke up screaming in agony. She didn't think she had it in her to hold Jack down if he was thrashing or panicked. She couldn't move him, couldn't lift the beam, and couldn't do anything that might exacerbate a spinal or head injury.

Instead, she gave him what little comfort she could, reaching for his hand and squeezing it gently in hers. "I'm here," she told him. "You're going to be okay. They're coming to get you, and I won't let you go alone. I love you, Jack."

Jack had traveled all the way to Spain to hear those words from Remy's lips, and she spoke them because they were the truth. Had it been under any other circumstance, Remy wouldn't have dared to utter them in case Jack took it the wrong way. But she did love him, of course she did, and there was nothing more gut-wrenching than seeing someone you love so grievously hurt. Love was the most powerful language, and Remy channeled the emotion to Jack through their entwined hands and hoped that it would help.

Where is the ambulance? It should have been here by now. Hurry up, she thought. Was it just her imagination, or were Jack's fingers growing colder? Was that wheezing sound coming from his chest?

She couldn't wish. She didn't dare. But the words were on the tip of her tongue. *I wish for the ambulance to show up right now and for Jack to be okay.* A simple phrase would make everything better.

"The medical team is two minutes away, Remy," the emergency operator reassured her through speakerphone. "Are there any changes to Jack's condition?"

"No, none," Remy choked out. "The bleeding might be slowing down. I don't know. It's too hard to tell." Her voice rose an octave. "Tell them to hurry up!"

"Just stay calm, Remy, you're doing fine. Any minute now."

And then she heard the blessed sirens, their screech cutting through the air like an angel's song. Remy just had to hold on and be strong for a little while longer.

"Over here! Over here! We're in the main house!" Remy screamed until she heard footsteps on hardwood floor.

A uniformed team of four burst into view, carrying a stretcher between them. They spoke to each other in terse Spanish, and Remy couldn't follow the conversation. The EMTs set the stretcher down out of the way and approached Jack, stepping over the beam and being careful not to jostle anything. One man appeared to be in charge and said a few phrases into the radio attached to his lapel.

Nobody even looked at Remy; she might as well have been invisible. They were so focused on Jack that she had to scramble out of the way when they all knelt down around him at once. *Slow down,* she wanted to say. *What's happening? What do you see? Is he going to be okay?* The word "hospital" might have been included in their conversation, but the rest was a blur. Why wasn't anyone explaining anything to her?

The radio guy finally addressed her and barked a sharp sentence. Remy focused her dazed stare on him. "Huh?"

His lips tightened to a thin line and he pointed to the corner of the room. Remy got the hint—*Get the hell out of the way.* She was useless. There was nothing for her to do but watch.

With practiced movements, the team immobilized Jack's neck and body as best they could, and then positioned themselves to lift the beam off his legs. "*Uno, dos, tres.*"

Remy gasped when she saw his legs revealed. One knee was twisted backward, and the other ankle looked crushed. The EMTs must have given Jack a sedative of some kind, because he didn't groan or move once his body was free. His broken and mangled figure didn't cause the team any pause, because as soon as they set the beam down a safe distance away, they gently loaded Jack onto the stretcher and strapped him down.

Jack had always seemed so big. Larger than life, big money and big dreams, coupled with a booming laugh and broad shoulders. Jack was indestructible, her rock, even through the darkest parts of her marriage and depression. Nothing could take him down. To Remy, he still seemed twenty-two, no matter how old he got, but the village had snatched away this hero-worship of him in one afternoon. It revealed a vulnerable and older side of Jack, a man that could break physically as well as emotionally. He looked so small strapped to the stretcher. The lines in his face and the gray in his hair were thrown into sharp contrast by the bright blood on his head.

He was mortal. He might die. And it was all Remy's fault.

She followed the stretcher outside, where the EMTs loaded Jack into the waiting ambulance. Remy put her foot on the first step to follow him but was stopped by the female technician.

"No, I have to go with him," Remy said, close to shoving her way onboard.

The EMT hesitated for a split second while everyone else filed into the ambulance. It was a moment's pause, enough for her to see the desperation on Remy's face. "*¿Familia?*" she asked. *Are you* *family?*

"*Sí,*" Remy declared. "*Familia.*"

The woman gave her a quick nod and held out a hand to help Remy inside. Remy grabbed it. As long as she kept moving forward, she wouldn't have time to reflect on the accident.

Could that have just as easily happened to me? Remy wondered. Only it would have been days before anyone noticed she was missing. The vulnerability of her day to day life sent a shiver down Remy's already frayed nervous system. *Maybe Jack was right.* She had no business being up here all alone. Thoughts of her already reckless behavior—the drinking, running down cliffs, talking to strangers, sleeping outside—were put into a whole new perspective.

Remy had trusted the village to keep her safe, and it had done so thus far. But Jack had spent mere hours in the village and it almost killed him. How could the village have betrayed her like that? Sure, she hadn't wanted her ex-husband poking around there, and she had definitely wanted him gone as soon as possible, but that hadn't meant she'd wanted him *dead*. Jack had been at the wrong place at the wrong time, and the roof happened to fall on him. Was it pure luck or coincidence that Remy hadn't suffered the same fate? Did the village recognize those meant to be there and those who wished it ill will?

She shook her head. *The main house doesn't have motive, it doesn't have thoughts! It is a building, for God's sake.* But still, the thought of going back to the village, which had previously felt more like home than anywhere else, freaked her out. At that moment, she wanted to be surrounded by people, in a well-lit hospital, far away from that haunting red door. It was all too much to comprehend, and Remy felt that familiar desire to run away.

But she was in too deep now, and she especially couldn't abandon Jack. All plans of Maggie and Madrid were thrown out the window as the ambulance arrived at the biggest hospital in Coruña. Jack was whisked through automatic doors and past a threshold that Remy could not follow. Instead, she was directed to a waiting room where other wide-eyed family members sat in hope and silence.

One hunchbacked old woman sat with her eyes closed and a rosary clutched in her ancient hands, fingers running with practiced movements over the worn beads as she muttered fervently under her breath. Remy wanted to join her, to have the ability to ask and pray for things without risking a slip-up. To have fate completely out of her hands would be freeing, and to ask for something from an omnipotent power without waiting for backlash would be a gift.

All Remy could do, though, was help in whatever small ways she was allowed. *Phone calls,* she realized. *I need to let people know what happened.* She pulled out her cell phone and unlocked the screen, her thumb smearing a spot of blood that had congealed on the surface. The names in her address book stared back at her like strangers. Who did she trust enough to call? Most of the people in there were half a world away.

She couldn't call Jack's parents. They cut off contact with their son when he went to rehab for the first time, after his second drug arrest. Neither of his parents had attended their wedding, either, and Remy had met them a grand total of one time in all the years she spent as their daughter-in-law. Jack's grandparents had been more forgiving. They helped him with the auction house in its early days and gave him access to a substantial trust fund once he proved he wasn't going to blow it all on, well, blow. But they had passed away close to a decade ago, and Jack was an only child.

Remy couldn't call anyone in her family, obviously. They didn't even know that Remy had married Jack, much less divorced him and moved to Europe. She didn't have their contact information in her phone, though somehow her brain could recall her home phone number from twenty years ago. As ridiculous as it was, Remy couldn't help but feel that if she did dial those ten numbers, her mom would pick up on the other end. That thought clenched her stomach, and Remy started scrolling to distract herself.

My lawyer, she realized. *I can call my lawyer to tell Jack's lawyer what happened. He would know Jack's emergency contacts and who has power of attorney.* Remy placed the call and received the promise that Jack's lawyer would call once he had answers.

It didn't feel like enough. How could Jack and Remy, both in their late thirties, have no one close enough to call but their lawyers during a crisis? Remy needed someone who loved both her and Jack, someone who would have both their backs and fight for them. With a sigh, she scrolled up to the top to the *A*'s. Adding on a quick acknowledgment of total forgiveness, she clicked Anita's name. Her best friend had won again, and now was not the time to hold a grudge. When the chips were down, Anita would drop everything for her.

"Remy?"

"Neets, I need to talk to you. It's about Jack."

"Did he find you? I'm *so* sorry—"

"Anita. I need you. Jack was in an accident." Remy's voice cracked, and she tried to regain composure. "We're at a hospital in Coruña. Can you come? I just need…" Remy didn't know how to voice exactly what she needed, but Anita understood. By some miracle, Anita didn't even ask her customary one hundred questions and demand an explanation over the phone. Remy wondered how desperate she actually sounded.

"Tell me where and I'll see you soon."

When Remy hung up the phone, what was left of the adrenaline surged out. Exhausted, she collapsed against the plastic chair, which suddenly seemed like the most comfortable seat in the world. There was still blood on her clothes and her hands, but Remy couldn't summon the energy to get up and find a bathroom. *I need to be here when the doctors come out and tell me what's wrong,* she reasoned. *I'll sit right here until they let me go back and see Jack.*

But the minutes dragged into hours, and Remy's limbs and eyelids grew heavier. She hadn't realized she'd fallen asleep until a gentle pressure on her shoulder jolted her back into the world. Snorting with surprise, her eyes focused on a pair of scrubs standing in front of her.

"Is he awake?" she asked, once she could form words.

"No, *Señora*, but he has been transferred to the intensive care unit," the nurse said, in perfect English. Feeling relieved enough to weep that she had found someone to explain things to her in her native tongue, Remy said, "Oh, thank God!"

"The doctors have stabilized his vitals, but he has not woken up on his own. They need to run more tests and do additional brain scans." The nurse held out a clipboard to Remy. "Any medical information you can give us about the patient would be helpful. You are his wife, yes?"

"Ex-wife, actually," Remy said, looking down at the paperwork. "But I know his medical history."

"Oh, my mistake. I'm sorry. I can only give out patient information to family or next of kin." The nurse looked flustered and pulled the clipboard from Remy's hands. "Is there anyone else we can contact instead?"

Remy reached up and yanked the forms back down into her lap. "I *said* I can do it. I'm the only person here that Jack knows. And if this is going to help save his life, then you'd *damn* well better let me do it."

"But—"

Remy all but bared her teeth at the woman. "I could have filled them out by now. To start with, go tell the doctors that Jack is allergic to penicillin. I'll have the rest of his information ready for you when you get back."

The nurse scurried off while Remy filled in blood type, age, and medications, marveling at the fact that even though they were divorced, she could never "unknow" Jack. From allergies to childhood dreams to deep-seated fears, Remy knew there must be a reason why marriage was meant to last forever—it was just too damn hard to forget every detail of the partner you once loved.

Remy needed to make room to fit other parts of her

life, but Jack still took up far too much space. Both mentally and emotionally, he was just as entwined into Remy's personality as the most basic aspects of herself. The thought of how much time it would take to extract herself from his influence was overwhelming. She would one day have to realize who she was without him, but today could not be that day.

Today, she needed to be as close to Jack as she could bear to get him through this. Though it would be more painful for Remy later on, she needed to embrace their connection instead of trying to deny it. Would it weaken her enough to let Jack talk her into going back to New York? All that work, and all her weeks of distance and starting a new life—would it be wiped away, and eventually feel like a distant dream?

As if fate sensed her desperate need to feel grounded in her current life, Remy looked up from the paperwork just in time to see Sebastian burst into the waiting room, so out of breath it would have been comical had the circumstances been different. Waving his arms and full of his usual drama, he spotted Remy, frozen in her chair at the sight of one of the last people she ever expected to see in an emergency.

"*¡Señora! Madre de Dios, you're okay.*" He rushed over to her, taking her hand, pen and all, into his own. "It is a miracle," he babbled. "Rosa from the market saw the ambulance returning from your village, and she told Teresa at the salon, who knows my wife, who told me that you had been in an accident and were headed to Coruña. What has happened, my dear?"

Incredibly touched and a bit surprised at his concern, Remy relayed the incident to Sebastian. When she got to the part about the beam falling on Jack and his severe head injury, Sebastian clutched his heart and gasped. "And you found him? You thought he was dead, no?" His face paled, and he looked sick at the thought of stumbling across such a scene. "You are a very brave woman, Remy. It is because of you that he is here."

Remy knew that Sebastian meant his words to be comforting, but instead they engulfed her with another wave of guilt. She *was* the reason that Jack was here. Squirming in the hard seat, Remy changed the subject. "I had no idea word got around so fast in Ortigueira. Not that I'm not grateful for it today." She gave Sebastian a wan smile.

"Why, of course Galicians look out for their own," Sebastian said. "You are not alone here, now or ever. Word is spread to help those in need. I thought you might need a friend, and now that I know you are uninjured, I will ask you if there is any other way I can assist." He bowed his head, then straightened up again. "I know!" he said, and snapped his fingers. "You will come to my house for dinner and to stay the night. My wife will cook. She has been looking forward to meeting you for some time. She says she wants to meet the woman who embarks on crazy adventures. You inspire her, I think."

"Oh, Sebastian, that is very kind of you, but I think I'll stay here in case something happens. I just don't feel right about leaving Jack in a hospital all alone. There is probably a cafeteria here I can scrounge a semi-edible meal up in."

"I wish you would reconsider, *Señora* Remy. It will be a long night."

"It would be a long night regardless of where I

was, Sebastian," she said. "At least when I'm here, I feel a little bit more useful."

Sebastian seemed at a loss for what else to do. "I can sit with you," he offered.

"That's okay, I'll probably take a nap soon anyway. Thank you for coming. It meant the world to me."

Slightly cheered by Remy's admission, Sebastian realized he was being tactfully dismissed. At this point, Remy was too worn out to entertain anyone. "I will return in the morning, *Señora*. Please do not hesitate to call if your plans change tonight." He leaned over and gave her a spontaneous hug, seeming to surprise even himself. "I am truly grateful you were not in the accident," he said. "I thought to myself, 'No, it is not possible' when I heard the news. You belong in the village, I felt it the first time you saw it. It would not have hurt you. Yet, I did not suspect it would hurt you in a different way." He pulled away from the embrace looking troubled. "My prayers to you and Jack."

With much less fanfare than he entered the hospital, Sebastian left. The waiting room seemed to shrink without his presence, each family member returning to their own little world of worry instead of the blessed distraction of eavesdropping on a flamboyantly loud realtor. With no word of update on Jack's condition, Remy curled up in her chair and fell into a troubled sleep.

****

Around four in the morning, Remy's consciousness emerged from a foggy haze to realize that a doctor was speaking to her. "What?" she asked.

The translating nurse standing beside the doctor

answered for him. "Your husband is awake," she said.

Instantly alert, Remy was on her feet. "Can I see him? Which way to his room?"

The nurse and the doctor both shook their heads. "He will need to be monitored for a time, and then you can see him during visiting hours. But this is a good sign," the nurse reassured her. "Go home and rest. Come back later this morning."

Well, Remy didn't have anywhere else to go, and she wasn't about to wake up Sebastian and his family. She had no car, and taking a taxi all the way back to Ortigueira just to turn around and come back to Coruña a few hours later was pointless. But after the news that Jack was out of the woods, there was no way she could fall back asleep.

Keyed up and bursting with the odd energy that fills a person in the hours from two to five a.m., Remy paced the deserted hospital. Not even the sterile smells that trigged painful memories could bring her down at that moment.

Remy's hospital phobia started when she found out that not everyone who went into the hospital came out cured. That was what she had always assumed when she was a young child—that people went to the doctors when they got sick, and then the doctors could always make them better. The notion that people could go in and get *worse*, and then return to the outside world completely altered without so much as a "Sorry, we did the best we could," astounded Remy when Jameson returned home. From then on, a hospital was a place where bad things happened to Remy and those she loved.

Adding on the trauma of multiple pregnancy loss,

Remy had yet to experience an instance where it *wasn't* bad news at the hospital. She was honestly astounded that Jack had woken up. She quickly reviewed the events of the last eighteen hours. Had she accidentally slipped up? Had she made any sort of wish? She was sure she hadn't said the words, but had she tried to make any sort of bargain?

No, she reassured herself. It had been chaotic and scary, but she was almost one hundred percent sure that she hadn't been the cause behind Jack waking up. Which meant, miracle of miracles, it was the doctors, because it sure as hell wasn't Remy.

Jack is going to be okay. Tears streamed down her face as she meandered down unfamiliar hallways, not caring which direction she took. But now, more than ever, Remy was convinced that Jack needed to stay away from her. She was only good at bringing him pain and putting him in danger.

Maybe the right thing to do would be to stay and play nursemaid to Jack until he was healed enough to go back to New York. However, it would only entrench them deeper into each other's lives, and Remy couldn't risk more injury to Jack. He wouldn't understand, though. He would just assume that Remy abandoned him again when he needed her most.

Good. Maybe that will stop him from still chasing me, and he will finally get the point through his thick head, Remy told herself with venom, trying to ignore the sadness at giving Jack one more thing to hate her for. Hopefully this would be the final straw for him, and he would give up and move on. Remy could be the evil shrew for the rest of her life in his stories, as long as he was still alive to tell them.

Just then, her phone beeped with a text message. It was from Anita, and read

—Getting on a plane, I'll be there soon. It will all be okay. Love you.—

Over the past few months, Remy had forgotten that she was loved. She felt so alone all the time, wrapped up in her own life and drama. But this whole time, there were people—unexpected people—who loved and cared about her enough to drop everything in their lives to make sure she was supported. She had been ignoring the signs to wallow in her own self-interest. All of Ortigueira had been worried for her. Sebastian's family, too, and Anita. Jack had flown halfway around the world to prove to her that he still loved her.

And Bieito. That thought shocked Remy into a full stop. Bieito didn't love her, obviously. But he had shown that he cared, connected with her on a deeply emotional level to where it mattered most to Remy—in her art. She had been too insecure after their interaction, and brushed him off completely after a perceived slight, when really it had probably been a misunderstanding. She was surrounded by love in her new life, if only she could pull her head out of her ass long enough to appreciate it.

Remy felt her reserved exterior crack the slightest bit. *I can lean on people, and let them in,* she decided. After careful deliberation, Remy sent Anita back a simple text—*You are a true friend. I can't wait to see you. All my love.—*

Remy found it was actually true, too. She couldn't wait to see Anita, though it could have been under better circumstances. As far as Anita gossiping about her personal life, well, that was water under the bridge now in the face of such an important time. Though Anita had her faults, she could always be counted on as Remy's waiting room person.

Remy's growling stomach finally stopped her pacing feet. The hospital cafeteria was still dark, and seemed to follow the trend that no self-respecting cafe in Spain ever opened before nine a.m. If she wanted to get something to eat, she had to track down a vending machine. A couple wrong turns later, and Remy accidentally exited the hospital and found herself stuck outside.

The bright morning sun burned Remy's retinas. It seemed far too cheerful—mocking, even—in contrast of where she currently stood. Remy tried to turn around and go back inside, but questions kept popping up every time she tried to enter.

What could she say to Jack when she saw him? *I'm sorry* wasn't nearly enough. The more minutes that passed, the more anxious she grew. Visiting hours had to have started by now. Was he wondering where she was? Was he even cognizant of his surroundings? Could she face a one-on-one conversation with him about what had happened? Did he blame her for it all?

It is too hard to go back to him once I've left, Remy realized. She had been brave before, coming with Jack to the hospital and waiting for him all night. But it seemed like her dawn walk had done more than clear her head—it had stripped her of her courage. Now she was filled with too many doubts in herself to handle the situation alone. So Remy took the coward's way out, and waited. Anita's plane would be landing soon, and then she could act as a buffer between the former spouses.

Remy's head snapped up at the sound of squealing tires on asphalt. A taxi came barreling into view, heading straight for her. The car had hardly stopped when the side door flew open. A bright pink suitcase was thrown out of the back seat, landing with a thump on the asphalt. It was followed by a neck pillow, a bouquet of flowers, and a floppy designer purse. A set of sky-high heels hit the ground next, with a true force of nature wearing them. Remy could almost feel the impact reverberate through the parking lot to where she stood. A head of glossy brown hair popped up over the door frame, and then a set of giant sunglasses.

Reinforcement was here, and earlier than expected.

Chapter Six

Anita slammed the taxi door shut and held out her arms. "Remington! Baby girl, come here."

This was Anita's element—taking control of any situation and giving her clients exactly what they needed. Today the role called for supportive best friend with a heavy dose of sympathy. This was the same Anita that Remy had called on during her medical issues. It was odd, though, not being the patient for once, but this was the energy that Remy needed redirected toward Jack.

As Remy fell into Anita's embrace, she felt her autonomy disappear and mentally gave herself over to her friend. Finally, a person to give her directions and the chance to turn off her brain. It was just in time, too, seeing as Remy had gotten herself stuck in a guilt spiral in the parking lot. She couldn't leave the hospital, but her feet wouldn't let her go back inside.

Anita pulled away to grasp Remy by the shoulders. "First things first. How are you? You look terrible."

"Yes," Remy agreed. Autopilot was bliss.

"We won't hash out the past month; now is not the time," Anita said, and Remy nodded along mutely. "How is Jack doing?"

"He's awake. Or was awake. The doctors told me at four o'clock this morning."

"And you haven't been in to see him?"

Remy just stared at her like a deer caught in the headlights. "All right, then." Anita clapped her hands together once. "Baby steps. Let's get you inside." She looped her arm through Remy's, and they started toward the building. "Oh shit, my bags!" The agent turned back toward the tower of color sitting on the black parking lot. "Any valets here, by chance? Oh well, there has to be some place inside I can stash them for a little while, right?" Anita flipped her hair and gathered her things. Knowing Anita, she'd recruit some poor young intern to guard them for her.

As if begging not to be left behind, Anita's phone started ringing. She pulled it from her giant purse and hit "ignore." "They can wait. It all can wait. I'm here for you, as long as you need," she promised. "Now, who do I need to yell at so they take us to see Jack?"

If Anita found Remy's silence disturbing, she didn't show it. She was more than happy to fill the silence with whatever popped into her head. A stream of consciousness ran out of her mouth with no filter, bathing Remy with a pleasant numbness. When Anita instructed her to "Wait here," Remy obliged, trying very hard not to think about the fact that she was inside the hospital again. At least she didn't have to navigate on her own anymore.

"They're letting us back now," Anita said when she returned, appearing out of nowhere. That was enough to jump-start Remy's emotions again, and numbness was replaced by terror.

"I can't," Remy whispered.

"I'm coming with you," Anita said, and took Remy's hand. "Thinking about it just makes it worse. It's the anticipation, you know. You've built it up too much in your head. I don't know if you know this, but you tend to do that." Anita cocked an eyebrow at her, and Remy read the humor in her face. That was how Anita operated. She believed in jumping off a cliff and figuring out how to fly on the way down. Anything else was just a waste of time. Her motto was that life happened too quickly for hesitations. That was what made her such a good agent. Anita's confidence had gotten her everywhere in life and was always the fool-proof way to open doors that were locked to everyone else. Anita had sold Remy's first major painting with a similar strategy.

They were perfect for each other, really. An artist that nobody would take a chance on, and an agent who was looking for her first client at barely twenty-one years old. At first, no one took them seriously. But Anita charmed her way into a charity event auction and submitted one of Remy's most unique pieces, one that had failed to find a home among traditional buyers in the previous months.

People didn't necessarily want a painting entitled *Dead Dog Living* hanging up in their foyer. Remy's brushstrokes and style were too wild and untamed, her use of color was too jarring, and the painting defied any genre category. A "childish nightmare" was how one critic described it.

People felt unsettled when viewing Remy's early work. There just wasn't a market for what Remy and Anita were trying to sell. It wasn't political, it wasn't a statement piece, and it wasn't about technology or counter-culture. Nobody could connect with Remy's art because they had no foundation for common ground. Remy painted with her own unique perspective on the universe. Of course, she saw things differently than other people did, considering she could alter her reality with just a simple sentence. The burden of maintaining the karmic balance fell squarely on Remy's shoulders. That belief transferred over into her paintings and left those who viewed them feeling off-balance and deeply unsettled.

But for Anita, who was determined to make a name for herself finding the next big thing, Remy's style was a revelation; she just had to make other people see it. Anita loved the odd, empty feeling when she looked at Remy's paintings, like she was being left out of a secret. Any assigned value was in the eye of the beholder, and Anita needed to make rich people see the value in being comfortable with the uncomfortable, and that included a painting of a dead dog. All Anita needed was the right audience to launch Remy into the New York art world. Go big or go home was the only strategy she had, and the agent bided her time until she found her opening at the annual charity auction for the New York Foundation of the Arts.

If there was any chance that Anita could sell Remy's painting at top dollar, it was there. They just had to have one good sale and the rest would follow. Done correctly, the one foot in the door would be enough to pique the interest of the rest of the private collectors and make Remy's paintings an exclusive commodity. Done incorrectly, *Dead Dog Walking* would sell for a few hundred dollars, just enough to raise a little money from a sympathetic person who wouldn't even bother to take the painting home with them, forever creating a black mark next to Remy's name.

Most artists wouldn't put their faith in a newbie agent to have the connections to launch a career, especially one younger than the artist herself, but Remy was just happy to have someone else around who appreciated her work. It made her feel less crazy and alone, and Anita soon became Remy's closest friend in an unforgiving industry.

Remy's painting actually ended up being the most bid-on item of the night, thanks to a mysterious bidder in the back who kept upping the price. Once he started in on the offers, it seemed like everyone else in the audience wanted to get in on the action. Remy looked around the room in amazement as the auctioneer slammed his gavel on the final price—one hundred and seventy-five thousand dollars. Anita shrieked and threw her arms around Remy, causing more than a few stares their way, but neither woman cared. It was later that evening, during the cocktail hour, that Remy met Jack. The universe had decided to make a lot of things in her life collide that night.

And now, just as Remy had entrusted Anita to hold her hand while navigating her first big break, she trusted her best friend to keep her from falling apart as they approached the next scary hurdle in Remy's life.

While they navigated the bustling hallways, Remy kept reminding herself that there was nothing to be afraid of because she had nothing to lose. She had already lost Jack as a partner and had insisted that he leave her alone. But seeing him so broken would be a new and raw experience. Squeezing Anita's fingers like a lifeline, they entered the room.

He was asleep. Remy let out a sigh of relief and sagged against the door frame.

"What do you think? Should we wake him up? Let him know you're here?" Anita asked, looking a bit let down that the dramatic moment between Jack and Remy had been postponed. She'd come thousands of miles to witness it, after all.

A thick gauze wrapped around Jack's head, and purple bruises on his temples blossomed out from underneath the bandage. Small scratches raked bright against his pale face, but his expression remained serene. He didn't appear to be in any pain, and Remy gave a silent thanks for morphine. Tubes connecting to IVs and monitors spiraled out from him in every direction. The rest of Jack's body was covered by a blanket, though Remy could guess that damage to his legs was severe due to the bulky hints of what lay underneath.

"He needs to rest," Remy said. He was safe here, and in good hands. She didn't feel like the one who had to be solely responsible for keeping him alive anymore. Everything was under control. Anita was here, Jack was healing, and nothing truly disastrous had happened. Remy felt like she was finally waking up from her nightmare.

"He will be confused for a little while." A voice behind Remy and Anita made them jump at the same time. "But hopefully within a few days, he will regain most or all of his cognition and memories. There was not any lasting damage that could be seen on the MRI, but concussions are still serious."

Remy turned to face the doctor, the same one who had given her the good news at four in the morning. "Thank you—" she started to say, but the doctor barreled on, clearly in diagnostic mode.

"The damage to his head was what we were most concerned about, and he has a long road to recovery ahead, including physical therapy for his legs. His right leg was shattered from kneecap to ankle. He will require additional surgeries to regain full use of it. His left leg fared better, a clean break at the ankle, but there was some tendon damage—"

"How soon until he can travel?" Anita interrupted. "I mean, no offense, but it would probably be best for Jack to be seen by doctors in the U.S., right Remy?"

"I can't think that far ahead now, Anita. Jack might not be comfortable with that. Look at him; he's hardly even responsive." Though Jack's eyelids had flickered when the doctor had come into the room, they didn't open. "He doesn't even know we're here right now."

"I'm just trying to do what's best for you both," Anita said. "And I think that would be getting the hell out of here and back to New York as fast as possible. They have the best physicians in the world. This is why you had me come out, right? To have your back?" Anita turned back to the doctor, who had kept his calm and professional composure while being interrogated, but now looked more than a little irritated.

He spoke again. "Recovery will be a slow process, like I said. Are you a family member?"

"I'm Remy's sister."

The doctor gave them a dubious once-over. "Jack should really only have one visitor at a time…"

"I'll sit here with him while you talk to the doctor, Remy," Anita announced, already crossing the room to Jack's bedside. Remy was surprised but followed the doctor out into the hallway.

"Jack was very lucky you found him when you

did," the doctor said. "He lost a lot of blood. It was touch and go seeing if he would wake up—"

Remy's heart started to pound, and her vision blurred. *My fault.* The guilt came back with a roaring vengeance. *I shouldn't be here. I need to stay away from Jack.*

"I, uh, have to go to the bathroom," Remy mumbled, and pushed past the doctor, trying her hardest not to sprint down the hall. *It's too hard to breathe in here.* The walls were closing in on her. She needed to get some fresh air before she could tackle the logistics of Jack's treatment.

But Remy's feet had other ideas. They carried her at a run once she burst out of the hospital doors and pounded down the sidewalk. *Have to get away,* a voice whispered. It was all too much. *Anita is there, he won't wake up alone,* her conscience reassured her. *You did all you could.*

When she started to think about turning around, her arm flew up on its own accord to hail a taxi. Only instead of telling the driver to take her back to the hospital, she gave him the address of the village.

"Ortigueira?" the driver asked. It would be a substantial fare.

"*Sí,*" Remy said, her mouth forming the words while the angel on her shoulder yelled at her to go back to check on Jack.

Home. Remy needed to know if the village would still feel like home after Jack's accident. Her happy place had been tarnished, and she didn't know if she could look at it the same way again. Would she ever be able to enter the main house? Would she feel jumpy and haunted as she tried to restore the village, waiting for another roof to cave in on her? The only way to know was to go back. Then, she would know if she had to return to New York with Jack and Anita.

As the taxi wove its way up her driveway, raindrops spattered the windshield. The sky grew overcast and gray, matching Remy's somber mood. When she paid the driver and got out of the car, Remy waited a beat before turning around to take in the sight of her property.

It felt like it was weeping with the rain. Depressed and wet, the buildings had never looked drabber. Though it was the last place Remy wanted to go, she forced herself to approach the main house. The red door was still open, as if hopeful of her eventual return.

A thump followed by a muffled curse made every hair on Remy's body stand up. *Another trespasser? Doesn't everyone know that this is my village now?* For the time being, at least. Unless she decided to chicken out and flee to New York.

"Who's there?" Remy demanded. "Being here is a good way to get yourself almost killed."

"Remy?" The voice came from the same room as the accident. The last room in the world that Remy wanted to go investigate.

"Sebastian? What are you doing here?"

"I thought you would be at the hospital, *Señora.* I wanted to finish before you saw…" Sebastian's voice grew louder as Remy approached the room. She rounded the corner to see a very dirty real estate agent, clutching a dripping mop.

He looked from Remy to a sudsy bucket and back to her face. His cheeks flushed red, and he explained, "You should not have had to clean this up. I did not want you to return to this horrible…" He couldn't think of the right words to describe the immense pool of blood that had been left behind and tracked through the house on the EMT workers' shoes. Remy vaguely remembered what it had looked like—a scene from a cheesy horror movie, with an overly enthusiastic director who loved fake blood. Only it hadn't been cheesy, and you couldn't fake the vomit-inducing metallic smell of the real thing.

"I can't believe you did this for me, Sebastian." Remy could only imagine how much of an ordeal it was for her friend. It was probably a bigger job than he had anticipated. Most of the blood had already been cleaned up, save for a few shoe prints in the corner that were Remy's own.

"I was thinking you were at the hospital this morning. Is Jack awake?"

"He's out of the woods for now. A pretty bad concussion and broken leg, as well as a broken ankle, but he's getting better. No long-term damage."

Sebastian's face broke into a grin. "That is wonderful news! Did he speak to you? Did he say what happened?"

Shifting her weight back and forth on the balls of her feet while she hesitated, Remy finally answered. "No, not yet. He was asleep when I left. But the doctors told me he had woken up and would be okay."

"Ah." Sebastian looked confused, but too polite to pry further. Remy could tell he was wondering what she was doing back at the village. "I can drive you back to the hospital," he offered. "I am almost done in here."

"My friend from New York flew in overnight. She is with Jack at the hospital now. He isn't alone or anything," Remy rushed to explain.

Sebastian held up a hand. "No need. I am just a phone call away if you decide that you need anything else."

"You've already done so much," she assured him. "Really, it was more than I could have asked for. Thank you for thinking of this." She gestured to the damp floor. "I honestly don't know what I would have done about it on my own."

Now that the visceral reminder of the accident had disappeared, it didn't seem as terrifying being in the main house as she would have thought.

Already Remy could feel her memories restructuring themselves in order to protect her from the pain. It had been the same with her miscarriages. A blur of blood, pain, cramping, and screaming as that potential little life met an undignified end in the bathroom. The details always became hazier as time went on, until months later she would decide that she should risk it all again because *what if this time it works out?* And in trying again, she would block out everything that had traumatized her the previous times.

So out of habit, she didn't try to fight the numbing calm as it took over. She embraced the comfort that it gave her and accepted that the worst was over. Remy recalled an article she read about how the best time to travel was immediately after a terrorist attack. Cities and airports were the safest then, because citizens were on such high alert. The worst time to get on a plane was when everyone was lulled into a false sense of security. Remy's security had been stripped from her, but the debt had been paid. Whatever karmic balance she owed, it would be quite a while before anything bad like that happened again. The village would be safe for a while, at least, if it adhered to this bizarre logic. Evidence to the contrary screamed at her, but the longer she spent in the village, the quieter the screams became, until they were just little whispers in her mind.

Sebastian peered at her, witnessing the change that dropped over Remy's face. "Do you still want to stay here?" he asked, point blank. "My wife has offered the spare room in our house—"

The words left her mouth of their own accord. "Yes. I will stay in the cottage, though. This house isn't safe yet, as we all now know." Her heart spoke, overruling the last of the fear and apprehension in her brain. *I don't belong anywhere else.*

"Are you sure that you will not be frightened? And it is a long way from the hospital."

"It won't be an issue," she said, refusing to explain further. "I'll meet you back outside. I have some of the camping gear you loaned me." Giving the room one last cursory glance, almost disinterested now, Remy exited the house.

The pile of supplies was exactly where she had left it while packing the day before. She had dropped the camping gear right beside the wheelbarrow due to her crisis en-route to the cottage. It was soaking wet from the rain. Thankfully, the tent had been on top, and had deflected much of the water from the gear underneath. Remy took it up onto the sheltered front porch and shook out the light canvas. While organizing the stack, Remy realized that she had left some very important books that were *not* waterproof on the ground.

"Shit!" Looking closer, she was relieved to find that they were only a little damp and the pages were slightly wrinkled, so she set them standing up to air out. The historical scrapbook one, however, looked like it had received the brunt of the damage. Remy groaned, wondering how much trouble she was going to get in with the cranky librarian when she tried to return it. Somehow, she didn't think that "My ex-husband almost died" was going to fly as an excuse with him.

Cautious fingers turned the pages, and a few of the letters peeled off. Some of the ink ran, but most of the book was still legible. *Or it would be, if I could read Spanish.*

Sebastian joined her out on the porch, mop and bucket in hand. "You are sure you want me to take this back?" he asked, gesturing at the soggy pile. "You can borrow the tent for as long as you need. I think it would be better."

"No, staying in the cottage will give me the incentive to fix it up faster," Remy said. *And distract me from Jack,* but she didn't say that out loud. Anything to avoid going back to the hospital for a while. It used to be that she would paint to distract herself, and let the hours and days pass in the blink of an eye. Now, she needed a different way to become immersed in a reality other than this one, and translating a Spanish architecture book and pounding nails might be her only way to do it.

She held up her books to Sebastian. "I've got everything I need right here," she said. "If I have any translation questions, though, I'll call you," she promised.

Sebastian's eyes skimmed the titles. "I don't mean to offend, but I do not believe that a book about the Camino de Santiago is going to help you rebuild your cottage."

"Aren't you the one who told me that the miracles in the village are tied to the Camino?" Remy reminded him. "I'm going to need some miracle help to fix up my cottage, and the rest of the buildings."

"But the accident...I do not think that was a miracle from the village." Sebastian shuddered. "After all of this, maybe I was wrong about this place."

"I'll hire a crew for the structural stuff," Remy conceded. "But statistically, there shouldn't be another accident like that." Sebastian didn't argue with her but looked skeptical. "If you'll excuse me, I really need to organize some stuff. You know, before I have to go back to the hospital to see Jack," Remy lied, but Sebastian nodded in understanding.

"Do you want me to wait while you pack your bag?" he asked. "Then you won't have to drive your moped in the rain."

"Ah, no. Really, it's okay. I need to call Anita and see what she wants me to bring back for her, too. I might be a while." *Just leave,* she thought. She had done a good job of blocking the memories out, and Sebastian insisted on reminding her all over again. She didn't want to keep up the ruse of handling it all like an adult. Her growing irritation toward him was unfair, but impossible to stop. Forcing a small smile to her lips, she said, "Thank you again for cleaning up. It was very kind of you. You've done too much to help already."

The urgent need for Sebastian to leave began to overwhelm her, and she basically pushed him to his car with arms full of wet camping gear. "I'll call you later," she promised, "with an update about Jack."

Once Sebastian left, the rain immediately stopped.

Remy breathed in the smell of damp earth and stared up at the clouds, transfixed at their movement as the wind picked up and carried them away. The sun broke through suddenly, blinding Remy with a flash. "Ouch!" Broken from her trance, Remy squeezed her eyelids shut and felt the sting of salty tears on her cheeks. Rubbing her eyes to clear the spots that kaleidoscoped across her vision, Remy waited for the pain to dissipate.

When she was able to see again, she looked across her village to see, of all things, a horse and rider plodding along through town square.

"Hey!" she yelled from the driveway. The rider didn't appear to hear her at all, so she started speed-walking in his direction. "I said *hey!*"

Though the rider didn't react, the horse clearly heard her shouts. The plodding hooves started dancing and its ears flattened to its head. The rider grabbed onto the reins and spun the animal around.

"Bieito?" Remy asked. That caused the rider to snap to attention.

"Hello? Do I know you?" he called.

Remy jogged closer so that he could clearly see her face. "Remy!" he said, and a joyful smile broke out on his features.

"What are you doing?" she asked, confused.

"Taking Blanco back to the barn," Bieito said, as if it was the most obvious thing in the world.

"My barn?"

"I do not understand what you mean," he said politely. "But I have been searching for you on the beach these past days. I have been hoping to see you again. You left rather suddenly during our first encounter. And now you are here! Right in my family's village. I am very glad you have found me."

Remy felt a little flutter in her chest when she heard that Bieito had been searching for her, but as he continued talking, she felt her heart sink. He was a nice man, but obviously confused. *Just my luck, I always crush on the crazy ones.* Regardless, she could not let this unstable man stable a horse in her ramshackle barn. After what happened to Jack, Remy wasn't going to let anyone wander around her property.

"Where did you get that horse, Bieito?"

"He is mine. I raised him from a foal, when his mother rejected him. I ride him to the port when my father does not need him on our little farm. Would you like to say hello? I will make the introductions." In one fluid movement, Bieito dismounted. Running his hands along the horse's velvet nose, Bieito whispered into the animal's ear.

"Really, I think you'd better get him home—oh!" The horse bowed his head low in Remy's direction, making a graceful curtsy to the ground. Then with a snort, the horse tossed his head high and trotted off down the hill.

"Your horse is running away!"

"*Señora* Remy, do not worry. He is just following your instructions. You told him to go home!" Bieito gave her a teasing wink and offered his hand to her. Remy held it out, surprised when Bieito bowed much like his horse had, and his lips grazed the back of her hand. "I might have told him to leave us alone," he confessed. "Have you been thinking of me as often as I have thought of you? You are a hard woman to find."

Don't get flustered, Remy told herself. *Stay on track. Find out where this guy actually lives.* "I haven't been down to the beach of late, unfortunately. I've been busy with...out of town visitors."

"More Americans?" Bieito asked excitedly. "I told my brother and father that I had met an American painter on the beach. They had heard of no such woman, though, and teased me mercilessly for my fantasy. Just wait until they meet you!"

"And when can I expect to meet your family?" Remy asked, getting caught up in his enthusiasm despite herself. Bieito had a way about him that made everything else in the world fall away. Nothing seemed as important, and Remy found it harder and harder to question the logistics or reality of her situation the longer she was in his presence.

Talking to him made her want to throw caution to the wind and not over-analyze, so she found herself playing along that this was his home, rather than her own. Remy became lost in his face as he grinned and chatted, and the main square became a blur as they walked. He took her elbow and guided her over the ruts in the street, flattering Remy with his gentlemanly attentions. He was just as courteous to her as he had been on the beach, and Remy no longer questioned if he talked to her out of politeness rather than interest. His delight at running into her seemed genuine, and that in and of itself gave Remy a boost of confidence.

When he halted in front of the cottage, Remy squeezed her eyes shut. *No, no, no,* she thought, internally screaming. When she regained feeling in her diaphragm to gasp for air, she said, "What? How?"

"Are you feeling all right, Remy?" Bieito asked, brow furrowed. "It is nothing special. Just my home."

Am I on drugs? she wondered. "Pinch me," she

ordered Bieito.

"I could do no such thing!"

Much to Bieito's dismay, Remy pinched herself, hard. Hard enough to leave half-moons of red blood on the back of her hand. "Are you feeling faint? Come inside and sit down. You are very pale."

I'll bet, Remy thought, and allowed herself to be led inside without protest. The cozy cottage looked almost exactly how Remy planned to renovate it. The biggest deviation from Remy's open concept design was the fact that this version of the cottage was divided into three small, but tidy, spaces. It was simple but functional, with all of the old-world charm she could have hoped for. With the rustic exposed beams, the antique wood-burning stove, and the farmer's sink underneath the window, it looked like a page straight out of a *Homes and Gardens* magazine. *Farmer chic.* The kitchen had a thick wood table situated right in front of the fireplace. A door opened up to one of the bedrooms off to the side, which housed two twin beds and a wardrobe.

"It is not much, but it is home," Bieito said, as he watched Remy take it all in.

"This is your home? You live here?" Remy whispered, hardly daring to speak aloud. As if by startling the cottage, she could make it all disappear. "How long?"

"I've always lived here," Bieito said. "My father and brother should be home soon. Would you stay for dinner?" Bieito's eyes pleaded with her to say yes.

"All right," Remy agreed, silencing the part of her that told her to run. Her cottage didn't—couldn't—look like this in real life. But if Bieito was actually the sane one, what did that make her? Not ready to face that possibility, Remy decided that staying for a hot meal was better than questioning her mental state. Plus, she could get some great ideas on how to restore the cottage. Her version of the cottage? Bieito's cottage? She didn't know.

When Bieito motioned for her to sit and poured her a glass of wine to "restore her color" as he delicately put it, Remy gulped it down without tasting it. As the wine tingled in her stomach and through her limbs, Remy relaxed into the moment.

Wait a minute. Remy sniffed her glass and did a double take at the bottle Bieito had poured from. It couldn't be, could it? Tilting the glass up to her lips again, she swallowed the last drop, and the flavor exploded on her tongue. *My mystery bottle!*

"Bieito, where on earth did you buy this? I've been searching for it for weeks! What is the brand name?"

"Name?" Bieito shrugged. "It is local wine from the vineyard. Last year's harvest."

"It is incredible." Sticking her nose in, she inhaled deeply. "Truly amazing."

Bieito chuckled and handed Remy the bottle. "I was nervous to cook for you, but since you are so excitable about our wine, I do not think I need to worry about our simple fare."

"You'd better cook a lot if your food is as good as this wine," Remy said, pouring herself another glass and savoring it this time. After tasting it again, she recalled drinking all those other wines during her quest for this one. Not even the most expensive bottles had come close. "I need to stock up on this." Try as she might to pace herself, Remy found herself staring at the bottom of her empty glass yet again and reached to pour a third. It was addicting, and she couldn't help it. *Don't look like a lush in front of Bieito,* she reminded herself. But her host didn't seem to mind or comment as she sipped and watched him work.

As Bieito moved around the kitchen with ease, Remy wondered if all Spanish men knew how to cook, or if it was just because there wasn't a female presence in the house. "What are you making?" Remy asked, face glowing and warm.

"A surprise for you," he said, giving her a grin. "I like watching you enjoy yourself. You seem much more content than during our first meeting. Relaxed. You have settled into life in Galicia, then?"

Through her slight intoxication, Remy tried to remember what she had been so stressed about. *Jack. I was upset about my ex-husband.* But instead of remembering Jack's accident, Remy could only focus on those memories of her and Bieito at the beach. Drawing in the sand, watching the sun go down, feeling the waves lap against her feet... *There is no reason to be tense.* Being here, totally comfortable in Bieito's home, was the only thing that mattered at the moment.

"All of my worries are so far away," Remy answered honestly, and tried not to slur. Her eyelids felt heavy as she watched Bieito light the wood stove. Such a simple life, so full of content. This was what was important, not whatever was happening out in the real world. "Galicia is a happy place."

"For the moment," Bieito said, and opened his mouth to continue, but the front door slammed open.

A straight-haired, younger version of Bieito walked in, taking long strides and shouting back over his shoulder at a barrel-chested, graying man who followed behind him. They appeared to be mid-argument, talking so fast that Remy couldn't follow. Both were gesturing wildly with their arms, the younger man holding a loaf of fresh bread that looked dangerously close to being thrown across the room.

Then she saw that they were both smiling, and what she mistook for anger was actually good-natured bantering. Without glancing in Remy's direction, the pair clapped Bieito on the back and started unloading their rucksacks.

"It was about time you two came home. I thought you had gotten lost on the way. Not that I would have minded if you had," Bieito said, and began pulling fresh produce out of the old man's bag.

"What's that now?" the old man demanded.

"Turn around, Father."

Remy shifted in her seat and sat up a little straighter. "Hello," she said.

The old man's eyes widened, and he hit Bieito on the shoulder. "A special guest?" he asked.

"Father, meet Remy. Remy, meet my father, Afonso, and my brother, Lino."

Both men were starting at her with naked appraisal, until Lino remembered his manners when Bieito nudged him. Remy stood as the young man approached, and he leaned over and kissed both her cheeks. "A pleasure," he said. "You are the American that has captivated my brother so."

Remy laughed. "I'm not sure 'captivated' is the right word. I think rather 'stunned' or 'confused' might be more appropriate. Either way, it is nice to meet you. Bieito has spoken very fondly of you and your father."

"When did you arrive in our village?" Lino asked with rapt attention. He gazed at Remy as though he didn't believe she was real.

"I came to Spain about a month ago."

"We thought that Bieito was telling tales when he came back from the beach," Bieito's father confessed.

"You thought I made up a fantasy girl because I didn't want to go to the wedding with Isabella!" Bieito interjected.

Lino shook his head at his brother. "You've spun crazier stories before."

"I *did* see that smoking ship out in the bay!"

"Yes, yes, and it was the size of the entire village. And it had no sails. And it was as high as the cliffs. We've heard it before."

A cruise ship? Remy thought. *Why don't they believe Bieito saw a cruise ship? Are they that rare in the bay? They must get big shipments into the port all the time.*

By the time Remy opened her mouth to speak, the conversation had moved on. "You are staying for the wedding, yes?" Afonso asked.

"What wedding?"

"My wedding!" Lino said, blushing with pride.

Bieito laughed. "He finally convinced María to marry him. After asking, and asking, and asking again."

"I would have proposed a hundred times to win her over. She is the most beautiful woman in the world, the light of my life. I would not go on living without her."

"Always the romantic one in the family," their father said. "A wedding brings such joy and celebration. My wife and I had hoped for years that Bieito would marry, and never thought that Lino would be first, but…" He shrugged, and a flicker of sadness passed over his face. "I will live to see one of my boys marry and find happiness. That is more than I could ask for."

Remy turned to Bieito and was surprised to find that he wouldn't meet her eyes. He appeared deep in thought, staring at the kitchen counter as he continued chopping vegetables. "An eternal bachelor, then?" she asked.

But it was Lino who answered, "Only because his face frightens women!" That earned him a slap on the side of his head from his father. Still, he possessed a boyish enthusiasm that would not be snuffed out. "Remy, you must come to the wedding. Bieito will escort you."

"Oh, I don't know—"

"I will talk to María, and she will insist that you come. You cannot refuse the bride!"

Remy was torn. She had just met these people, and already they were inviting her to attend such an intimate event. She didn't know if Bieito even wanted her there, much less as his date. It would be completely understandable if he refused such a pathetic attempt at a set up. Hesitating, she waited for Bieito to jump in one way or another and let her gracefully accept or decline. "Well," she said, stalling. "That would be quite the honor. Tell me about your beautiful wife-to-be."

Lino launched into his tale of the woman who captured his heart down in Ortigueira, and how he couldn't wait to move her into the village so they could finally live together. He was apparently hard at work saving enough money for them to build their own little cottage next door.

"All three of you work as fishermen in the port, right?"

"I have been a fisherman for forty years," the father said, pounding his finger into his chest. "And I will one day die a fisherman, for the sea has half my soul. My late wife Catarina, God rest her, has the other half."

"And you say I'm the romantic one!" Lino said. "The obsession with the sea, you and Bieito both. I prefer to take my opportunities and set down roots on land."

"Bah! There is salt water in your veins. Less than your brother, maybe, but it is there all the same."

"I haven't been down to the port yet," Remy said, interrupting their blossoming argument. "I was planning to drive down soon." *And stalk Bieito, but whatever.* "It seems like such a fascinating cultural piece of Ortigueira."

"*Por favor, no Señora.* It is no place for a lady. There are many rough men and it is very unsafe," Lino said. "There are many travelers that come through looking for work. It is also a good place for people to disappear. Not like our village, where everyone looks out for their neighbors. It would be wiser to stay here instead."

Remy scoffed. "It can't be *that* bad. I can take care of myself."

"Now is not a good time, Remy," Bieito said quietly. "There is talk among the men, of discontent—"

"As there should be!" Lino said. "The idea that proud Galicians should be ruled by—"

"That's enough!" Afonso silenced his sons in one sharp phrase. "There will be no talk of such things in

115

this house. You know it is dangerous to even think of the changes that they want to bring about. I will not have my children involved in it. You will work hard, settle down, and live happy lives. Or I will stay alive forever to ensure it," he threatened.

"Yes, Father."

"Sorry, Father."

What the hell was that about? Remy wondered. She made a mental note to ask Bieito more about it later. She had to know whatever it was that struck such fear into this grizzled old man's heart.

"Supper is ready," Bieito said, serving up heaping mounds of steaming rice onto chipped ceramic dishes. To each plate, he added a seasoned whole fish and steamed green vegetables. Remy scooted her chair back to rise and help him, but Lino gestured for her to stay put. He took the plates from Bieito and brought them over to the table while Remy tried to get over the head rush that standing up had induced. *No more wine for me,* she thought.

Unfortunately, the boys' father had taken it upon himself to pour them all a generous amount of wine from an additional bottle that seemed to appear out of nowhere. *Well, I can't be rude,* Remy thought, and giggled out loud.

Who were these people, this entire family, who said they lived in her village? She sat among them as she would any neighbors, eating and drinking, and speaking Spanish of all things, though she wasn't quite sure about that last part. She wasn't sure how it all worked and how she was communicating with them, but she just relaxed and let it happen. *I should be more concerned,   more   worried   about…something?*

Questioning the logistics of it all? It was impossible to remember.

It felt like she belonged here, with these men, sharing their supper. There was no time or place outside the little cottage. The welcoming spirit inside this dwelling was strong.

It was unclear how long they all sat around the table, eating and drinking and laughing. Once the sun went down, Bieito lit a merry fire in the fireplace and they all continued where they had left off. Nobody seemed in any hurry to end the evening and go to bed, least of all Remy herself. Empty dishes were left on the table and there was no discussion about work the next day. Everyone was simply content to live in the moment and make it last as long as possible.

The flickering firelight wrapped around Remy like a hug, and her eyelids grew heavy. Just before she began to drift off, she wondered if there would ever be a time when she actually slept in a bed again. *The only sleep I've gotten in the past few days has been in a chair*, she realized. *But why is that, again?* Her brain was turning itself off, and she couldn't outrun the alcohol. Sleep washed over her, and the last thing she heard was Bieito's rumbling voice asking her a question, but it was too late.

Chapter Seven

Remy awoke with a gasp on a hard dirt floor. Someone outside was calling her name, but her dusty throat could barely manage a "Hello?" from inside the cottage. Her head throbbed and her tongue felt swollen and sticky in her mouth. Squinting against the bright light permeating dirty windows, she tried to get a grip on her surroundings.

There was no table, no food on kitchen counters, no brightly woven rugs on the floor. There was no Lino, or Bieito, or their father. The air wasn't filled with the smoky scent of burning wood and fish and wine. The only thing in the cottage was Remy, shivering on the cold ground, still her clothes from the day before, only with a hangover from hell.

She cleared her throat and tried again. "Hello?" she called, sitting up slowly.

"Remy?" The door pushed open and Anita walked in.

"Remy, what the hell?"

Self-consciously, Remy stood up and brushed the dirt off her clothes. Her hand reached up to smooth her hair, only to discover it was a tangled rat's nest.

"Have you been drinking?" Anita asked.

"Just a little," Remy lied.

Anita shook her head. "Look, I know it's been a terrible time, but you can't just go on a bender! Not with Jack at the hospital. He's been asking for you. I can't believe you would just disappear on him. And me. I've been calling you all day. You've been MIA for two days, since you freaking walked out and left me with Jack and the doctors. Thanks for that, by the way—"

Oh shit, Jack! A rush of memories bombarded Remy and cleared her foggy head. "Is he okay?"

Anita let out a huff. "You'd know that if you bothered to pick up your phone! Do you know how long it took me to find this place? Nobody would freaking tell me where it was! Then I couldn't leave Jack all by himself, so it took forever until I could get over here—"

Remy cut Anita off mid-rant. "What do you mean two days? I left the hospital yesterday morning."

"No, you didn't. Today is the sixth. What the hell happened to you?"

It can't be the sixth, Remy thought. She had come back to the village yesterday morning, found Sebastian there, then saw Bieito, and had dinner with him and his family. "I didn't lose a day," she whispered.

"Damn right you did."

Her best friend would have understood if Remy wanted to get away for the night. Hell, she would have understood if Remy didn't want to answer her phone for a few hours. But the only way that Anita would be *this* irritated with Remy was if what she claimed was true; Remy *had* been gone for two days. She had abandoned her ex-husband and best friend at the hospital without so much as a heads up.

Anita was still ranting. "So not only was I trying to keep it together for Jack—who, by the way, *probably* won't suffer from long-term memory loss, if you care—

Taylor Hobbs

I had to wonder if my best friend had been abducted or murdered or whatever and then try to track you down in the middle of *nowhere!"*

"I'm so sorry, Anita," Remy said. Emotion usually surged forth with a heartfelt apology, but the words sounded robotic to Remy's ears. "I—I don't know what happened to me. Honestly. I should never have put you in this position."

Anita sighed. "I came here to help you, and I understand why you wanted to escape for a while, but can you *please* not do it again?" Anita gestured to Remy's rumpled appearance. "Time to get it together, girl."

"I will. I promise I will."

"Good. That starts with visiting Jack at the hospital. But first, you need to clean up." Remy nodded meekly and allowed herself to be tugged from the cottage. "Where exactly do you shower around here?"

Without a word, Remy pointed over to the well, and the bucket sitting on top of the cover. Anita rolled her eyes. "You have got to be kidding me."

"It isn't so bad…"

"Once you aren't so disgusting, you and I are going to have a sit down, come-to-Jesus chat about everything. I know you said that this place was a fixer-upper, but now that I see it, I just have to ask, what on earth possessed you to buy this heap?"

"It's coming along." Remy defended her village. "You just can't see my vision."

"You are living like a hobo up in the mountains! When are you going to have an actual house?"

"I'm moving into the cottage, as soon as I fix it up. It's my favorite."

"Yeah? And what about the rest of this? What are you going to do with all these extra buildings and so much space? It is like one giant code violation. How are you getting any of your painting done?"

Remy didn't want to tell her, almost as if by saying it out loud she was setting herself up for failure, but she needed Anita to understand. "I'm turning it into an art school."

"You think people are going to want to come stay here?"

"I want to turn it into an intensive program. For children like me whose parents have no idea what to do with them."

Anita's eyes widened. "Do you have any idea what a place like that would cost to run?"

"Sort of," Remy confessed.

"And are parents paying for their kids to attend your 'school'?"

"Well, I was thinking it could be an outreach program. With scholarship funds for the kids who deserve to come but can't afford it."

"Okay, I doubted your sanity before—you disappeared for two days—but now I know you're crazy."

"What's wrong with my idea?" Remy demanded.

Anita considered her words carefully before speaking. "I just don't think you're in the best place right now to take something like this on. Especially when it involves kids…"

"What's that supposed to mean?"

"Well, how is your next collection coming? Have you started? You need to be honest with me. I'm your agent and pretty much the only person in your court right now."

"I told you, this place is inspiring me—"

"You aren't even painting right now, Remy! How are you going to teach when you can't even do?"

That very thought had been haunting Remy, but she liked living in the land of denial. "I'll get back to it, I know it."

"And meanwhile, what am I supposed to do?" Anita demanded. "You aren't selling anything new, which means neither you or I are making any money. How long until you run out of cash? Are you even going to make a dent in the repairs with the money you have access to?"

Remy's fingers clutched her temples. "Stop! Just stop! Why did you come here to attack me?"

"I'm not attacking you, Remy. I just want you to be realistic and see this for what it is. Your little project almost killed Jack. It's a time and money suck, and it is preventing you from working on your art. You're never going to get this place up and running, much less as a *scholarship* program so you can be 'pretend mom' to a bunch of needy kids. This isn't the life you're supposed to be leading. Why are you so determined to fuck everything up?"

"Fuck everything up?" Remy's anger surged. "I thought you were happy for me. That you understood why I needed to get away and start over. You're my best friend, and you're supposed to be supportive—"

"Well, I guess I stopped being supportive when I spent all day yesterday taking care of *your* ex-husband in a foreign country while you were lost doing God-knows-what." Anita's voice softened as she changed tactics and continued. "Seeing you this morning, girl,

I'm worried. Not gonna lie. I really don't think you're in the best place right now to be here alone, physically or mentally."

Remy opened her mouth to argue, but she couldn't think of an effective retort. What leg did she have to stand on, really? She hadn't even known what day it was when she woke up this morning. It had been a month and she had yet to paint anything. The entire village was one big liability, as evidenced by Jack's injuries. Was Anita right to question everything? Did it take someone with an outsider's perspective to see what was really happening here? *I'm in too deep,* Remy decided. Too deep to see the truth, but also too deep to back out now. "I just know that I'm supposed to be here, Anita."

"Then you aren't living in the real world."

"Maybe not," Remy conceded. "And maybe you're right, about all of it. But I won't know for sure until I've tried. I need more time."

"I want you to come back to the States with me and Jack. I can't leave you here knowing that you're like…this. So lost."

"Are the doctors going to let Jack travel home soon?" Remy felt relief at that for two different reasons—one, because Jack was okay, and two, because Anita and Jack would leave soon, and she could be alone in her village again.

"In a few days, maybe a week, depending on how he does on the follow up tests. He says he wants his leg surgeries done in the U.S. You would know all of this if you showed up and talked to him. He's been asking for you. I've had to dodge so many of his questions. He deserves better than how you've treated him, Remy."

Really? Anita wants to start in on this now? "I already feel guilty enough that I walked out yesterday. I mean, two days ago. I'll go see him today."

"I don't just mean the accident, Remy. I mean the whole thing. You should have seen him back home. He's been a wreck. I know you won't even talk about the divorce with me, but you need to give him some answers."

Remy bristled at being ordered around more. "It's complicated."

"I just hate to see him hurting so much."

He's hurting so much? What about me? I am too! Remy wanted to scream. *He wouldn't even be here and hurt if you hadn't opened your big mouth and told him where I was!* But now was not the time to open that can of worms, especially because Anita looked done dealing with Remy's shit.

"Clean yourself up," Anita said. "I'll be in the car. You know, the one I rented to drive all over the place looking for you."

Message received. Remy was in no position to argue with her friend anymore. She changed into some clean clothes after washing off at the well and started to head up to the driveway. Unable to help herself, she turned around to give the cottage one last, confused look. Before she left, she had to know if anything had been changed, if there was truly any evidence of Bieito and his family living there.

Remy entered the cottage again, fully expecting to find at least a shred of proof. Last time she'd talked to Bieito, the door on the main house turned red. *He would have left me a sign.*

There was nothing. The cottage was still as empty

as it had been this morning when Remy woke up.

"Seriously?" she said out loud. No hints of her evening and no clues to understand why. "Fine." She slammed the cottage door shut and walked through the square. As always, the red door taunted her. *My books!* she remembered. They were still stacked on the front porch of the main house from when she had talked with Sebastian.

"Hurry up Remy!" she heard Anita call.

Considering all the damage that had already been done to the books, Remy couldn't very well leave them out in the open again. There looked like more rain on the horizon, maybe even a summer storm. She stacked up her treasures and walked them to the car.

"What are those?"

"Reading material. For when I'm stuck at the hospital and Jack is asleep."

Anita cocked an eyebrow and pursed her lips at Remy's choice of words but didn't press further. In fact, the two friends hardly exchanged a word on the half an hour drive to Coruña.

When Anita pulled into the hospital parking lot and killed the engine, she seemed to be waiting for Remy to make the first move. When Remy remained in her seat, Anita sighed and turned to her.

"I'm sorry I snapped at you this morning. But you have to understand. I'm worried about the choices you are making lately. I know you need my help with Jack, but you have to show that you're trying, too. Otherwise it is just too hard."

Remy nodded. "I will. I promise. I don't know what I would do if you weren't around."

"That's what I'm afraid of," Anita said. "I don't

know if I'm helping, or helping you fall apart. You might be better off if I wasn't here…"

Desperation struck Remy. "No, please! I need you here. Jack needs you. I'll do better."

"Well, that starts with you getting out of the car."

"Oh, right."

****

Jack was awake when the women walked into his room, and more alert than Remy had anticipated. He managed to give them a wry smile, but it was Anita to whom he spoke first. "So, you managed to find her, I see."

He didn't sound confused or concussed to Remy, until Anita continued the conversation. "And what's her name?"

There was a long pause as Jack struggled to come up with the answer. "She's my wife. My ex-wife."

"But what's her name, Jack?" Anita gently prompted.

Oh my God, Remy thought. *Answer her! You know my name!*

"Remy!" Remy blurted out.

Anita spun around to her. "You're supposed to let *him* answer. Details and memories might be slow and fuzzy for a little while, but he needs to practice recalling them. He will get better every day, but you can't just answer things for him."

Remy might have been in the wrong, but Jack looked relieved to have an answer, and rested back onto his pillows with a sigh. "Remy," he said. "Where did you go?"

"I, uh, had to go home for a while. I'm sorry I took so long, Jack. I'm glad to hear you're feeling better,

126

though."

"I think it's the drugs," he said, and gave her a wink. It reminded Remy so much of when they were married that it hit her like a punch in the gut. The guilt from avoiding him, and the guilt that overwhelmed her when she got too close to him were fighting it out in her consciousness. It was too hard to know which was the right choice. Staying, and staying away, both felt wrong.

But you're here now, so suck it up, she told herself.

"There was something I wanted to ask you," he said, motioning for Remy to come closer. "I was wondering if you would—"

Remy interrupted his question, sensing that it was leading down a road she wasn't prepared to deal with yet. "Do you remember what happened at the village, Jack? With the accident?"

Jack's face twisted into a grimace, as if the memory caused him physical pain. "I remember that I wanted to help you. To prove...something...important. Then I was inside a house. An old house. I thought it was empty, but I heard noises farther back. Like people talking, or fighting. So I followed it. Then I heard a loud noise, like a crack. I felt something heavy hit me."

Remy's heart started to pound. "You heard people talking in my village? What did they say?"

"Be careful not to push him, Remy," Anita warned.

Jack's brow furrowed. "I don't know."

"You couldn't understand them?"

"I don't remember."

"Did you *see* anyone?"

"No," Jack said, closing his eyes. "I don't remember. The next thing I remember was waking up here. My body hurts."

Anita held Jack's hand. "You need to rest. Get better. Otherwise you won't be allowed to travel home."

"But—" Remy protested, and Anita cut her off with a meaningful glare. *Jack heard voices? In the main house?* That didn't make sense. No one else should have been there. No one else, including Jack. He shouldn't have been there in the first place.

What was going on with her village? If Jack had experienced some weird stuff too, then maybe it wasn't all in Remy's head. Her mind started to spin with possible explanations, but each one sounded more far-fetched than the last. There really was no way to explain what had been happening to her, but Remy knew one thing for sure—the answers lay within the property itself.

Everything led back to the village. She hadn't experienced anything out of the ordinary anywhere else in Spain. The instances of weird occurrences were when she was alone among the buildings.

Remy felt a burst of hopeful energy shake the last of her hangover away. She felt more alert than she had in hours, filled with new determination to find a real explanation. Of course, there was always the chance she was completely wrong, taking the word of a severely concussed and injured man as the only additional evidence to her own experiences.

"I'm tired, Remy," Jack mumbled, closing his eyes. "I'm sorry. I can't remember what you need me to remember."

"Oh Jack, it's okay. Rest for a few more days, and then you'll be on a plane home before you know it.

You'll be up walking again in no time."

"And you'll come with me? You won't leave me alone?"

Remy didn't know what to say to that. She didn't want to coddle him but didn't know how to let him down gently. She was almost one hundred percent sure now that she wasn't going to be leaving with him. She settled for dodging the point. "You won't be alone." It wasn't a lie, per se, because Anita would technically be with him.

Anita, however, seemed to visibly relax at her words, no doubt misinterpreting them as Jack did. She reached over to give Remy a half-hug with one arm, her other hand still grasping Jack's. "You're making the right decision," she whispered to Remy. "Jack needs you."

Is it technically a lie? I still have a week to break it to them gently that I'm not going, Remy reassured herself. There was no point in getting everyone worked up about it now. Maybe if she got a grip on everything in the next few days—her painting, her career, the renovation—the rest of her life would fall into place. *That won't happen, though, until I stop seeing things that aren't there and disappearing for days a time. But if I can figure out why it's happening, then I can fix it.*

Unable to sit still, Remy jumped up and began pacing the room. Jack's eyes tracked her, but he didn't ask any more questions. She wanted to go research her village right now and get answers, and the hospital walls felt like they were closing in on her again. Jack was being taken care of, and there was nothing she could really do here anyway. All she could do was sit and stare at him, which didn't feel very productive.

"Remy, don't you have some books out in the car that you brought to read to Jack?" Anita prompted.

"They're in Spanish," Remy said. Anita just gave her a bewildered stare but dropped the subject. Remy was unable to think of anything else to talk about, especially because she couldn't pester Jack about the accident, so she paced in silence until Anita grew exasperated.

"Remy, will you go pick us up some lunch, please? I'm sure Jack could use a change from the hospital food, and you're keeping him from resting right now."

"She's not," Jack mumbled. His eyes were closed, but he wasn't asleep. Remy's energy could not be contained in that little room, and even the patient felt her stimulating effect.

"Okay," Remy agreed, and held out her hand.

"What do you need? Money?" Anita asked, looking offended.

"No, your car keys."

Anita fished them out of her purse. "Come right back, okay?"

"I will," Remy said, with every intent to fulfill her promise.

Once Remy left the hospital, though, all thoughts of food flew out the window. The need to know about her village consumed her. There didn't seem to be any real answers in the village itself, just more riddles. Remy decided she would have to change tactics. *I'll drive and take Maggie the books.*

For whatever reason, this seemed like a perfectly reasonable thing to do at the time. Later, when Anita made her opinion known over the phone while Remy was in Madrid, it would seem like a less brilliant plan.

Remy ended up using her last chance with Anita without a second thought, and the scary part was, she didn't even feel that bad about it.

They are trying to convince me to abandon my home, she rationalized. Remy wasn't going to give up that easily, not until she knew for sure what was happening to her. Like adopting a stray dog from the shelter, Remy couldn't just abandon her village at the first sign of trouble. The place itself might be a little more complicated than she originally thought, and Remy needed to be equipped to deal with it.

Driving south, Remy remembered seeing this countryside for the first time with Maggie. Jet-lagged, confused, and trusting a stranger to bring her home. If she had known then what a headache the village would bring, would she have done everything the same? *Yes.* Even more so now, because now Remy had a puzzle to solve. *Once I figure it out, it will all fall into place and things won't be so hard anymore. The balance will be restored.* First, she would find out what the village wanted, and then there would be no more obstacles for her art school.

Mostly, Remy needed to find the true explanation for her mental breaks. In her experience, artists were not the most stable of the general populace. Over the years, Remy had lost friends to suicide, depression, and drugs. She was determined not to go over that edge, no matter how frustrated she was with her art, or how disappointed she was in herself for causing pain to others. Even through her darkest days, Remy had been able to hold onto her sense of self. The thought that that part of her was disappearing terrified her.

Taking responsibility for her mental health was the

most important step in making sure she didn't spiral. And that's what she was doing now by driving to Madrid—taking responsibility, for her village, for what happened to Jack, and for her own well-being.

****

The countryside flew by, and soon the city enveloped Remy. After so long in isolation among her village, with only side trips into Ortigueira and Coruña, Remy had forgotten what a big city was like, how it pulsed with its own unique energy. It flowed around the people, shaping their lives and intertwining them into one collective experience, but at the same time separated by individual perceptions. Everyone was leaving their mark on the city by living, seeing, and breathing in a slightly different way.

Now Remy added to it, bringing her own form of crazy to Madrid. But among such a dense population, her problems diffused and seemed infinitely smaller. She wove Anita's car in and out of narrow streets, deciding to drive until she either reached a dead end or found somewhere she recognized. *That plaza has to be around here somewhere.* It turned out that the dead end was her first option, and she parked.

Thinking ahead for once, Remy snapped a photo of the street she left the car on. If she brought it back in one piece, maybe Anita wouldn't list grand theft auto onto her many sins from the past few days.

Remy hailed the next taxi that came by, handing the driver Maggie's business card with her office address. "Take me here, *por favor*," she said, juggling the stack of books she held in her arms.

"Okay," the driver said, surprisingly in English. He gave her a smile, and motioned for her to get in. "I help you with the books?" he asked, eager to practice his new language skills.

"No, thank you," Remy said. The driver tried twice more to engage her in conversation on the drive to the plaza, but Remy's monotone answers soon discouraged him. Her thoughts were preoccupied with how to explain the situation to Maggie. She had an ex-husband problem, a—possibly ex-—best friend problem, a new man problem, and a village problem. There were too many places to begin her story, and she couldn't decide which was most important. Should she try to tell her the whole truth, exactly how she had experienced it? Or should she just get Maggie to translate the books for her and leave the rest out? Addressing the village first would be the most helpful, but Remy was dying to talk to someone about Jack and Bieito. *How do I explain Bieito without sounding like a nutjob?*

Remy shouldn't have worried, because the moment she walked into the realtor's office and saw Maggie, she collapsed into her arms, and the story released in a flood of tears. The arms around her were not Maggie's, but Nana's. They held Remy with an iron grip, anchoring her to reality, and allowed Remy to stick to the facts. Just as she had run to her Nana to confess her sins on that first fateful night, she poured out the events of the last three days to a bewildered Englishwoman, who, to her credit, took it all in stride.

Maggie let Remy ramble through her tale, waiting until the end to ask questions and trying to understand exactly what the artist was telling her.

"Your ex-husband came looking for you? And he got hurt at the village?"

Remy sniffed, trying to get her tears under control

while they soaked into the back of Maggie's shirt. "Yeah," she said, the hint of a southern twang creeping into her cracked voice.

"But he's okay. And your friend Anita is there with him."

"Uh-huh."

Maggie gently untangled Remy's hands from around her neck and guided her to a chair. "That must have been very scary. But, child, it wasn't your fault. Don't ever think that. It was an accident."

"But if he hadn't come, then he wouldn't be hurt!"

Maggie looked at her sternly. "He is an adult who made his own decision. Put it from your mind for now; there's no point in worrying about it when you can't change it. He will be good as new, and he will heal in more ways than one without you being there."

Remy hiccupped, already feeling less guilty now that she had been absolved by the older and wiser woman. *Sometimes, you just need someone else to forgive you when you can't forgive yourself.*

"Now, you couldn't have come all the way down here just for this, not that I'm not overjoyed to see you. Are you unhappy in your new home, or afraid, after what happened?"

"I—I needed your advice about something. I may have met someone." Remy blushed.

"A significant someone?"

"Maybe. Sort of. I don't know! It's just, when I'm with him, I lose myself. And I'm not sure if I'm losing myself in a good way."

"What do you mean? Is he a bad person?"

"No! Bieito is a wonderful person. That's the problem. When I'm with him, it is like nothing else matters. I lose track of time and place, and I find myself not caring one bit."

"It sounds like you are just in the honeymoon stage of young love," Maggie said. "Perhaps you've forgotten what it is like to feel this way. And now you are feeling guilty about having feelings for another man while Jack is hurt."

Remy didn't know how to fully explain it to Maggie and shrugged hopelessly. "I'm not even sure what I feel for Bieito right now, honestly. I think I'm interested, it's just that something feels *wrong.* Off-balance. I don't trust myself when I'm with him. He makes me so happy, but what if I lose everything else that matters to me in the process?"

"How long have you known this Bieito?"

"That's the thing. I've only ever been with him twice. I met him at the beach, and then again at my...his family's cottage. I need to know more about him, but when I'm with him, all of my questions and doubts fade away and before I know it, he's gone again, and I feel empty."

Maggie's eyes were bright as she considered Remy's despondent gaze. "He sounds like a special person, Remy, for you to feel this deeply so quickly. Take caution, though, for I, too, fell for a man such as that, and he broke my heart. It comes along once in a lifetime. All you can do is cut off all ties with him now and save yourself, or grab on for the ride, and hope you hold onto enough of yourself to rebuild from the wreckage at the end."

Remy shook her head. "I am already such a wreck. I know I should just walk away, but..." Remy couldn't very well explain that somehow Bieito and his family were residing on her property, but only part of the time. She took a deep breath. "I thought Jack was my forever. He *should* have been my forever. But walking away and starting over was easier than I thought. But this...this would be different." *I am already more entangled with Bieito than I thought.*

Maggie nodded in understanding while Remy gathered steam. "I don't know who I am anymore," Remy said, voice thick with emotion. "The village was supposed to be mine, a place for me to find myself. Now it's causing more complications, stirring up things between me, my past, and my future, and throwing in two men who couldn't be more different just for the fun of it. I hate not being in control. That leads to bad things."

Thankfully, Maggie ignored the last part of Remy's comment, and didn't ask for clarification on the "bad things" she was talking about. "You can't exist in a bubble. The village is just that—a village. It is the people inside who matter."

Remy let out a harsh laugh. "It was supposed to be my *milagro de Santiago*. My miracle."

"Just give yourself more time. Jack's accident was unfortunate, yes, and you are understandably cautious with Bieito, but have more faith in yourself. The universe is unfolding as it should."

"I just wish I knew why."

"What would be the fun in that?" Maggie asked. "I, for one, am so proud of you. I was actually planning on making a visit up to Ortigueira in the next few weeks to see what you've done with the place."

"I haven't made a lot of progress, I'm afraid," Remy confessed. "I had hoped to have more done by now, but I really don't know what I'm doing. It is mostly trial and error so far. I jump from project to project, when I need to just focus my energies on one thing in particular and see it through to the end." She hesitated. "Plus, I want to be as true to the integrity of the village as I can be. You know, preserving its true character. I want to do it right, but I just don't know enough about the history of the place to be authentic."

"I'm afraid I can't help you very much on the authenticity. You'd be better off asking Sebastian for that, or talking to some locals. But I understand wanting to get it right."

"Actually, I think you can help me with something. How are your translation skills?" Remy gestured to the books she'd thrown onto Maggie's desk when she had embraced the older woman. They had been through quite the adventure—from the library, to the village, to the hospital, and finally to Madrid. Now, Remy was hopeful that their secrets could be unlocked and help her make sense of her life in more ways than one, starting with construction.

"My Spanish should probably be better than it is, considering I've lived here for more than enough time, but I'm willing to take a stab at it."

"Can we start with the history book?"

"If I'm going to do this, we're going to get comfortable. Come on, I'll close up my shop and we can head to my flat. You look like you could use a siesta anyway."

****

At Maggie's insistence, Remy took a nap at the apartment. By handing over the books to Maggie and relinquishing responsibility, Remy was finally able to rest. When she woke up four hours later, both confused and very hungry, Maggie was finishing up the obscure little history book about the Kingdom of Galicia.

"How do you feel?" Maggie asked, closing the worn cover.

"I think I could have slept all the way through until tomorrow," Remy confessed. "Are the books useful?"

"It was difficult to find anything referencing your village. It was just too small to be of any real significance. I did, however, learn some interesting facts about the area. And there *might* be a small mention of your village in the part about the Martyrs of Carral, but it was hard to tell. I'm afraid I can't help very much except to give you a general summary, though I don't know if it will help with your restoration project."

"Well, I have to start somewhere. What I was doing wasn't working, so you might as well tell me," Remy decided. "Even a little bit might inspire me."

Maggie gathered her thoughts for a moment, deciding where to start. "You've seen how proud Galicians are of their heritage first-hand, haven't you?" Remy nodded, and Maggie continued. "This is because up until eighteen thirty-three, Galicia was not part of Spain and was its own kingdom, dating all the way back to the Middle Ages.

"In eighteen forty-six, a colonel by the name of Miguel Solís y Cuentos rebelled against the new Spanish rule. Though the uprising spread to surrounding cities, the rebels were squashed in only twenty-four days by a vastly superior force from the Spanish Royal Council. The colonel was executed by a firing squad, and the eleven other soldiers were put to death in the Forest of Rin, their bodies dumped into an unmarked tomb.

"Miguel Solís y Cuentos had many sympathizers in Coruña, which is why the general feared executing the rebels within the town. That didn't stop the people from turning Miguel and his eleven soldiers into the twelve Martyrs of Carral, though. They are remembered as the first wave of Galician nationalism and regionalism."

"Wow, I had no idea. I mean, I knew that Galicia used to be called the Kingdom of Galicia, but I never really thought about what that meant for all the people here to have their identity absorbed by Spanish rule. No wonder they like to be known as Galician rather than Spanish. What did you find out about the rebels?" Remy asked.

"That's the part that connects to your village. There's a list of names of the soldiers that were executed, and one of them lists Ortigueira as his home. So, someone living in your village may have been a part of the Galician uprising!"

Remy raised an eyebrow. "That seems like a pretty far stretch. It sounds like a lot of these details are fuzzy at best, and probably aren't all that accurate. Was there anything else of historical significance I can incorporate with the renovation? No descriptions of what the village used to look like?"

"I'm afraid not, dear. This was the best I could do. Like I said, your village is very small; it doesn't even have a name other than its extension to Ortigueira."

Remy sighed. "Thanks for trying. The rebellion was kind of cool, I guess. Too bad it was only three weeks long and didn't have much of an impact. No wonder I hadn't heard about it before. Were you able to translate the architecture book at least?"

"There were a few good chapters about historical homes. Here, come sit by me and we can go through them together." Maggie scooted over and Remy sat down on the couch next to her. "Now, with these old buildings, you definitely need to start from the bottom and move up…"

Remy and Maggie lost track of time as they came up with designs and floor plans for the buildings. With rough sketches, Remy added rooms and windows to the buildings she knew by heart now, having spent weeks living among them. When Remy confided that she wanted to turn the larger houses into dormitories for her school, Maggie was enthusiastic.

Though she was nervous at first to pick up her pen, Maggie's chattering kept Remy distracted enough for her to forget her mental blocks. The outlines came effortlessly, flowing onto the paper almost as easily as her paintings used to.

It's getting better, Remy thought, relieved. She pulled forth the distorted memory of her drunken run through the village, and of her night in the cottage with Bieito's family. *Authenticity.* That's what she needed to focus on to get into her flow state, and then the best ideas would come.

During the hours spent immersed in future plans for her art school, Remy forgot about all the complications surrounding the village. What she saw on paper were her dreams turning into reality, and she was determined not to let anything stand in her way. Anita could try to freak out Remy with skepticism about logistics, funds, and permits, but she would not succeed in forcing Remy to move backward in life.

She realized she had been obsessing over the wrong things all along—the mystery of Bieito, the drama of Jack, the accident, and, most of all, paralyzing indecision about which direction to go with the village. It was time to get serious about it all, put her plans into motion, and get back to the real reason she bought the village in the first place.

As she made up a very grown-up plan for her future and the people it would affect, Remy decided to be an adult and call Anita first, before Anita inevitably tracked her down and reamed her out. She already felt more self-assured than she had during these last few confusing and chaotic days. "Thanks for helping me get my head on straight," Remy told Maggie while turning on her phone. "I need to have an important conversation right now."

"I'll step out and bring us back some carryout for dinner. Best of luck with Anita." Maggie was halfway out the door when she turned around. "Remember, Remy, you came here to start over. Your past has not only followed you here, but made a mess of your present as well. Don't let it define your future."

While Maggie's words burned a new confidence within Remy's chest, she dialed Anita. To her surprise, the phone rang and rang and eventually went to voice mail. She had fully expected her best friend to jump all over her at the first ring. Prepared for an interrogation interspersed with outrage and demands, Remy didn't know how to leave a message at the polite request of Anita Lopez, artist agent and specialized publicist who promised to call back as soon as she was available. Remy took a deep breath, and then hung up.

Staring at her phone screen, Remy debated whether

or not to call back right away and try to explain over voicemail, or if she should wait for Anita to see she had a missed call. Remy wondered which was worse, sucking it up now or waiting in agony over the next few hours for Anita to call back.

The result, however, was neither. The blow came in the form of a text, cold and impersonal, about as far from emotionally removed from the situation as Anita could be.

—Whatever your explanation is, Remy, save it. I can no longer listen to your excuses. Return the rental car when you're done with it. Jack and I don't want to see you again while we're here. You can also consider this the end of our professional relationship as well. I cannot associate with clients whose moral character I question. I hope you find whatever it is you're looking for, and you realize that it wasn't worth all of this.—

Remy read the message three times until the words finally sank in. *So that's it then. Almost two decades of friendship and this was the final straw?* She had been expecting Anita to be pissed, of course, but she had never expected that Anita would fire her as a client. Like most close friends, they had weathered their share of fights over the years, but one thing was always certain—they were better as a team.

Remy was Anita's number one client, the one who had propelled both of them out of obscurity. To have one woman without the other was unthinkable. Anita lived and breathed her job, just as Remy lived and breathed to paint. Their careers were so intertwined that their "divorce" would be more complicated than Remy's split from Jack.

But here they were, actually splitting up *because* of

Jack, just not in the way one would expect a husband to come between two best friends. *My constant avoidance and running away caused all of this.* If she hadn't called Anita out of desperation, they would probably still be working together and Remy would have some way to make an income. *What am I going to do now?*

As the blunt words stared up at her from a blindingly bright screen, Maggie's advice overrode the searing image. *Don't let your past define your future.* Remy could either fight Anita's words and refuse to accept the end of their friendship and partnership, of which Remy was sure Anita would eventually cave in, or she could just let it go. *The end.*

This time, she could have an *actual* fresh start, without having to worry about reporting back to Anita and hearing her overblown opinions all the time. No more cajoling to return to New York, no more avoiding Jack's mopey gaze, no more hospital obligations...Did it make her a terrible person to be relieved?

An enormous weight felt like it had been removed from Remy's shoulders. She was no longer beholden to Anita and didn't have to answer to her any longer. Any painting she decided to do would be on her own schedule. Remy's personal business would be her own. Nobody would be nosing around looking for the next big story and leaking it "for her own good" to boost her career. Granted, Remy wasn't even sure she would be able to have a career anymore, but that was beside the point.

When Maggie returned, she asked, "Everything squared away with your friend?"

Remy looked up from the sketches she had been flipping through, imagining her completed renovation.

"Oh yes," she said, with a huge smile. "I'll probably go broke soon."

"There's a certain freedom in that," Maggie agreed.

Chapter Eight

Full of renewed vigor, Remy left Madrid early the next morning, but not before extracting a promise from Maggie that she would visit soon. Though Maggie was disappointed that they couldn't spend a few days relaxing in the city, she had understood Remy's urgent need to return to the village and get started on the improvements as soon as possible.

Remy hummed with excited energy, clutching the architecture drawings in her lap on the way home, as though they would disappear at any moment. She felt as though she literally held her future in her hands, and she was not about to let it blow away out the open window. *I'm in control,* she reminded herself. *I can do this.* Part of being able to do it was knowing when to ask for help, and she was on her way to meet with a renowned architect in Coruña. But first, Remy couldn't help stopping by the village, just to see if it had missed her during her absence.

Remy parked at the top of the drive and stared down at the quiet buildings. She stepped out of the driver's seat, frowning as she felt her muscles tense in anticipation. *Why am I so high strung?* It was a confusing contrast amid her tranquil surroundings. Remy slammed the car door shut, locking it with a beep, and took a step forward.

Quick as a blink, her village went from being

completely empty to swarming with people. They were coming out of buildings, chatting in the streets, children and chickens running around underfoot. Remy screamed in shock, and heads turned to stare. Still, there was enough general din that her outburst didn't attract as much attention as Remy feared as she prepared to hop back into her car.

The car was gone. Remy stared in confusion at the keys she held ready in her hand, to the empty space, and back again to the keys. Wild-eyed, she turned back to the crowd, some of whom were still studying her curiously.

What the fuck what the fuck what the fuck. "*¡Qué mierda!*" she shouted. *Wait, that wasn't "what the fuck."* Remy swallowed hard, and her legs gave out from underneath her. People she didn't recognize filled a space that was supposed to be solely hers. Well, hers and Bieito's family's, if only on occasion. But this— this was too much.

Taking shallow breaths, Remy wondered how on earth she was going to kick this many people off her property. It looked like they were some sort of weird Renaissance freaks. *No, not Renaissance, exactly. Pilgrims?* Whatever group they were in, they apparently liked to dress up in crazy costumes and trespass onto abandoned villages. Well, that just wasn't going to fly with Remy. Before Remy could stand to confront the unwelcome guests, a familiar face was striding over to her.

"*Señora* Remy! There you are." Lino beamed at her. "What are you doing on the ground? My brother will be so pleased you have returned. He has been searching everywhere for you. I told him not to worry, you had promised to attend my wedding, and here you are!"

"Your wedding?" Remy asked, dazed. "You're having the wedding here?" *Nobody asked my opinion about it!*

"Come," Lino ordered, extending his hand down to her. "You must meet my beautiful bride."

What else could she do? Remy took Lino's hand and he hauled her up. "Then we shall track down that infernal brother of mine so he can stop moping about on this joyous occasion!"

Lino's exuberance was so endearing that Remy felt her anger and frustration slipping away, replaced by that same sense of calm and contentment she had felt while in their cottage. *Maybe it wasn't just the wine,* she conceded, as logic and reason seemed determined to slip out of her brain. Instead, she focused on the infectious excitement all around her as everyone busied themselves with wedding day tasks.

A new archway stood in the center of town square, woven with bright wildflowers. Two women holding more flowers in woven baskets worked together, adding to the riot of color. A gaggle of children ran laps around and through the arch until the women shooed them off to make mischief elsewhere. Men tipped their hats at Remy as they hauled barrels of wine up from cellars and through the streets. The smell of freshly baked bread poured out with the hot air from the bakery's open door. Tables were being loaded with cured meats, cheeses, and fresh fruit in a never-ending stream of platters carefully carried out from the houses. A young man stopped Lino and handed him an overflowing glass of sweet purple liquid. "For the groom!" he shouted.

"I cannot, I fear," Lino said. "But soon. I am on my way to find my bride. And my brother. Have you seen either?"

"Ay," the man said, and pointed to the main house. "Your lovely María is with her mother, getting ready for the ceremony." He then shook his head with a warning. "Wouldn't try to go in there if I were you. Anyone who tries to peek is thrown out!"

Just then a group of gossiping young women filed outside, dressed in their wedding finery. Remy had never seen the style of dress they wore. *Maybe Lino and María are doing a themed wedding, almost like the Renaissance wedding Jack and I went to upstate.* It had been for an eclectic friend of theirs, and Jack had moaned the whole time about having to wear a 'costume'. Remy hadn't minded; it was sweet and seemed like a fun way to celebrate, but most of the other guests had done the bare minimum to fit the theme. Here, however, it looked like everyone had gone all out.

Each woman wore a different color, swallowed in lace and satin up to their chins, their hair pulled back with intricate braids and curls. They all shared the same high cheekbones and thick eyebrows, and when they smiled as they talked over one another, it was easy to see that they were all related by blood.

One of the women spotted him. "Lino! Shoo! You are not supposed to be waiting about here. María will see you."

Lino settled his face into a mask of innocence. "I was delivering Remy to my brother. Have you seen him?"

The girls lapsed into silence as they took in Remy's

ragtag appearance, sticking out like a sore thumb amid the theme of the wedding. One of the older women, an auntie, maybe, remembered her manners and hurried forward to kiss Remy on both cheeks. "Welcome, my dear! We are thrilled that you're here. María told us you might be coming. We adore our dear Bieito and have been looking forward to meeting you. Come, come inside, please. Bieito left a gift in my care for you, if you were able celebrate with us."

The women engulfed Remy in a sea of fabric and herded her toward the house. One of the most beautiful women Remy had ever seen sat serenely on a settee inside, while an elderly woman fussed and prodded her fiery red hair to lay flat underneath a gauzy veil. The bride looked to be in her late teens, but with the poise of a much more mature woman. Her creamy complexion set off the white of her dress, and instead of making her look pale and washed out, she simply glowed like an angel. María radiated pure happiness and contentment, and Remy could only stare at her in awe.

While everyone else fussed about, clucking like chickens, the bride looked to be at peace. *This is a woman who knows she's making the right choice,* Remy thought. Had she looked like that on her wedding day to Jack? She doubted it. Remy remembered being so nervous she had to vomit, and the entire walk down the aisle she was afraid Jack was going to change his mind. Forever seemed like such a long time. How did someone know for *certain* that they wanted to be with someone until the end of their days? Had some part of Remy known, even way back then, that their marriage was doomed from the start? Would she have done anything differently, or gone through with the ceremony just the same? *If I had wished back then for a happily ever after, could I have prevented all of our heartache? Would my happily-ever-after even include Jack in the first place?* Remy shook the dark cloud of contemplation and regret away. This was María's big day, and not the time to reflect on her own failures.

María's serene face lit up once she realized who Remy was, and she crossed the room to wave away the relatives still encircling the new guest. "You came!" she said, and embraced Remy like a sister. Dumbstruck, Remy tried to delicately return the favor, aware of her travel-weary condition and more than a little thankful she had at least borrowed one of Maggie's conservative sundresses to drive home in earlier that day.

"Bieito has talked much of the American girl who has stolen his heart," the bride gushed.

"Stolen his heart?" Remy asked, skeptical.

María laughed. "Well, not in so many words. You know how he is." Linking her elbow through Remy's, the pair walked back over to the couch. "Sit, sit. My Aunt Rose has gone to fetch something of yours for today."

"Congratulations, by the way. Lino is a very lucky man. You are simply lovely."

Red flush graced the bride's face, and her eyes lit up. "He is the love of my life," she said, stating a simple fact. "How fortunate I am that he loves me the way I love him! And today we will share our love in front of the world."

"It was very kind of Lino to invite me," Remy said, feeling a bit awkward to be in the middle of such a life-altering day when she barely knew the bride. "Are you sure it is okay that I'm here? I don't mean to intrude. I'm not even really sure how I got in here. I know you're busy getting ready for the ceremony—"

María held up her hand, cutting Remy off. "Of course, you are not intruding. You must understand, I love my Lino, but I also love his family as well. Sweet Bieito—he has been alone for so long. You cannot imagine how my heart sang to hear that he wanted you to be present for today. I care for him like my own brother, and I worry for him. He is happy for me and Lino, I know he is, but I also know that a part of him yearns to find the same, though he will never admit it. Now with you here, I will be able to watch him dancing and laughing as Lino and I do the same. There will be no melancholy on my wedding day. You have brought the sunshine with you, and I am excited to see the shadow lift over Bieito when he sees that you are here."

Um, whoa. That's a lot of pressure.

"If you still need convincing, then look no further than the dress that Bieito bought you."

"What dress?" Remy asked, and turned around to see where María pointed.

Aunt Rose had returned, holding a rich red bundle of fabric in her arms. She smiled at Remy and held it out to her. "Bieito thought that you might need it."

Remy reached out with trembling fingers. She had owned many gorgeous dresses over the years—gala dresses, charity dresses, auction dresses, and one very fine wedding dress—but hadn't worn any since the fateful night she had hopped on a plane to Spain. The dress she arrived in last month and the gift in front of her were the exact same vibrant shade.

"Oh," Remy gasped. "It's absolutely beautiful."

She turned to María with troubled eyes. "Why would he do something like this? This dress must have cost a fortune!"

"He wanted to give you something special, something that you would never forget," María said, taking the dress from Aunt Rose carefully and shaking it out. She held it up to Remy's front. "An almost perfect fit, I think. You two will make a fine couple tonight."

Her first instinct was to refuse the gift. It felt like too much too fast, and another part of her was reminded of Jack, and his lavish gifts while they were dating. But at the same time, the dress felt like it held a different meaning. Whereas Jack had thrown money around to woo her, Remy was sure that for Bieito to afford a dress like that, he must have worked hours and hours, scrimping and saving just to do something nice. It was much more than a gift, and Remy didn't want to let Bieito, or any of his family, down today.

It felt *right* to be here with these people, who welcomed her into their hearts without a moment's hesitation. Her village felt whole and complete with everyone here, and Remy didn't want to dwell on what it felt like to be alone in an echoing reminder of a time gone by. What were the downsides of "just going with it," as Anita would say?

The thought of her friend stung, and Remy quickly retreated to her happy place in the present. She took the dress from the bride as though it were made of glass, and asked, "Where can I change?"

María pointed upstairs, to a place in the main house that Remy hadn't explored on her property yet. "My cousin, Isabella, will assist you." María looked around until she spotted a woman who looked to be about Remy's age. "Please help my guest into her dress for the evening, dear cousin."

"But I was going to finish my hair—" Isabella protested, but María shot her an expectant stare, effectively reminding her who this day was really about. Although, Remy felt like it was gradually turning into *her* day and felt uncomfortable with all the unnecessary attention. Escaping upstairs for a while sounded like a great plan to her.

Isabella inclined her head at the bride. "I apologize. Of course, I will help. Please let me know if you need anything else in the meantime." She turned and marched past Remy. Halfway up the stairs, she turned to where Remy had remained frozen at the bottom and asked, "Are you coming?"

Putting aside the fear that the second floor might collapse, Remy scurried up behind María's cousin and Isabella motioned her into a nearby bedroom. "This is my family's house, you know," she said, as they both entered the lavishly decorated room.

"It is lovely. I've been wanting to see the upstairs for some time," Remy said, trying to smooth over whatever animosity Isabella seemed to have toward her.

"What a strange thing to say," Isabella said. "Is it customary in America for visitors to want to snoop around the house of their host?"

"What? No! I just meant—"

"You should take off those...clothes." Isabella sniffed with disdain at Remy's sundress. "It is not appropriate for a wedding. Though why Bieito would go through all this trouble—"

All right, I've had enough. Remy took a deep

breath and stood up tall. "Excuse me," she interrupted. "Just what the hell kind of problem do you have with me?"

Isabella went pale at her words, but whether it was the tone or the directness that caught her off guard, Remy didn't know. It only took Isabella a few seconds to get her feet back underneath her, though. She turned red, and stared Remy down with fearful intensity. With clenched fists she said, "You Americans think you can have everything. But you can't. I won't let you. I've been waiting a long time—"

"Listen," Remy said. "I don't know what you have against me, but I don't think the bride needs this right now." She turned her back on the other woman and started undressing. Whatever grudge Isabella apparently had against her, she really didn't care. Remy had dealt with mean girls all her life, and the best way to handle it was to make them see that they couldn't ruffle her, especially because she wasn't an insecure teenager anymore. Remy rolled her eyes at the thought of how much it used to matter that she didn't fit in. That was one of the best things that came with passing thirty-five—the complete inability to give a shit about petty people.

Isabella, however, had apparently not learned that lesson yet. "Yes, it is all about my precious and beautiful cousin," she spat. "Her first marriage. May it last forever. One could be so lucky."

Still turned away, Remy heard Isabella stomp out of the room and slam the door behind her. *Whoa, that lady has some issues.* There was obviously jealousy, but it had to be more than that. *First marriage,* Remy thought. What had happened to Isabella to make her so bitter? Remy's marriage hadn't worked out, but that didn't mean she went around stomping on other people's happiness. Was Isabella upset that Remy had swooped in and caught the eye of the town's handsome bachelor?

Focusing on the task at hand, she fingered the soft fabric before pulling the full skirt over her head. *Yes, this would definitely be easier if I had help.* After twisting and turning and a couple of false starts, Remy finally secured the dress around the correct limbs, then struggled to catch her breath. All of the layers were exhausting and cumbersome, but when she caught a glimpse of herself in the mirror, it was obvious that it was worth it.

The dress Bieito had chosen looked like it was pulled out of the past. The neck scooped delicately around her collar bone and into the short sleeves that draped off her shoulders. The waist was cinched in, but Remy could still breathe after tightening it up by herself, which had required a certain amount of skeletal contortion. A thick, full skirt blossomed from her waist and fell to the floor, just skimming her feet. It wasn't a dress that screamed, "Look at me!" It was a dress that pulled eyes from across the room, with a subtlety that suggested, "Look at the beautiful person *wearing* the dress."

Bieito had chosen a dress that showed off Remy for who she was, and not what she looked like. Just as she was thinking about him, she walked over to the window and looked outside, and there he stood. Remy's heart leaped in her chest and she suppressed the urge to shout down at him. He waited in the middle of the street, with the same lost, yearning look he had when he stared out at the ocean. He was as removed from the festivities as Remy herself had felt, an observer but not a participant. Other people floated around him, but he remained immobile.

He's waiting for me! Remy thought, and ran for the door. She pulled on the handle only to find that the door wouldn't budge. She tried pushing it. Nothing. With both hands, Remy grabbed the stiff handle and gave it a shake with all her might.

"That bitch locked me in." The realization that a grown woman could be so petty and immature flared Remy's anger. *"Seriously?"* she yelled, hoping someone downstairs could hear her. There were no footsteps in the hallway to bring her hope. Was she stuck until someone remembered she existed and came to find her?

She ran back over to the window, and of course Isabella was now outside talking to Bieito. The other woman flirtatiously fingered the necklace she wore while attempting to get his attention, but Remy could see that he was distracted. *Good,* she thought, and smirked.

Having had just about enough of all the drama she could stand for the day, Remy rapped sharply on the window. When that didn't garner a response from either Bieito or Isabella down below, Remy turned her fist and started banging. *"Hey!"* she yelled.

That worked. Bieito turned around in confusion, before finally looking up. Remy stopped banging and gave him a wave and a smile. Bieito waved back hesitatingly, as if he didn't believe what he was seeing. Remy pointed to her dress and then gave him a thumbs up. *Could I be more awkward?* she thought, and rolled her eyes. "Oh wait, not you!" she tried to explain, as Bieito's face fell. She motioned for him to come into the house, and as he started to move forward, Isabella blocked him.

"Remy?" María called through the closed door. "Are you still in there?"

"I'm here! The door is stuck."

"Isabella said you'd already snuck out to go and find my brother-in-law, but when I saw her outside—"

"Can you get the door open?" She gritted her teeth for her next lie. "I guess I accidentally locked myself in once I told Isabella I was fine to finish getting ready on my own."

Remy heard a click and then a creak. "Oh, you look stunning!" María said.

"Nothing compared to the bride," Remy said, smiling at her new friend's radiance. "But, I have to go."

"I'm sorry, Remy," María confessed. "I shouldn't have sent you up here with her. I thought that she was past all this, but I guess not. You'll have to excuse my cousin. She's been through a lot this past year, with the death of her husband."

Oh. That explains a lot. "I won't think twice about it," Remy promised. She gave a twirl on top of the landing. "Everything in place?" she asked.

"Bieito will think you're a dream."

Remy decided to take it as a compliment, but, having had difficulty distinguishing between dreams and reality of late, she didn't know if being someone's dream was a good thing.

"Now go!" María laughed at her. Remy didn't need to be told twice.

When Remy got down to the street, Bieito was still trying to politely extract himself from the conversation with Isabella. "...If you'll excuse me, I really must—" he was saying.

"If I could just get your help with one thing—" Isabella interrupted him.

Bieito inhaled sharply when his eyes landed on Remy. "Remy," he said, almost as a sigh. And just like that, Remy and Bieito were the only two people in the world. Everything else faded away as Remy saw herself through his eyes. Any worries she had about not being welcome at the wedding disappeared, because she just *fit* right here—wherever "here" really was—with him.

Isabella must have seen herself off, because Remy couldn't remember her leaving. She could barely remember her own name. In more clothing than she had ever worn, she had never felt more naked in her life. Remy swallowed before she spoke. "Thank you for the dress. You really didn't have to..."

"You came," he said, direct as ever. "I was worried that you wouldn't."

"Then why did you buy me this dress?"

"Because I hoped you would." He cleared his throat. "I tried to find you the past couple of days, to apologize for my family's brash behavior at dinner. I may have had too much to drink; my memories are confused. I feared you had left..."

"Not by choice," Remy mumbled, before she spoke up and said, "I'm just happy I found my way back here in time." *"Found" being the operative word. How do I keep getting back here?* she asked herself, but her brain felt like it was fighting her from questioning it too closely. *More importantly, can I control when I leave?*

Trying to ask that question almost made Remy black out. She shook her head to clear her vision and focused on the man in front of her.

What did it matter, if she was here now? She held out her hand as an invitation, and Bieito took it, flipping her palm upward. He bent down to kiss the inside of her wrist, a gentle, even chaste touch that sent tremors through Remy's body. It felt strangely intimate out in the middle of the street where anyone could see.

Bieito straightened up. "Forgive me," he said, but the twinkle in his eye showed that he was anything but remorseful. "I've been waiting to do that since...well, I met you." Seeing that Remy had accepted both his gift and invitation had emboldened Bieito, and Remy could see his flirtatious side starting to emerge. *This wedding is about to get really interesting.*

Chapter Nine

The ceremony was a little long and religious for Remy's taste, but the bride and groom looked so smitten with each other that Remy could ignore the hard seat under her butt while the priest droned on. When Bieito gave Remy a wink after Lino and María sealed their marriage with a kiss, Remy felt the giddy excitement of being twenty-three again. How long had it been since she felt this carefree?

When the time came to celebrate out in the square, Remy dove in headfirst into the festivities with abandon. She filled herself to the brim with wine and food and conversation as though she had been starving for weeks, which in a way, she had been. Remy lost her self-consciousness and feeling of being an outsider while at Bieito's side. He seemed more than happy to show off his American date and introduced her to the rest of the villagers, all of whom Remy was not surprised to find out lived somewhere on her property.

Remy was seeing and experiencing her village as how it should be, bursting with life, and not as the lonely, abandoned property she was determined to fix by herself. It didn't bother her that all these people weren't really supposed to be here. It just felt right, until Bieito led her into the middle of the street for a dance. That's when Remy felt like a fish out of water again.

The haunting cry of bagpipes reached Remy's ears, and she looked around for the source as the townspeople lined up, men on one side and women on the other. The folk music picked up the pace with the addition of a tambourine, while Bieito took her by the shoulders and set her in place across from him.

"What's happening?" she asked.

"Follow along as best you can. I trust you'll be fine, this is in your blood."

"But I don't dance—" she tried to protest, but now she was surrounded on all sides by celebrating Galicians, and there was no way she could escape the revelry. *I'll just have to suck it up and try not to trip anyone or fall flat on my face.*

"It's the *muiñeira*," Bieito said, as he started to kick his feet. "You feel it inside of you, and you just move." Remy watched carefully as Bieito moved his feet in the semblance of an Irish jig, only more loosely and free-formed. His arms raised above his head like he was holding castanets, and he twirled counter-clockwise. When he saw that she remained frozen in place, trying to analyze his movements, he laughed. "Like your art, Remy. Don't think too hard. Just let your mind rest and your body take over."

Dubiously, Remy stared down the line of villagers and saw everyone doing some variation of Bieito's movements, but nobody seemed particularly concerned about the technicalities of the dance. Each person had their own flair, but their bodies all held the same lightness and joy as the music flowed through them.

She waited for the right beat to come in on and gave her foot a tentative kick in time with the rest of the women. Fumbling a bit while she tried to keep time with their footwork, her feet tangled up in her unfamiliar skirts and she staggered backward. Down the line, she felt eyes on her and turned to see Isabella's judgmental stare and smirk. The woman tossed her head and gave an extra-graceful twirl just to rub it in.

Remy straightened up and got back in line. Her eyes found Bieito's, and held in their trance-like intensity, she blocked everything else out and started to dance. Once she started moving and stopped thinking, Remy was swept away with the rest of the dancers. Like the Romans and their worship of Dionysus, the swirling mass of bodies was caught up in the ecstasy of celebration.

Until María came over to interrupt the pair, Remy hadn't even realized she was getting tired. When the bride grabbed Remy's outstretched hand, it jarred her like a scratch on a record player. Everything halted as Remy's consciousness returned from the collective and catapulted back into her own body. The link that connected her to Bieito on a fundamental level was severed, and the aftershock left her cold, though she still sweated from exertion. Wild-eyed, she stared at the bride, trying to remember where she was.

María grinned at her. "Watching you and Bieito was everything I had hoped!" she said, glowing with happiness. "Now, my new husband apparently has to talk to his brother about something that cannot wait until later, so please come join me at my table and have some refreshments! You have been dancing for quite some time."

Remy turned around to look for her date, but Lino was already dragging Bieito off to the far side of the party, toward a table where a rough group of men were sitting.

"Where is he going?" Remy asked the bride.

María waved a hand, unconcerned. "They might be new workers at the port. From what Bieito told me, Lino has been so excited about the wedding that he was telling everyone. That boy cannot keep anything to himself! They might have just decided to come by."

"You don't mind that they crashed your wedding?"

"Crashed?"

"Arrived uninvited," Remy explained.

"If they want to celebrate with us, then I am happy they came!"

They didn't look much in the mood to celebrate to Remy. They weren't joining in the festivities like everyone else, keeping themselves separated and secluded. The setting sun cast long shadows that hid their faces, but their stiff posture indicated that something was wrong. The way Bieito was resisting being towed along by his brother told Remy that these men probably weren't port workers, and if they were, then Bieito probably didn't care for them, but didn't want to make a scene.

When María stopped to talk to an elderly couple who were bestowing best wishes and kisses on the young woman while telling her to have lots of babies, Remy decided to gracefully excuse herself. *Don't want to taint her with my bad luck,* she thought, and then immediately felt guilty for being so bitter. Why, after all these years, couldn't she be happy for another woman's situation without thinking about herself? María had been nothing but sweet to Remy, and she and Lino deserved to have a family, if that's what they wanted. Still, Remy wondered why old people never considered that their words could be hurtful, and that not everyone had the option to have lots of babies. María was graciously accepting the grandparents' advice when Remy mumbled an excuse and bolted before the bride could protest.

Remy hid around the back of the bakery and collected her thoughts for a moment. She needed a distraction. Actually, what she really needed was to go back to dancing with Bieito, and not thinking about anything at all.

She walked the back way around the buildings, instead of through the village, to the table where the men still sat. Uncaring of how they eyeballed her disapprovingly as she approached, Remy realized she liked the look of them even less up close. They just looked—shifty. That was the word for it. Like they were prepared to bolt at any moment. Remy didn't trust people like that. Bieito, on the other hand, looked almost afraid when she walked up, and placed his body in between Remy and the other men.

"What are you gentlemen up to?" she asked. Bieito wrapped an arm protectively around her waist and leaned in close to her ear.

"This is not good time," he said, low but without malice. Bieito gestured his head over to Lino, who just looked like a little boy caught by his mother with a hand in the cookie jar. Whatever they were up to, Lino looked in over his head.

"Your wife was asking for you," Remy said to the groom. "It's urgent." She felt the tension ease slightly out of Bieito's posture. *Relief, then, about being given an exit.*

Lino addressed the men. "My apologies. It appears

I'm being summoned. We can continue this conversation later, but in the meantime, please stay and enjoy the party."

One of the men stood up, shaking his head. "We will be in touch." At his cue, the other five men rose without saying anything. The leader gave Lino a handshake, gripping until Lino's fingers turned white. "I trust you and your brother will think about our proposal." He then turned to Bieito, as if to shake his hand as well, but thought better of it.

With light feet and swift movements, the men disappeared down the quiet path toward Ortigueira, swallowed by the trees and the rapidly dimming light. Remy thought she saw them mount up on horses, but it was too dark to be sure. "Why didn't they just drive?" she muttered to herself. Everyone seemed to be taking this themed wedding very seriously.

Once they were gone, Remy said, "People you work with? They don't seem like fishermen."

Lino laughed nervously and dodged the question. "Where is María?"

"Over by the refreshments." It seemed that Remy wasn't going to get any information out of Lino, but she might have better luck with Bieito once they were alone. As the interrogation plan blossomed in her brain, Lino and Bieito's father tracked them down.

While he had been puffed up with pride at the ceremony, gazing with unashamed adoration at his youngest child while he said his vows, Afonso just looked pissed now. "Lino!" he said, storming over to them. "What is going on?"

Bieito stepped in front of his little brother, blocking him from his father's less-than-sober wrath. "Don't tell me you knew about this," Afonso said.

Bieito held up his hands. "Nothing, Father. I swear it."

"And you, Lino?" Afonso demanded.

Lino peeked over Bieito's shoulder. "No harm was done, Father. They just needed to speak with me."

"And you thought that bringing them here to our family's *wedding* was an appropriate time to do so?"

"I didn't invite them," Lino insisted. "But they didn't interrupt anything. Look," he said, gesturing to the party still in full swing in the town square. "No one even noticed they were here."

"You endanger yourself, you endanger your bride, you endanger our village—" Afonso stopped himself, realizing that Remy bore witness while he berated his sons like children. Struggling with himself to find the words, he finally said, "This is enough. You will not associate with them anymore. I don't care about their cause. No sons of mine will be caught up in their madness. Think of your new wife, Lino. She would be heartbroken."

What cause? What madness? Remy wanted to know more but bit her tongue. Lino stared straight ahead, fists clenched and bright red with either embarrassment or rage, maybe both. He took a deep breath and stormed off toward the square, without looking back at his father or brother.

Afonso shook his head. "I thought getting married would put these foolish ideas out of his mind," he said to Bieito. "Bah. Look at him. At his own wedding…"

"He has María to look after now, Father. He will come to the realization himself. Eventually."

"We'll keep an eye on him until he does, eh

Bieito?" Afonso sighed. "Family."

"It was a wonderful wedding, though," Remy assured the old man. "Really, I don't think anyone noticed the interruption. María didn't seem too bothered by it."

"Of course, she wasn't," Afonso said. "That María—her heart is as big as the sun. I am lucky to call her daughter now."

"If only the rest of her family was the same," Bieito pointed out.

Afonso chuckled. "Yes, let us be grateful we are not here for *your* wedding to Isabella."

Remy felt a flash of jealousy. Bieito and Isabella? Was that ever a possibility? She had assumed that Isabella's interest hadn't been reciprocated, but maybe once upon a time...

None of my business, she reminded herself. *Be an adult and change the subject.* "So, when are you guys doing family photos?" Remy had been surprised that the wedding went straight from the ceremony and into the reception without making the guests wait for the bridal party portraits. She hadn't seen a photographer or videographer among the crowd during the ceremony, but they could have just been skilled at blending in. Other traditions had been ignored too. There wasn't a wedding cake on display, no name cards on the tables in the square, no guest signing book. All of the formulaic components that had become commonplace in the American wedding industry were nowhere in sight. It was refreshing, but odd.

It might have been cultural difference, but it was also rather surprising that none of the guests had even whipped out their cameras or phones for some selfies.

Remy hadn't had her phone with her since getting back to the village but hadn't missed it at all the entire day. In fact, she had completely forgotten about it until now. *Maybe that's the point? Enjoy the moment instead of worrying how it will look on social media?* It was also entirely possible that Lino and María had asked the guests not to bring them as to fit in more seamlessly with the theme. *Still, there should be at least a few rule breakers among them.*

Remy snapped awake from her pondering to see Bieito and Afonso looking at her curiously. "Photos?" Bieito asked. "What is a photo?"

Remy laughed. "Seriously, stop. I know that you guys will probably grumble your way through it, but I'm sure María will want at least a few good photos of the whole family. You can be a good sport for her."

The two men exchanged a quick glance. "*Señora* Remy, are you talking about something American? I'm afraid we are unfamiliar with that word," Afonso said delicately.

Was the language barrier back up? Remy had been confident in her Spanish abilities all day, but now doubted herself. "You know," she tried again to explain, "like portrait pictures?"

"Oh no, we would never afford to have the family sit for a portrait painting," Afonso said.

"No, not a painting." Remy looked to Bieito for support. Hopefully it was just a generational miscommunication, but she was beginning to feel ridiculous having to explain to Bieito's father what a photograph was. Were they making fun of her? Was it a joke?

"Bieito, what kind of phone do you have? I don't

have mine on me." Instead of reaching into his pocket, Bieito looked just as confused as his father.

"Phone?"

"Oh, for God's sake!" Remy said. "I know we're isolated back here, but this has to be a prank."

Bieito set his hands on Remy's shoulders. "Take deep breaths, Remy. It is our fault we do not understand your words, but don't worry, we will figure it out together."

But Remy was not in the mood to be placated anymore. "Photos! Phone!" she said, like she was speaking to a toddler. Then she froze. Hypnotized, she turned around to look back at the village. *No cars. No phones. Horses. Costumes, but not costumes? Losing track of time. Populated village. My village but not. What is this?*

There were things in life that Remy accepted that most people would not be willing to wrap their heads around. She believed her wishes could actually make stuff happen, and that there was always a cost. She believed herself to be cursed. She was willing to believe there were some odd things about her village that she would need to eventually sort out. She believed that by some miracle, she could occasionally count on her foreign language skills to kick in when necessary.

What she was not prepared to deal with, however, was Bieito's answer to her next question. "Bieito, what year is it?"

"What year is it?" he repeated. "Eighteen forty-six."

Chapter Ten

Remy burst out laughing. Of course it was eighteen forty-six. What else would make sense? It made more sense than a theme wedding gone too far. Her giggles dissolved into full-blown hyperventilation. Bieito, not caring who saw, gathered Remy up in his arms and clutched her to him.

From a very faraway place, Remy heard Bieito order his father to fetch Remy something cool to drink. Then, he resumed murmuring sweet Spanish endearments into her ear, begging her to breathe and to tell him what was wrong.

Remy gasped for air, both her mind and body betraying her at the same time. She couldn't get control of her lungs or the thoughts careening around as her brain tried to make sense of it all. As with Bieito's cottage, when Remy tried too hard to analyze the village and any confusing events, her thoughts refused to connect. It was like trying to read Shakespeare while drunk. No matter how many times she went over the facts in her head, they slipped through the cracks like sand. It was futile to try and hold onto any sort of logic.

But she was determined to figure it out this time. And by focusing totally on her mental state, she released her physical body completely and let herself fall limp against Bieito, eyes unfocused. With her attention less divided, this strategy seemed to work, and allowed her to put all of her energy into figuring out what was happening to her.

I've apparently gone back in time. This is also not the first time. Either that, or I've completely lost my mind, this is a psychotic break, and none of these people are here. It is all just a figment of my imagination.

Remy decided she would much rather it be the first choice than the second, even as impossible as time travel might be.

Oh God, I might be stuck here forever. I haven't had any control over when I come and go here, past and present. It just always sort of...happens. When I'm upset or feeling strongly about something. Does that influence on how and when I get back here? Have I ever done this before, somewhere else?

Plenty of weird things had happened to Remy, but she was firm in her belief that she had never time traveled before. What was the catalyst?

The village. It only happens when I'm alone in my village. Well, that didn't bode well for her "it's not a psychotic break" theory.

But why here, and now? Why this time? The village had been around for hundreds of years, yet brought Remy here to this particular snapshot in time. What was so important about these wonderful people? Her experiences had only gotten more powerful and sustained the longer she resided in her new property. What began as a chance meeting with Bieito on the beach for an hour had lengthened each time Remy had been "brought back." Her fears and doubts had been soothed by time, wine, and company as the past drew her away from her everyday concerns. The longer she was back in the past, the less important her life in the present seemed. It was harder to remember small details about her normal life while she experienced the village in full glory.

Now that she was more attuned to her strange reality, Remy became aware of an underlying pull on her emotions. It was the same yearning that she ached to fulfill when she threw caution to the wind and bought the village. Something had been manipulating her. The choices Remy had been making since coming to Ortigueira had not been entirely her own.

A shiver went up her spine, and Remy's thoughts were cut off by a blinding migraine that made her cry out in pain. White lights flashed behind her eyelids and she couldn't feel her limbs anymore. Cool darkness washed over and released her from agony.

****

When Remy came to, she was buckled in to the front seat of a car. *I don't own a car.* She blinked and squinted through the windshield, trying to discern where she was parked. The clock on the dashboard glowed, informing her that it was close to midnight.

I'm in the middle of the square. At the village. This is Anita's rental car. Details started to come back to her, but they didn't explain why she would have no memory of driving the car into her home. *I thought I parked at the top of the drive?*

Remy unbuckled her seat belt and opened the door, a musical dinging reminding her to remove the keys as well before getting out of the vehicle.

Why am I here? she wondered, looking around. It felt wrong. The square looked wrong. What was missing? *Lights. There should be lights. And food. And a gazebo over here…*

Remy gasped as it all came pouring back. *The wedding was just here. It should still be here.* The memories of Bieito were sharp, clearer than her previous encounters with him. The ghost of his embrace still wrapped around her arms, protecting her against the night's chill. One minute she had been with him, and the next she was here. He had told her that it was eighteen forty-six. *I went back in time.*

But there had been something else, something important that she had been thinking about before the fairy tale night had been ripped away from her. It had been so hard to realize, she remembered that much. It was an epiphany within a dream, one she couldn't remember when she woke up.

However, she felt grounded in the certainty that whatever she had experienced, it *was* real. Bieito was real, he just wasn't *here.* Well, he was, in a sense, but not in this time. They were connected through the village. The village had brought them together.

A sense of deep loss and emptiness hit her, but she couldn't determine if it was coming from within her or some external force. A tear rolled down her cheek, and it was accompanied by a scattering of raindrops falling from the sky. The village was crying with her.

Do you see? it seemed to say to her. *Do you see how lonely it is?*

Instead of relief at not being stuck in the past, Remy only thought, *I need to go back. How do I get back?*

Remy was being torn in two. Her current plans of an art school and trying to resurrect her career just didn't seem as important any longer. The present only held a bitter ex-husband, an angry ex-best friend, an embarrassing career slump, and hemorrhaging finances. The only thing she loved about her current situation was the village.

Maybe the past is the real future for me. Maybe a simple, happy life was all that she needed. Her escape. The village was either her Miracle of Santiago, or her undoing, unraveling her mental state beyond repair.

Exhaustion dropped over her, and she needed to sleep before doing any more theorizing. Without thinking twice, Remy turned and headed for the cottage. *Home.* Dark red skirts swirled around her ankles, the soft swishing the only sound that accompanied Remy as she made her way down the empty path. Wherever she had been pulled from—eighteen forty-six or some parallel universe of it—would still be celebrating the wedding in full swing.

Experimentally, Remy kicked up her feet just like she had when dancing with Bieito and danced her way to the cabin door. She pulled the handle, and a note on the door caught her eye. For a wild moment, she thought maybe Bieito had found a way to reach her. However, she felt more than foolish as she read the note, followed by a deeper sense of guilt.

Remy,

I have tried calling you many times over the last few days. Maggie informed me that you left her apartment three days ago and she has not heard from you since, either. We do not know what has happened to you. The police have been unable to find your rental car, but your friend Anita told us not to file a missing person's report yet. She said you have a tendency to disappear, and that we should wait for you to contact

*us when you are ready. But please, please call me or
Maggie when you have returned.*

   Your friend,

   Sebastian

Remy hated to think she had put Sebastian or
Maggie through any sort of ordeal. She reread the note
and wondered how she could excuse her behavior. It
had been selfish of her to make them worry...*Wait, did
he say a few days?* How was that even possible? Remy
had woken up at Maggie's apartment that morning and
driven back from Madrid to Ortigueira. Though it was
the middle of the night, Remy was certain she had only
been gone in the "other" time for a few hours.

She recalled how Anita yelled at her for
disappearing for an extra day. She assumed she had lost
time because of the alcohol, but there was no way she
had disappeared for three days. Each time she went
back to the "other" village, she lost crucial periods in
her real life. As her trips got longer and the more time
she spent away from the present, it was progressively
more difficult for her to adjust.

There is always a cost, Remy reminded herself. It
worked that way with wishes, why not with time travel?
Am I aging faster here now? There were so many
technical questions running through her head she
needed a sci-fi geek to explain things to her. *I need to
move away from the 'how' and focus on the 'why'.*

But, before she could even begin to tackle that, she
needed to call Sebastian and tell him that she was alive.
Shit, I don't have my purse or my phone, Remy
realized. Everything was up in the car, which seemed
miles away at the moment. *I'll call him in the morning.
It's too late now anyway,* Remy thought, as she

clutched Sebastian's note and walked inside. *At least my sleeping bag is still here.*

As her eyes drifted closed, she suddenly remembered the drawing plans she had made with Maggie were still in the rental car, too, and it was almost enough to motivate her to get up. All of her dreams for the village, laid out on paper. The surrounding bare walls called to her to fix them and promised new life inside the cottage. She still had a lot of work to do in the present, and maybe she wasn't quite ready to give it all up to live in the past just yet.

Please let me wake up in my own time, she thought, on top of her sleeping bag, still fully clothed. *I need to sort out my mess on this end. I owe it to my friends, and I can't afford to lose any more time.*

If Jack and Anita still weren't speaking to her, then that was probably for the best. She wouldn't have to explain herself or her random disappearances, which was a relief. Instead, Remy just had to come up with a way to apologize to Sebastian and Maggie. It was very disconcerting being yanked back and forth, but at least she knew for certain that the present was real. She hoped.

Lying there, she missed Bieito with a starving longing.

She couldn't control or even anticipate what was happening in the past, or if she would ever find her way back there.

Could I have both? If Remy could figure out a way to control her travel, could she have everything she ever wanted? The village and the career in the present, but the love and acceptance she found in the past? Was it even possible?

She had never been able to reconcile her family dreams with her career aspirations, but what if it was because the two were never meant to coexist in the same time? The strangeness of the village, its removal from the laws of time and space, might just be the very miracle that she was waiting for from the Camino de Santiago.

Remy's heart lurched in her chest as it filled with hope, before the negative side weighed in. *What if I can't control it?* That would be even worse. Her life would be split in two, at the whim of forces outside of her control. She would be forced to live a half-life, unable to be secure in either of her realities.

The only factor she could be sure of was that the village had to remain the central part of this equation. Her fate and her life were inextricably tied to it now. The village would never be abandoned again.

Mind spinning with so many scenarios, Remy's thoughts kept circling back around to Bieito. *If I dream about him, will that take me back?* The temptation to test it out was overwhelming, but the persistent urge to do the right thing and talk to Sebastian and Maggie first was still on Remy's mind. If it worked, great, then she could go back to Bieito, but there were no guarantees when she might make it back into her own time again.

I can't sleep yet. I can't risk it. Not until I can control these time hops. Shaking off her fatigue, Remy got up and left the cottage.

I need something more to ground me to the present, she realized. Crumbling buildings and far-off dreams of reconstruction were not enough, the pull to be back with Bieito was too strong. If there was nothing for her to pull her back to the present, how would she go back and forth?

Fire and determination raced through her veins as she paced the streets of her village, seeing it both as it was and how it should be. The urgent need to do something great and impact the village at that very moment overpowered her, and a familiar itching started behind her eyes.

Remy stopped in her tracks, letting her eyes glaze over as she waited for the flash of inspiration that was about to pop into her mind. It was almost like preparing to sneeze. Think about it too hard, and the urge goes away, but the itching doesn't stop. A very unsatisfactory result. The best thing to do was to wait quietly for the inspiration to take over on its own.

Don't over think it. It had been so long—forever, it felt like—since Remy had felt the itch. Her sketch in the sand with Bieito was child's play compared to the drowning visions that used to inspire her artwork back in New York. The tickle that teased her mind was so close to surfacing, and Remy could already tell that the picture would be the accumulation of patiently waiting for months for her skill to come back.

A minute passed, and then two, as Remy paced the dirt path outside the cottage. When her feet did an abrupt ninety-degree turn and started walking toward the main house, she didn't fight it. Her arms swung free of their own accord, feet almost dancing as they had with Bieito just hours ago—or was it days? Remy's mind floated free from her body as she released the iron grip of control.

Remy had missed this feeling with a painful ache. A deep exhaustion from trying to be rigidly in control all the time melted off her shoulders and she realized how much it affected her day to day happiness. She hadn't been truly happy since she had painted her last collection. Sure, there were fleeting moments here and there, in the village and with Bieito and her friends, but there was something singular and special about the moments she spent with a brush in her hand, the real world closed off by canvas as she created her own.

Light as a feather, Remy climbed the front porch stairs to the main house and found the tool she was looking for—a can of black spray paint, used weeks ago to mark the other possibly dangerous areas inside.

Remy always used color, no matter how dark the theme of her paintings. She also only ever used acrylic paints that she mixed herself. The can in her hand, cold and industrial, was an artistic medium she had never considered before.

Its weight in her hand felt right, filled with the color of shadows, paint that appeared and disappeared in the blink of an eye, activated by the lightest touch of a finger. The tool of degenerates and rebels, gang bangers marking territory, or sending a message. However, spray paint had also launched the enigma that was Banksy, forcing people to see his perspective of the world in a way that everyone could connect with.

No, spray paint was not Remy's typical choice for a painting, but neither was the side of a building. In a bold jump from canvas to one hundred-year-old walls, Remy decided to make her mark. The piece would have to be big and meaningful enough in order to pull her back here, a symbol of past and present merged. *A metaphorical gateway.*

She considered all of the possible walls for her mural and settled on the wall at the back of the main house. The one outside, underneath the window where she saw Bieito standing on the street before the wedding. There were some crumbling parts, but as a whole, the main part of the structure was smooth and intact.

As she raised her hand to start, Remy hesitated. It was one thing to be able to return to her art, it was quite another to return in such a large and new way. But the longer she stared at her life-size canvas, the greater the itching behind her eyes became, until her eyes watered in protest. The image was there, in her brain, and she just needed to let go of self-doubt and press her finger down.

The soft *shhhhh* of the can in the silent night made her fumble it in surprise. It was hard to see the black paint in the dark, but Remy could see the results clearly in her mind. She was painting blind, but her fingers and hand knew what to do, so she let herself go.

With bold strokes, she passed over large swaths of the wall, never letting go of the picture she held in her mind. She was painting the shadows, learning to create figures and emotions using the empty space that emerged from them. It was backward to what she usually did. She was looking to reveal the life using the shadows, not using the colors as a way to force life into her work.

Remy worked the balance from the other end, discovering a side of herself she hadn't known she was capable of reaching. She had never approached her art, or life, from the side of the darkness before. Hours passed, and as pink light tinged the horizon, Remy finally started to slow down.

When the sun hit the wall with a golden glow, she

stepped back and shook herself from her fog. With a sob, Remy dropped her now-empty can onto the ground.

Two figures, neither male nor female, intertwined in a connected embrace. They appeared to be floating, either in the air or under water. They spiraled around each other, no end and no beginning, locked in place, one not being able to exist without the other. All brought to life in the negative of the shadows.

Who are these people? Remy had created them from the deepest and most intimate part of herself, but she had no idea. For an instant, she pictured having to explain the piece at an auction or come up with a title for a gallery display. Something that would get the people talking and speculating, all while Anita buzzed around the party and added kindling to the fire.

No, she didn't have to worry about any of that. For the first time in a long time, she could let the piece just be what it was, a snapshot into her psyche at that given time. Something beautiful that didn't need to be analyzed or sold. It was just for Remy, and she was proud of it. There was no paint left in the can even for her to sign the bottom corner of it. It was hers, but she didn't need to take credit for it.

She almost laughed when she thought about Sebastian or Anita or Maggie stumbling upon it. Would they know it was her, or would they think some vandal had trespassed on the village while she was gone?

No, Maggie would know that I did it. I was here, and okay. The older woman would connect instantly with the artwork. The mural was the first truly meaningful way that Remy had tried to make the village in this time period her own. A part of her soul was now up on the walls for all to see, that she could belong in both this time and the past. It was the first real step to taking control of her situation.

Now, should I test it out? There were a million things that Remy should be doing, including reassuring her friends that she was not, in fact, a missing person, but it was still early, and the urge was too strong. *I know what's happening to me now,* she reasoned. *I can get back to this time. I know I can. I just want to check on Bieito and the family. They are probably really worried about me right now, too. I'll just pop in for a second, to see if it works, see if I really can control it.*

Remy sat on the ground in front of her mural, took a deep breath, and closed her eyes. She thought hard about Bieito, the way his arms felt around her, his lips on her wrist, the joy she felt when his eyes lit up when she spoke.

Holding onto all the memories, she popped open her eyes and looked around expectantly. No change. She was still in front of the mural.

Panic set in almost immediately as her mind automatically jumped to the worst-case scenario. *What if the wedding was all I got? What if I can never get back to him?* Remy squeezed her eyes shut and tried again, but this time there were doubts infringing on her concentration.

When the mural appeared in front of her again, Remy realized what she was trying to do. *I'm actively trying to go back in time.* Ridiculous. She burst out in a half-laugh, half-sob and started to doubt Bieito's actual existence. *What am I doing here?* As always, the dark option floated its temptation—*you could wish for it.*

In the harsh light of day, her decision to paint a

mural as a portal through time seemed like a bad dream. "I need to get out of here," she said aloud. But as soon as she said the words, dizziness overcame her and the earth lurched underneath, like a rug pulled out from under her butt. Remy fell over backward and looked up at the morning glow.

Then, like a miracle, Bieito's concerned face appeared above her, perfectly framed by a cloudless blue, late-afternoon sky.

"Remy?" he said, and, throwing away all self-imposed inhibitions, took her face in between two callused hands, and leaned down.

It wasn't a slow-motion, epic-music, movie-climax kind of kiss. It wasn't the gentle, hesitant touch of a man brought up in a traditional society. There was nothing old-fashioned or demure about Bieito's kiss, and it wasn't at all what Remy had expected from him.

It was raw. Urgent. Filled with panic, but not at the thought of her possible rejection. More like he was afraid she was going to disappear any second. Bieito wasn't taking any chances this time as his lips found hers, desperate to keep hold of her for as long as he could.

Remy's lips parted as she molded her mouth to his, inviting him to go deeper. Bieito's hands moved from her cheeks to the back of her head and neck, clutching her to him. Remy's fingers found his hair, and she tangled them in his dark curls. Nothing was going to tear them apart this time. Bieito's body crushed into hers, leaving no space between them.

Air didn't matter, nothing mattered but the magic Bieito's tongue was working in her mouth. Who cared if he was real or not? *This* was what pulled Remy across time and space. Him.

With a groan, Bieito pulled himself off Remy and sat up, face flushed. He stared at her through dark eyelashes, afraid to look away in case she vanished again, but also waiting to gauge her reaction.

"Why'd you stop?" Remy struggled to form words, drunk from the unexpected kiss.

"Where did you go?" Bieito asked, dodging the question but reaching out to help Remy sit up. His hands didn't pull away even after her butt was firmly planted.

"How did I get to the beach?" That seemed like the more pressing question at the moment. Remy's fancy red dress was completely covered in salty wet sand, her hair a caked mess. "Huh. I thought for sure I'd end up in the square again. But you're here too! Why are you at the beach and not at the wedding?"

Bieito's eyes narrowed with concern. "*Mi amor,* the wedding was a week ago. I have been searching for you since that night. I even feared that the revolutionaries—" Overcome, he leaned forward and locked his lips to hers once more, hard and fast. He released her and took a deep breath.

"My apologies. This is not proper."

"Hey, I'm not complaining!" Remy said, and moved to pull his face back down, but the look in his eyes stopped her.

Their foreheads gently rested together, and he asked again, "Where did you go? You are making me crazy, Remy."

"If you're insane, then so am I. I don't know what's happening, either."

"Promise me you will not leave like that again."

Remy swallowed hard. "I can't promise that. I'm sorry, but I can't. But I don't want to leave you, either. I-I don't have control. I wish I did."

"Just stay with me. All the time. Stay in my village, do not return to your home. I want us to be together."

"I want to be with you all the time, too, Bieito. But I am—literally—torn between worlds right now. Can we just be thankful right now that I'm here with you? I'm so relieved I could make it back." Short of telling Bieito the rest of the story, she changed the subject. "So, I lost a week, huh? Interesting."

Now that Bieito knew Remy was safe, his worry turned to anger. "Interesting? I've been searching for days, in all the surrounding villages. The beaches. The port. I thought something terrible had happened to you."

"I've been home, technically. Bieito, please don't think too hard about it right now. I couldn't explain, even if I wanted to. And I don't know if you'd believe me." True regret reflected in her eyes, and Bieito immediately softened.

"The tide is rising," he said. "We will get wet soon."

"Where do you suggest we go?" Remy asked, determined to live in the moment and appreciate the time they had together. Bieito wouldn't be placated forever, but it bought Remy a little time to come up with some sort of explanation. "You know, I really should get out of this dirty dress."

Bieito's eyebrows shot up with surprise, and he let out a booming laugh. "*Mi amor,* you certainly have an American way about you, but with the passion of a Galician woman."

"I think I can wear this a little longer, if you don't think it will get too ruined."

"I will take you home, and you can be comfortable," Bieito insisted. "Though I am flattered to see that you like the dress so much you have continued to wear it."

She didn't want to go back to the village just yet, in case she got yanked out again to her own time. Part of her experiment, in addition to controlling her jumps, was to see if she could be in the past but remain outside of the village. To break out of the bubble and see more of Bieito's world, to understand if it was just the village itself that held the power or if Remy had it within her.

"Let's go to the port," she said.

Bieito pulled back, horrified. "I should think not!"

"I want to see where you work." *And there seems to be a lot of interesting activity around there,* but she didn't say that part out loud.

"It is much too rough to bring you there. It is not safe."

"Because of the revolutionaries?" Remy asked with wide, innocent eyes.

Bieito jumped at her words, and instinctively looked around. He lowered his voice to answer. "Yes, because of the revolutionaries. But we cannot speak of them."

"Why?"

"The wrong people may be listening."

"Bieito, you're being paranoid! We are the only people on this beach. Please just explain to me what's going on."

He set his jaw and turned away. "There must be no suspicion turned on my family. You are putting me in a difficult place."

Remy flushed red, seeing how scared and uncomfortable her causal questions were making him. "You know you can trust me, right?"

"Your life must be much different in America," Bieito said, and looked like he wanted to continue, but stopped himself. Remy watched him struggle to find the right words and jumped in to interrupt him.

"You know what? Never mind. We don't have to go to the port."

Bieito bowed his head and wrung his hands, hating to disappoint her. It was starting to get awkward. Couldn't they just go back to the kissing part?

"Ah!" Bieito said, brightening. "I know what we will do." He offered his hand to Remy. "Come with me."

Considering her dress a lost cause, Remy didn't bother hiking up her hem. "Is it a surprise?" she asked, interlacing her fingers with Bieito's callused ones. Not that walking hand in hand down the beach with a handsome Spanish man wasn't a romance novel in itself, but Remy was hoping for a bit more action.

It had been a long time since Remy had felt this part of her come alive. A very long time since she and Jack had been intimate. Even longer since she hadn't associated physical closeness with the stress of trying desperately for a baby. Once they decided not to try anymore, and attempted to separate sex from the heartbreaking devastation of either a miscarriage or another month of failure, they found that they couldn't go back to the carefree early days.

Jack's closeness, or attempt at physical connection, was just a sad reminder of an anxious time. It held no hope or fun, just tinged with a sadness that Remy knew they would never move past. That was why Jack had been so surprised the final time Remy seduced him, after making her fateful wish. When she came to him that night, there had also been a spark inside of her that he hadn't seen in a long time. The spark of hope and fire that had been missing from their marriage.

He had given into her advances without protest, hardly willing to believe his good luck. He asked her afterward, as they lay on their bed without space between them for the first time in years, if they should go away together, and take another honeymoon. A rebirth of their marriage.

Remy, in order to placate him, had agreed noncommittally, but already her mind was spinning with the possibilities of what the next few months would bring instead. The line had been crossed that night. She had made her wish, and there was no going back. She wanted to confess at that moment, as her head rested on Jack's shoulder, held up in his arms but weighed down by her decision. It hadn't been on purpose. She hadn't meant to give Jack that amount of hope for them, the assumption that the two of them could go back to normal, but she was unwilling to crush and bring him down to her level of desperation. For her, it was the exact moment where she betrayed herself, and everything fell apart.

So she said nothing, and that was the last time between them. Remy knew that they probably remembered it quite differently, given their difference in context. Maybe that was why he had had such a hard time letting go and signing the divorce papers, following her all the way to Spain because of a different interpretation of their last close memory together.

Seeing him in her village had put her into a tailspin, and the physical temptation to re-explore the familiar reared up, but Remy was grateful she had resisted. A rebirth wasn't been possible with Jack, but she could start something new and pure with Bieito.

A cool breeze whipped across the bay and Remy shivered. Her feet and dress were covered in salt spray and wet sand. She was raw, exposed, and possessed nothing from her former life, not even the clothes on her back. Fresh and untainted by the past, she felt ready to try again.

The feeling of Bieito's urgent kiss still tingled on her lips, and Remy risked a glance over at him. He gave her an easy, uncomplicated smile, eyes lit up in excitement for her surprise. Instead of feeling like a wanton, experienced woman approaching forty, Remy found herself as shy as a teenager, too nervous to make the first move. Deep down, was Remy afraid she would curse him like she had cursed Jack, and everything would blow up in her face the moment she decided to take that next step?

Being with Bieito wasn't like dating in the twenty-first century. There was something about him that told her if she took the plunge, then there was no going back. She felt strongly for him, sure, and the thought of being without him or unable to get back to him made her panic, but was she really ready for a 'forever' type of thing? This was a different kind of line than the one she faced with Jack, but a line all the same, and Remy had to be certain this time before she crossed it. That would lead to a free-fall, and Remy still wanted to hang onto her control, even if she was clawing at it with her fingernails.

She had painted that mural in her own time for a reason. It wasn't time yet to let go. But oh, how she wanted to. But the last time she had let herself do what she wanted without regard for consequence, her life had imploded. Walking this tightrope was exhausting.

"You are quiet, *mi amor*," Bieito said, breaking Remy from her destructive thought cycle. "I hope I did not frighten you earlier."

"It has just been an overwhelming last few hours," Remy said.

"For me, it was an anxious few days," Bieito admitted. "But now, I feel calm. You are by my side, so nothing will go wrong."

*If only you knew...*Remy squeezed his hand and stepped closer to him, so her shoulder brushed his arm. "Will you tell me where we're going?"

"Around the bend a little farther. I would like to share something with you."

"Do you want me to guess?"

He chuckled. "You can try, but I think this is something new for you."

New for me? Well, I think I can be certain he isn't planning on seducing me, then. As they rounded the beach, a little sailboat sat upon the sand. It was tucked up a ways on the bank, out of reach of the tide, nestled in between some large boulders. A long rope ran from the bow, securing it to a scraggly tree poking out from the rocks.

Remy let go of Bieito and ran up to it. The wood was smooth, cared for and sanded by hand for years. The boat was small, but obviously loved. "Is this yours?" Remy asked. "Did you make this?"

Bieito ducked his head. "Yes, my brother and I made it years ago."

"It's beautiful!"

"I thought you would like it."

"Do I get to ride in it?"

"If you would like."

"I've been on row boats and skiffs before, but never on a sailboat. How do you make it work?"

He untied the bow line, moved it to the stern, and began digging a channel in the sand to drag the boat out to the water. "You have to listen to the water, and the air. You have to dance with both of them, and not be in a rush to get to a destination."

That sounded pretty doable to Remy. In fact, it sounded like the perfect way to travel. "Did your father teach you how to sail?"

"He did. My mother loved to sail. They used to go out all the time together. It was the one activity my mother would put away all else for. If the winds were right, she would look at us and say, 'No more work today. Go get your father. We are going to the boat.'"

"And you guys would take this out?"

"It was another boat. One my father made for my mother."

"He didn't help you make this one?"

"No. Sailing makes him miss her too much." Bieito grasped the stern rope and began to tug the boat behind him down to the water.

"Did something happen?"

Bieito pulled the boat down to the white foam before he stood up to answer. "My mother was dying of an illness. It took her quickly, and she had mere hours left. My father, in his grief, took both her and the sailboat out to sea, intending not to live without her. The worst storm in fifty years struck the bay and capsized him. My father washed ashore, barely alive, but the boat and my mother's body were gone. He regrets it to this day that he has no grave site to visit, and that his madness blinded him to his responsibilities to his children. So, he vowed never to go out on the water again. He is a fisherman still, at heart, but does his work dockside while my brother and I bring in the catch. He believes it to be his penance."

"Bieito, I am so sorry. That must have been tragic for your whole family. I don't know what to say."

He shrugged. "It was a long time ago. We all handle grief differently. I am thankful that my brother was small when it happened, and he is not as weighed down by it as my father and I are."

"But you still take to the water," Remy noticed. "Do you feel close to Catarina here?"

"This is where I feel my mother's spirit. I do not run from it; I embrace it. I think it was fitting that the waters took her body. It was where she was happiest. I do not mourn that she did not have a proper Christian burial, though I know that it deeply offends some. She is exactly where she belongs, and watches over me when I am out there."

"I completely believe that," Remy agreed. "And I think she would be happy to know that her son still finds such joy in the same thing that she did."

Bieito busied himself with the boat once more, but Remy could tell that her statement touched him. She was grateful that Bieito had opened up, and the dynamic between him and his brother and father suddenly made all the more sense. The way Bieito took care of the two of them, why Lino had fallen in love and gotten married, but Bieito kept himself on the outside. He chose never to get too close, to watch over his family instead.

Wanting him to feel comfortable opening up to her some more, Remy decided to give Bieito something of herself in return. "I have not lost a parent, but I never fit into my family, and I don't think they mourned me when I left, even though I might as well have died in their eyes. I almost lost my brother when I was young, and things were never the same after that. Moving away and actually doing something with my life was considered the ultimate betrayal. I can't say I've been through what you've been through, but I *have* lost something precious to me. Precious somethings. Irreplaceable. And each loss took a part of my heart I can never get back. I admire you, Bieito, for how you've held everything together. You are a remarkable man."

The sailboat was now in the water, and Bieito held the line so tight his knuckles were white. Remy saw him swallow hard, his throat bobbing with emotion. "No one else has ever been on this boat besides me and Lino," he told her.

"I'm honored to be your first guest."

He held out his hand to her, and Remy grabbed it like a lifeline. They stood knee deep in the freezing surf, the waves breaking around them but neither one feeling the cold. "I think the ocean brought you to me," Bieito whispered, so low that Remy could barely catch his words.

"The ocean. Or the village. Or the Camino." Bieito heaved Remy aboard, her wet skirts a heavy tangle around her legs. "Or maybe, a combination of all three. Because no matter what, we were meant to find each other."

Chapter Eleven

Bieito transformed at the helm. Holding onto the tiller, he expertly steered them through the breaking waves, showing no hint of fear. He was right—it was a dance. Remy tried to stay out of the way as he raised and trimmed the sail. Soon they were flying. The little sailboat skipped over the choppy waves, riding on moonlight.

Their serious conversation from earlier was placed on an indefinite hold. Remy couldn't speak right now even if she wanted to. The entire experience stole her breath away, and all she could do was hold on tight, smiling from ear to ear until her cheeks ached.

Let's sail forever. Remy longed to just keep moving forward, into the unknown. To never see land again, and to live in the waves and at the whim of the wind. It blew all the thoughts and worries straight out of her head.

This was Bieito's version of painting. The release of consciousness as he let his body live in the moment, just as Remy did with a brush. She looked back at him from her seat across the cockpit. The lines on his face were completely smoothed out in the silver light, and she could see the boy he used to be; a boy who got his love of the sea from his mother, and the respect of the sea when he learned how to ride it.

Remy could picture him as a teenager. When all of

the other kids were preoccupied with courting and flirting, Bieito would escape down to the beach, and out onto the water. She bet he disappeared from sunup to well after sundown, only to return with sunburned skin and untamed hair. Not even the responsibilities and drudgery of adulthood in the coming years could keep him away from what he loved. Fishing all day on a working boat wouldn't be the same, and Bieito would still crave the solitude and freedom of his own small sailboat.

This is the real reason that Bieito never married. Nobody else can understand this passion. The sea was his mistress, and he would return to it every time. No other woman could understand always coming in second place.

It was the same problem with Jack. He could never reach Remy while she was lost in her own world, no matter how much he begged to be let in. Jack never got over the fact that there was a piece of Remy he could never touch. There was nothing in his life that drove him like painting drove Remy, and she believed that a part of him deeply resented her for it. Maybe even blamed her for it. It took walking away from her marriage to see that Remy needed a partner in life, not another person to complete her. Jack wanted to fill the role as her other half, but she was already a whole person. Painting was already her other half, her true soul mate.

Watching Bieito now, Remy's hand itched to hold a brush, to preserve the wild and distant look in his eyes forever. Bieito had never found his other half because he didn't need one.

The coastline was rapidly disappearing behind her.

The only evidence of land was the white foam crashing onto the shore, and somewhere far up the cliffs, lay Remy's village. Would they land back on shore in Bieito's time, or Remy's? Would she walk up onto the sand, only to find herself alone again?

The wind shifted, bringing up a large wave that crashed over Remy and into the boat. The shock of the water only added to her adrenaline.

"How far can we go?" she shouted.

"All night, if you want."

"How far have you sailed by yourself?" Remy asked, scooting closer to him.

"By accident or on purpose?"

"You've gotten lost before?"

"Many times. But you do not have to worry. Because of all those times, I can find my way back home wherever I am, no matter the weather."

How nice it must be to always be able to find your way back home. Technically, his home is my home. So if I'm with Bieito, I guess I can always find my way back home, too.

"Right now, we are sailing upwind," Bieito explained. "Feel how the wind pulls the sail forward? When we turn around, we will be sailing downwind. That's when the ocean and the wind will push us back to shore."

"Oh, so upwind pulls you, like an airplane wing."

Bieito looked confused. "A what?"

"Never mind."

"Is that a type of sail? Or a boat?"

"It's a complicated explanation. Tell me more about sailing."

"When I move the tiller, it turns the rudder

underneath the boat. Would you like to try?"

"Am I going to capsize us?"

"I will be here the whole time," Bieito promised.

Remy tentatively gripped the wooden stick, surprised by the immediate feel of drag underneath it due to the current. "It's fighting me!" She almost let go when it yanked her sideways. Bieito's arms latched around her waist and he pulled her back down onto his lap. Placing his hand behind hers, they steered the boat together, and Remy got a feel for it.

"I can see why this is addicting," she said into his ear. She couldn't help but give it a nuzzle with her cold nose and laughed when she felt him jump. "There's no roads or anything to restrict you. You can just go wherever you feel like, day or night."

"That's why my mother loved it. The one place in her life that there were no restrictions, no judging eyes. The rest of the village never truly understood her. They thought she was odd. You remind me of her."

Remy leaned away. "I remind you of your mother?"

"Only in the way that you care not what others think. You live by your own schedule and whims. It is frustrating for me, especially when you disappear for days on end, but I am beginning to trust that you will always find your way back to me. That is all I could hope for."

Well, when he puts it that way, it doesn't sound so bad.

Another wave burst above the boat, spraying Remy again. She shivered and felt Bieito's arms tighten around her. "We have been out too long. You are cold. This was thoughtless of me to take you out in the dark.

You should be sailing in the sunlight, comfortable." He cranked the tiller to the right and the boat spun around, bobbing like a cork, insignificant in the sheer amount of water surrounding them.

"Downwind, then?" Remy asked, and Bieito looked pleased that she had been paying attention.

"Yes, downwind. We should be back to shore in much less time."

"I still can't believe you can get us back to where we left. I can't see anything!"

"I can feel it calling to me. Stay warm, *mi amor.* Stay close. We will be there soon."

Remy didn't need to be told twice, and was lulled into a trance by the waves, darkness, and Bieito's unending warmth. Yawning against Bieito's shoulder, she said, "Do you promise we can do this again soon?"

"Anytime you like, *mi amor.* I would be overjoyed to share this with you."

"Do you think she'll be jealous?"

"Who will be jealous?"

"The sea. Having to share you."

Bieito kissed her temple, and Remy closed her eyes. The next thing she knew, she felt a bump on the bottom of the boat and her eyes flew open. They were at the beach once again. Bieito gently disentangled himself from her and leaped off to pull the boat in.

Remy, not wanting to be additional weight, jumped off as well, and grabbed onto the rope to help. Together, they hauled the boat out of the water and up onto the sand. In the boat's usual spot, however, there was already somebody occupying it.

"Father?" Bieito asked, incredulous.

The figure, who had been laying down, popped his

head up at his name. "Where have you been, son?" Afonso demanded. "I have been waiting here for hours for you to return."

"What happened? Is something wrong?"

"We need to discuss Lino," he said. Then, seeing that Remy stood next to Bieito, remembered his manners. "My dear, you should not let my daft son talk you into sailing at night!" He turned to Bieito. "And you! She will catch her death of cold out here. I thought you were trying to woo this woman?"

"It was my idea," Remy said, feeling a bit ridiculous that two middle-aged, consenting adults needed to justify their choice of date to a father waiting up for them.

Bieito moved forward to help his father out of the sand and onto his feet. "We are not the only ones who will catch a sickness out here. Why on earth could you not have waited for me at home?" Bieito demanded.

"Bah! You have been gone at all hours lately. I had no idea when you would return. I thought to check the beach, and when I saw the boat was missing, I knew you would at least be back here, though I did not know you would be bringing Remy along." He paused and turned to her. "It *is* good to see you again. You had us all worried."

"What about Lino?" Bieito asked. "Is he in trouble?"

His father hesitated, looking around the deserted beach cloaked in darkness. "I am not comfortable discussing it in the open."

"Father," Bieito said, exasperated. "There is nobody else around. Remy will not breathe a word, either."

"You never know who is listening. They could be anywhere."

"We saw nobody else earlier, and you have been guarding the beach for quite some time. Unless you heard anyone, I doubt they are down here in the middle of the night."

His father shook his head. "You have your head in the clouds most days, Bieito. You do not realize just how bad it has become lately. I am afraid there has been much more than just talk and grumbling. Are you even listening at the port and in Ortigueira? People are angry, and they are ready to take action. Have you been looking out for your brother?"

"Of course, Father. We spend every day together on the fishing boat, then he goes home to María. They are newlyweds, and together you and I decided to give them time alone—"

"María came to me tonight. She was quite distraught, asking why we were making Lino work extra hours. I told her that we had been sending him home to her early, and she said she knew nothing about that. Bieito, your brother has been disappearing, leaving his new wife alone at home. Lying to her and us. I fear the worst."

Remy couldn't keep her mouth shut anymore. "I can't believe he's having an affair!"

"No, *Señora* Remy. My son would never break his vows. I fear it is much worse than that. Politics."

Bieito's eyes were dark and stormy. "We do not know for sure what he is tangled up in, Father. We need to tread carefully. If he is involved somehow, these are dangerous people we need to get him away from."

"What do they want?" Remy asked.

"Independence," Bieito's father whispered.

"And they need Lino to help them get it?"

"They need sympathizers," Bieito explained. "People to spread their message. Give them supplies. Help with the movement in any way they can."

"A revolution?"

"Yes."

Remy remembered being on Maggie's couch, warm, sleepy, and full of takeout. Maggie had been reading to her from her Galician history book. *A revolution. Martyrs of something. Martyrs mean failure. Uh oh.*

"Oh shit," she said, and both Bieito and his father jumped at her curse. Then, Afonso nodded seriously. "*Mierda* is right," he agreed.

"You guys have got to talk him out of this. It is doomed to fail." They assumed she spoke out of fear for Lino, when really Remy was telling them an actual historical fact.

Bieito held up his hands, silencing the other two. "I will speak with him, and find out how involved he truly is, and what he has been doing for them."

"Bieito, he met with a group of them at his own wedding," Remy pointed out. "I think it is safe to say he's pretty involved. And going so far as to abandon María—though we all know how crazy he is about her—I think it is safe to say that Lino is in way over his head. Confronting him might not be the way to go; he will just get defensive. You might just have to follow him and see what he gets up to."

"Spy on my own brother?" Bieito managed to look both saddened and offended at her suggestion.

"I don't think you'll get the whole story or big

picture out of him any other way."

Bieito shook his head. "That is not what my brother would do. He trusts me. I need to trust him as well, to be honest with me. I expect he will want to confess. My brother has never been one for keeping secrets. He is also against violence."

"Even if he is the smallest bit involved with them, Bieito, isn't that still treason? You have to save him from himself!"

Bieito's voice rose. "You accuse my brother of being a traitor! Of already assuming he has committed the worst!"

"Well, no, I—" Remy sputtered, caught off guard at the vehemence of his outburst.

"My brother is an idealist, yes. He was probably tricked or pulled into this, but you cannot be certain he has committed a crime!"

He is also a grown-ass man, who is married to boot. I'm willing to bet he knows exactly what he's doing. Poor María...

"Bieito, maybe your father is right. We shouldn't be discussing this out in the open. Let's all go back to the cottage and see if we can't come up with a plan."

Bieito took a deep breath and looked over at his father, who had been watching the exchange between him and Remy without a word. His gaze must have spoken volumes to his son, though, because the next words out of Bieito's mouth stunned Remy. "I think my father and I need to handle this alone, as a family matter. I will make sure you get home safely, though."

"Bieito, seriously. I can help. I know more about this than you think, and if we are going to get Lino out of this alive—" Remy's vision started to tunnel, cutting off her plea. *Not now, not now,* she begged, trying to hold onto consciousness. *I need to stay here. I need to help them.*

****

Apparently her plea to the universe, the village, the Camino, or whatever else was yanking Remy around fell on deaf ears. "God damn it," she moaned, finding herself on the hard ground behind the main house once again. She sat up with a sigh, head pounding. Not only had she been yanked out before she could tell Bieito and his father what she knew, but it had been in the middle of her and Bieito's first fight. Double crap.

The date had been going so well, too. Seeing and experiencing that part of him...Remy was more sure now than ever that he was her match, and that she could truly build a life with him. Or a half-life, maybe, split between his time and hers. She would explain it one day and have the best of both worlds. That is, if she could ever figure out the rules of the village and learn to control this jumping back and forth. Not only was it frustrating, but it was starting to get dangerous.

Remy's heart ached for Lino, as well as for Bieito and Afonso. She couldn't let anything bad happen to them. Lino was headed down a path that was guaranteed to fail, if he really was as deeply involved with the separatist forces as she suspected.

"Take me back," she begged. Only silence answered her plea, her village devoid of any other signs of life. Why was it doing that to her? Giving her what she wanted, and then taking away? "Did I do something wrong?" she yelled. "I need an answer!"

The cool night that surrounded her while she was with Bieito moments before was gone. The sea breeze

204

that had wrapped around her like an ethereal cloak had been stripped away, leaving her raw and exposed. Now, Remy stood in the midday sun. Everything was too harsh, too bright, too *real*. The broken-down buildings in this hard light seemed more like a nightmare she needed to wake up from, rather than a familiar home. It was just too painful to be here, and she felt more alone than ever before.

She had no idea if it was mere moments after her time hop, or if weeks had gone by. The good news was that her village was still standing, and her painting was still up. Remy hoped it meant that people weren't worried about her too much. Either that, or they had given up completely that she would ever return.

"What did I do?" she yelled at the sky. Open palmed, she slapped the painting. "Let me back through! Don't take him from me now."

With all of the variables surrounding the time shifts, there were no guarantees when she would return to him. If her past luck was any indication, it might be too late already. If anything happened to Lino, it would destroy Bieito, and any semblance of a future with him would be gone as well. He would never recover or open his heart again.

Remy knew she had a role to play in all of this; she just couldn't figure out exactly was it was. As she clawed at her painting, trying to rip her way back through to Bieito, she replayed the last few moments with him.

I assumed my role was to tell them about the revolution, but as soon as I tried, I got yanked out. But if she wasn't supposed to be there to help, why had she traveled back in the first place? *Is it some grand 'spoiler alert'? I can't just be expected to witness and not say anything.* Remy held valuable knowledge about the future, and about the direction in which Galicia itself was taking. It was powerful, to be all-knowing. She could save lives. She could transform the future.

It hit her like a truck. *That's the problem.* Remy had been allowed to stay with Bieito until she opened her mouth and threatened to reveal too much. She thought back to all the other times she had been yanked out—asking for Bieito's phone number, talking about photography...

I need to play by the rules, she realized. The game was so obvious it about smacked her in the face. *I can be with Bieito, as long as I don't upset his time period.* The minute she broke the rules, she would be pulled into her own time again, as punishment until the powers-that-be let her in again.

Remy couldn't control her trips, not really, but she *could* control her actions in order not to get pulled out again. "All right," she announced. "I will do it your way. I won't tell him." At the same time, she also made a promise to herself. *I won't do anything to change too much, unless it comes down to life and death.*

Playing puppet master would be difficult, especially because Remy only had the most rudimentary knowledge of actual events from a small excerpt in an old history book. If she had time, Remy could have thrown herself into studying everything she could about the uprising—names, dates, places, and more. Instead, she only knew that some colonel organized a failed coup, there were lots of sympathizers in Ortigueira, and ultimately all of his followers were executed.

And Lino might be one of them. Being armed with the minimal knowledge that the revolution would fail would have to be enough. There was no time to become an expert on some obscure little rebellion in a tiny former kingdom of Spain. It had barely made a blip in the history books.

But Lino was real, not a piece of history. Dealing with flesh and blood altered the stakes. Remy had to get back and help any way she could, and subtly nudge and cajole Bieito's family to safety. The only rule was that she couldn't reveal too much.

Remy started to sweat, her heavy dress now dried in the sun but stiff from her sailing adventure. The essence of the sea mingled with the salt on her skin, and the stinging sensation brought Remy back to her body. It forced her to remember that, no matter how much she plotted, there was currently no way to get back right now.

"Argh!" *I have a plan, I understand the rules, and the more time I spend here, the greater the chances that something disastrous is happening on the other side!* Nothing in her own world mattered at the moment—the crumbling buildings, the time she had spent away, the messes she had to clean up, her worried friends, her angry ex-best friend and ex-husband…An event that happened more than a hundred years ago was the most pressing matter in her life. If she could help Bieito and his family, then she would be able once again to focus on the village in the present, but until she knew that the danger had passed, every waking moment of hers would be devoted to finding her way back to him as quickly as possible.

If anything happens to them while I'm gone, I will

never again be able to live in the village. "You know that?" she challenged. "I swear to God, if anything bad happens to them while I'm stuck here, I'm selling this crap heap and leaving for good!"

She slapped the main house for emphasis, and as soon as her hand hit worn stone, the earth lurched from underneath her once again. *Thank God.*

As an experiment, Remy tried to hold onto consciousness for as long as she could, to find out exactly what happened when she "disappeared," but her efforts proved futile. She caught a glimpse of a flash of light and felt a tingling sensation throughout her limbs. As the tingle moved up her spine and into her head, she blacked out. There was no fear or apprehension this time around. Remy felt more in control than she had been on her previous trips and felt confident she could stay longer this time by playing by the rules.

The forces of the universe severely underestimated her need to be in control. It was only a matter of time before Remy would be calling the shots. She just had to learn a little bit more and bide her time. The uncertain aspect now was where she would end up and how much time had passed. *Oh, and who I will scare the bejeezus out of by randomly appearing.*

****

Save Lino from being an idiot. That was her first thought when she could open her eyes again. Remy's brain wasn't as scrambled, probably because she had been anticipating the jump. *It's nice not being so confused.* But she wondered if her first thought also influenced who discovered her first, because María was the person who tripped over her.

The newlywed stumbled, throwing her basket of

freshly baked bread into the dirt in one spectacular arc. "Ayyyyy!" she shouted, hands coming to hit the ground.

"I'm sorry!" Remy said, coming from her butt to her knees to help the poor girl.

"Remy! What? How? Why are you in the middle of the street?" María took a shaky breath and held a scraped hand to her heart. "You gave me a fright! I did not mean to stumble over you as if you weren't there. My head has been in the clouds lately, I apologize."

"It was completely my fault. You couldn't have seen me."

María looked apprehensive, and Remy reminded herself to be more cautious with her words. Any slip could send her away.

"How are the brothers?" Remy asked, knowing full well that was what had María so distracted. The other woman's face went from apologetic to closed-off in an instant, like a mask had slipped over her face. *Is she mad at me?* After the day she'd had, Remy was in no mood to play games. She needed information, quickly. Namely, what day it was and what she'd already missed.

"Did I do something wrong?" Remy asked.

María's face flushed, obviously not used to any sort of confrontation. "My brother-in-law has been very concerned about you."

"I know you are loyal to them, so you feel like you have to be short with me. I haven't been the most reliable of late, and I know you have a lot to worry about without adding me and my drama into the mix. But I would really appreciate it if you would give me one more chance. I had a wonderful time at your wedding; it was absolutely beautiful. You treated me like a sister, and then I disappeared without a word. I'm so sorry."

María's big brown eyes filled with tears, and she looked away, trying to brush them off. "I know you don't mean harm. There is so much happening, and no one will speak frankly with me...Your honesty is refreshing. No one here is speaking honestly anymore, and it is driving me crazy!"

Her outburst turned a few heads across the street, the other villagers noticing the two women sprawled on the ground for the first time. A young boy rushed over to them. "*Señoras!* Are you hurt?"

María waved him off. "We are fine, thank you."

"Yeah," Remy chimed in. "You've never seen two people having a conversation in the dirt?"

The boy pointed a little way up the road, where a cart and horse were approaching.

Remy sighed. "I guess we'd better get up unless we want to get run over. María, can we go to the cottage?"

Remy witnessed as the other woman held an internal battle with herself, longing to have another female to talk to, but worried for the safety of her family. "I need to go to the bakery again, first," she compromised. "Would you like to come with me?"

"I would love to."

They picked up the scattered loaves of bread. "Food for the chickens and pigs now," María said, brushing off the clumps of mud and what Remy suspected was a little bit of horse manure. She offered to carry the dirty bread, which María handed over without much protest. *I deserve it,* Remy conceded. She would have to earn her way back into the woman's good graces, after what she put Bieito through. María was fiercely protective of her family and her new brother-in-law, and from what Remy had heard from their father on the beach, her disappearance from the wedding had put Bieito into a tailspin.

During their walk over to the bakery, however, María's frosty exterior began to crack. By the time they stood inside the oven-warmed building, María was happily chatting with Remy as though no time had passed.

"Isabella was furious with me after the wedding." She giggled. "She wouldn't speak to me for days! It was this past Sunday that she finally spoke to me in church. Informed me that I had ruined my own wedding and cursed my marriage by including 'the American.' That's what she called you."

"What a charming woman. What did you say to her? I hope it was 'thanks for the best wishes'!"

María gave a small, scandalized shriek. "I could do no such thing! I wish I could, though. I was speechless in the moment. Lino pulled me away and told me not to give her any more thought."

"Does she hate me because of Bieito?"

"Yes, and now she hates *me* because I allowed you two to be together."

"Well, she was probably ecstatic when I left." As soon as she said it, Remy regretted it. The last thing she wanted to do was bring attention to her weird behavior in public. María, thankfully, seemed to have the same aversion to speaking about Remy's disappearances in front of others, because the two lapsed into an awkward silence while the baker handed her the fresh loaves.

"So, um, back to the cottage?" Remy suggested.

The wall was back up between them, but common sense and courtesy still ruled María, and she couldn't turn Remy away. "Yes. We have much to discuss."

Remy wasn't sure she liked the sound of that, but she would have to pay the price and listen to the lecture in order to get back into Bieito's family's good graces. They needed to trust her if she was going to have any chance of getting Lino out of the danger he was unknowingly dragging himself, his family, and his village into.

Remy was not surprised that the cottage was empty when María opened the door. The men were still at work down at the port. It would be at least a few hours before she would see Bieito again.

"So," Remy said, but María interrupted her before Remy could step inside. "You can take the bread out to the chicken coop."

"Got it," Remy said, and did as she was asked. Walking back to the cottage, she wiped her hands on her near-unrecognizable dress and gathered her thoughts for the imminent conversation. Cringing, she marveled at María's manners not to say anything about her attire, even though she was probably dying to ask. There was no way she didn't recognize the dress from the wedding. What sane person would still be wearing the same dress, possibly weeks later?

That's my first order of business. Find out what day it is.

Full of purpose, Remy opened the door and let herself in. María jumped in surprise at the unexpected entrance.

"Can I help you prepare dinner?" Remy asked. This would be easier if they both had something to do with their hands.

María gestured over to the freshly washed carrots that sat on the counter. "You could chop these, if you want."

Once they were both at work with their task, the silence between them transformed from strained to comfortable, but neither of them appeared to know where to start. Remy thought maybe she should let María lead the conversation, considering she was the wronged party, but the young woman seemed unwilling to begin.

"Like what I've done with my dress?" Remy asked.

María's eyebrows flew up and her knife stopped moving. "I—ah—"

"Totally kidding. I'm a freaking mess. No need to be so polite about it."

María gave a nervous giggle. "I didn't know how to ask—"

"Ask how I got to be so fashionable? Easy, I spend a lot of time in the dirt."

Now María's face broke into a full-blown smile. "I think it is still salvageable."

"Only with your help. I think I'll make it worse."

"Tonight," she promised.

"Just exactly what day is 'tonight'?" Remy ventured.

"Thursday, of course. You mean to say you don't know the date?"

"Ah, yeah. That too."

"April fourth."

"Shit," Remy said. "Bieito is going to kill me. If he even wants to talk to me, after last time."

"He has been rather occupied with my husband, so

I doubt he has room in his heart for anger," María said, with a sting of bitterness.

"Is Lino still being a dick?"

María's jaw dropped open. "A what?"

Remy tried to backtrack. "I mean, is he treating you okay? Now that you're newlyweds and all?"

The other woman's brain still seemed to be stuck on the fact that Remy called her husband a dick. "A dick," María repeated, trying the word out on her tongue. "Yes," she decided. "That's exactly what he has been!"

Seeing the sweet, conservative girl say the word "dick" had Remy doing all she could not to burst out laughing. "María," Remy said. "You are adorable."

The young woman flushed, pleased with the compliment. "Now if only you could remind my husband of that."

Remy set the knife she had been using on the counter and reached across for María's arm. "I don't think his behavior has anything to do with you."

María shook herself free and slammed a pot down on the stove. "That is exactly what Bieito told me. And my father-in-law. But they don't understand. Lino is not the same man that I married. When he is here, he is not really here. Like he would rather be somewhere else, far away from me. I speak, and he doesn't listen. He agrees with whatever I say, gives me whatever I want, but it doesn't feel real. I tell him what I want is for his old self to return, but he denies anything is different. Then he disappears for hours on end! I never thought…it is simply that…Remy, has he grown tired of me already? Is there someone else?"

Remy wanted to punch Lino for putting his wife in

this position. It wasn't fair to her, but Remy didn't know what to say in order to prove to María that it wasn't about a lack of happiness in the home. After watching Bieito and Afonso discuss the revolutionaries' ideas in such a hushed, fearful way, Remy decided to keep her mouth shut. Telling María anything could put her in danger.

If I tell her, though, maybe it would force Lino to reconsider his involvement. Maybe he would extract himself without us having to intervene any more. That would be the ideal situation—Lino would decide on his own that this failed coup wasn't worth the risk. It would force him to evaluate what he would be giving up if he decided to rebel against the Spanish crown. If anyone could talk him out of it, it was María.

Remy took a deep breath and was about to reveal what she knew to her friend when the cottage door slammed open.

"Lino? *Lino!*" Bieito yelled. He stopped short when he saw Remy there, standing in his home without apology. "You're here?" he said, more question than statement.

"Ta-daaaa."

Bieito crossed the threshold in three great strides and swooped Remy up in his arms. He clutched her tightly and whispered, "I'm sorry, my love."

Guess I'm forgiven. The warmth that spread from Remy's chest threatened to ignite them. "I'm sorry too. I don't like fighting with you. And I'm especially sorry that I left again in the middle of it. It wasn't planned."

Bieito set her feet back down on the ground. He gave her a meaningful look. "You were right," he told her.

Remy's heart sank, even though she knew the news was coming. Lino was heavily involved in the coup, no doubts about it now if Bieito was admitting this to her. María, however, had no idea what they were talking about. "Remy was right about what?" she asked. "Why isn't Lino with you? What happened to my husband?" She looked at both of them with wide, fearful eyes.

"It isn't what you think, María." Remy rushed to console her.

"Why do you know more than I do?" she asked, betrayed. "Bieito, why didn't Lino come home with you? Where is your father?"

"Lino didn't come to work today," Bieito said. "He said he had some business to do in the port, and that Father and I should walk on ahead without him and get the nets ready."

"And you let him go alone?" Remy asked. The subtext of, *I told you he was up to something* was clear in her tone, and Bieito hung his head.

"I trusted him. He's my brother," he said, by way of explanation. "I watched him carefully all week at the port, and there was *nothing* suspicious. I thought that whatever his involvement may have been, he was through."

"María told me that Lino had been disappearing for hours on end!" Remy said.

"What." Bieito rounded on his sister-in-law.

"He was having trouble sleeping. He left to go for walks to clear his head, often in the middle of the night."

"Why didn't you say anything?" Bieito demanded.

"I was ashamed! My husband was leaving our bed in the middle of the night. Why should I let that be known?" María burst into tears. "I knew something was wrong," she said, through her sobs. "But everyone— Lino, you, Afonso—kept saying everything was fine. Well, everything is obviously *not* fine!"

Bieito moved from Remy's side to embrace María. "It is my fault," he assured her. "You did nothing wrong."

"It isn't your fault," Remy said. "It's Lino's. He's already been gone for hours. If we have any hope of finding him, we need to move fast."

María hiccupped, her tears still flowing fast down her cheeks. Her voice, however, was steady when she said, "Nobody is going anywhere until they explain to me what is going on."

Bieito swallowed.

"She deserves to know," Remy said.

María looked back and forth between them, becoming more enraged. "Why have the two of you been keeping secrets about my husband?" She stared them down.

After a beat of silence, Bieito broke first. "We think Lino may be involved with some dangerous men."

"Not maybe," Remy corrected him. "Most definitely."

"What sort of men?"

"Separatists," Bieito said. "Those who want to go back to the old days of the Kingdom of Galicia. People who want independence from Spain."

María gasped. "Why on earth would you think Lino was involved in treason? He isn't a soldier, he is a fisherman, for God's sake! He has never ventured outside Ortigueira! He is a sweet and hardworking man, no matter how he has been acting lately. You must be mistaken."

"I know this is difficult," Bieito said. "I didn't want to accept it at first, either. But you cannot deny the gossip and grumbling throughout Ortigueira and even our small village. People have been angry for a long time. No one will come out and declare it, but there are many sympathizers in the area. My little brother is an idealist; he always has been. He is a man of action, not just talk. Remember how he wooed you until you agreed to marry him? Lino doesn't give up. Now I fear he has latched onto some dangerous ideas and has not considered the consequences."

María shook her head. "He wouldn't. He just wouldn't. What would they want with him, anyway?"

Remy jumped in. "Quite a lot, actually. Lino works at the largest and most important port in the area. If they are smuggling things in—supplies, weapons, food—it would work out quite well to have a man on the inside. Something spooked him today, though, if he didn't show up for work, Bieito."

"I'll find him." Bieito's face set into a grimace.

"*We'll* find him," Remy corrected.

"You will stay with María," he said. "These are dangerous men."

"I will not." Remy stared at him without blinking. "I know more about this than you could possibly imagine." It was a risk, saying that, and internally Remy braced to be yanked out, but she had to level with Bieito. It must have been vague enough, however, to follow the "rules" set for Remy to be there, because she remained rooted in place. She let out a tentative sigh of relief.

"Then where is my brother?"

Bieito had a point. *If I had read the history books more closely, I could tell you exactly where he is,* Remy thought, cringing internally. Remy knew the outcome of the coup, but what good was that when Lino's life was on the line, and Remy didn't know his location? This was almost worse than not knowing anything at all about the revolution. Everyone else was navigating this blind, but Remy could see the train wreck coming, with no way to stop it.

"I—I don't know, exactly."

"Then you will stay here."

Remy drew her shoulders back, preparing for the inevitable argument. Bieito's eyes blazed with as much passion as her own, and they were about to launch into a fight when the door opened. It was Bieito's father, face drawn and white. "Did you hear? It has begun."

"What has begun?" Bieito asked, all readiness for the argument forgotten. "Did you find Lino?"

"The uprising. I know you didn't want me to do this, Bieito, and bring suspicion onto Lino, but when he didn't come to work today...He is my son. I need to do everything I can to find him. I was asking all of the dockworkers if they had any idea where Lino had disappeared to, or who he could have been consorting with."

Bieito motioned impatiently. "Yes, yes, I understand, Father. What exactly did you find out?"

"The port received word this afternoon. Two days ago, a colonel started an uprising in Lugo. We are ordered by the Spanish government to be on the lookout for any suspicious activity from boats in or out of the port. They don't know how far this insurrection has spread and are preparing to send armed forces into our province as a precaution."

"Lugo. But that is days from here. Even if we leave now…"

"Bieito, there is no guarantee that Lino is even in Lugo." *Where ever the hell that is,* Remy added internally. "You can't go running off to there. What if Lino is already at the next place they are planning on taking over? There is no way to know."

Bieito's lip curled in disgust, and he slumped down into the chair closest to the fireplace. "I cannot believe he would do this to us. His family." Turning to María, he said, "Most of all, I cannot believe Lino would do this to you."

María sighed, looking more resigned now that she knew the truth and the shock was beginning to pass. "I knew I married an optimist. It is what I love about him. Lino can make anything seem possible, if one wishes and tries hard enough."

"You shouldn't wish for anything," Remy said automatically. Three heads turned to stare at her. "Wishing is dangerous."

Bieito nodded, agreeing with her but for a different reason. "Wishing will not return Lino to us unharmed," he said. "María, did Lino ever say where he went on his midnight walks? Have you noticed anything out of place in your bedroom?"

She jumped up, grateful for something productive to do. "I will go look right now."

"Father, what other talk did you hear in the village about the coup?"

While Bieito's father launched into the gossip he had heard on the way home, Remy sat there silently, weighing her options. *I can go back right now, and find the exact information they need, but I don't know when I'll be able to return. Tomorrow? A week from now? And what if something bad happens to Bieito while I'm gone? I just want to take him with me, to know that he is safe. Damn it, Lino! Why did you have to go and screw everything up?*

Looking at the somber faces of Bieito and his father as they discussed the overwhelming situation, Remy knew what she had to do. *Shit.* She had to roll the dice, hope that the time jump wouldn't be too long, and that she would be able to get the information they needed before it was too late to find Lino.

"I'm sorry about this, Bieito. I promise I'll see you again as soon as I can. This will help in the long run."

"What do you mean?" he asked.

"iPod! Internet! Cellphone! Facebook!" Remy closed her eyes and braced to be yanked out. Nothing happened. She tried again. "Obama! Microwave. Cable TV..." Bieito stared at her like she had sprouted a second head. "What the hell, this should be working. I'm breaking the rules! I'm talking about stuff I'm not supposed to talk about! That means I go nighty-night now and wake up in *my* village!" Remy shouted at the ceiling.

Wide-eyed, Bieito's father poured a glass of wine, handing it to Bieito, who then tried to hand it to Remy.

"I don't get it," Remy whispered. "I'm not supposed to be stuck here. I need to get to *my* village and find out where Lino is. That's why I'm here, to help." *What if I'm stuck here forever?* The very real possibility that she could never return to her own time struck an icy fear through her limbs. *I've been playing with fire.* Remy thought she was in control, that she was special enough for the village to show her incredible things. But now, stuck here with no way back, Remy realized just how bad she had been played. "I don't know what you want from me!" She threw her glass into the unlit fireplace, where it shattered against the sooty stones.

María returned from the bedroom to find the two men watching Remy's breakdown. "What did you two do to her?" she demanded. Both men sat there, unable to move, mouths agape. What nobody could understand, however, was that Remy was currently fighting an internal battle with her greatest fear.

Make the wish, a voice inside her insisted. *You know it is foolproof. It is the only thing that will work.*

Remy hissed. "I won't be forced into doing that," she murmured, ignoring the stares around her.

The rules of the game have changed. It has been unfair to you. Time to even the score.

"It is never even. It will come with consequences."

But maybe not. You aren't in your own time. It could work differently here.

Remy began to pace around the room. "It is too great of a risk."

Lino is in trouble. You have the power to save him.

Had this been the plan all along? To force Remy into making a wish, to upset the universal balance for some other, greater goal that was even bigger than she could understand?

I have the power to change history in my hands. But should I? Remy felt it, deep in her gut, that a wish now could cause such an unbalance that it would ripple the consequences through space and time. It could alter her own reality in the future. Whatever the fallout would be from making such a request, Remy was sure it would be even greater than life or death.

You don't have to wish to save him, the voice reminded her. *Just to find him.*

Just his location. That couldn't be that bad, right? It seemed a far lesser request than wishing that Lino would return home, alive, this very instant. Information was all she was after. There would be no messing with the absolutes of life and death. This was not comparable to her brother and her beloved dog, or wishing for the creation of life inside of her. This exchange was more modest. Maybe it would be worth the consequences.

At least it would give them a place to start. Whatever happened after the wish would be up to Remy's actions in order to influence the future. Remy was sure she would eventually be punished, but the fallout would be significantly smaller with a simpler request.

Remy took a deep breath and stopped pacing. She turned to face her audience. "I wish we could find Lino." Finite. Clear. *No going back now.*

"I know, *mi amor,*" Bieito said, crossing the room to her. "I wish we could find him, too."

"No, that isn't what I mean." How could Remy make him understand? Make him see what she had just sacrificed, and hope he would still love her after all the pieces landed?

"I need some air," Remy said, and excused herself. Her knees were shaking, and the words "I wish" still lingered on her tongue. There was always a compulsion to say it again after she let it all out. It felt so *good* to be that uninhibited, even for a moment. Such a rush to make her mouth form the words that always caused immediate change, whether for good or bad.

Now standing outside, she watched as the villagers clustered in small groups, talking in hushed tones. People split off and ran to join other gossipers, spreading what they knew. Most looked proud, but afraid. They were Galicians, through and through, just like the people of Ortigueira that Remy had gotten to know in her own time. They were proud of their land and heritage. It was just that, like most average people, they had all been too cautious to do anything to take it back. Now that the colonel had started it for them, Galicians all proclaimed their love for their country, and felt validated enough to whisper that maybe the coup wasn't a bad thing after all.

Whispers hadn't been enough for Lino. As futile as Remy knew this coup was, she couldn't help but admire Lino's courage to actually fight for what he believed in. Granted, it pulled the rest of the family into a minefield to deal with it and try to save him, but at least Lino had acted.

Remy felt a chill pass over her skin and looked around to see what could have caused it. Isabella was staring at her from across the square, with murder in her eyes. *I should have known, my biggest fan.* Unable to help herself, Remy gave her a little wave and a wry smile. *Yep, I'm back. Deal with it, lady.*

To her surprise, instead of running away to spread nasty rumors about Remy, Isabella strode forward until the two women were almost nose-to-nose. Remy cocked an eyebrow, unwilling to deal with Isabella's attitude right now when she had Lino's life to worry about. "Can I help you?" Remy asked.

"Most women I know wouldn't dare show their faces again after causing such a scene at my poor cousin's wedding. And here you are, still wearing the same clothes, even! Such a display...You should be ashamed! Are all American women as barbaric and rude as you?"

"I don't know," Remy responded. "I would ask you the same thing, but so far *you're* the only Galician woman I've met who has a stick stuck up her butt, so I'm thinking it isn't a regional thing."

Isabella's hand flew to her mouth and she stepped back. Once she had gathered her wits enough about her, she didn't bother keeping her voice down while she said, "You stay away from Bieito. He deserves better than you."

"Honestly, Isabella, we have bigger things to worry about right now. I think your people's coup tops that list. And since I know you're the biggest gossip in the village, you'd better have useful intel for me."

"Like I would tell you anything!"

"Listen, if you really care about Bieito—truly care—then you'll tell me whatever you know."

Isabella sniffed. "I care a great deal more for him than *you.*"

"Then prove it. What have you heard? Anything about Lino?"

"Lino? What does he have to do—oh!" Isabella looked like she had just been given a juicy treat.

"If you won't tell me, then you need to tell your cousin. María is beside herself with worry that something has happened to him."

Isabella seemed to be weighing her options. "I'll help," she said. "But I will be the one to deliver the news to Bieito. Not you." The woman twitched with anticipation, having been given the information to put two and two together.

Remy sighed. "Whatever you want. I don't really care as long as he gets told." Though personally, she wondered at the glee in which Isabella seemed to be taking at possibly giving devastating news. Was Isabella punishing Bieito as well as Remy? Or did she just take perverse joy in starting drama?

Isabella reminded Remy a little bit of Anita, and the thought of that comparison to her former friend made Remy's stomach queasy. How had she put up with Anita's insatiable need for gossip all these years? Even going so far as to spread personal news about Remy. *And I forgave her for it!* Remy had always been the one to forgive Anita for her inappropriate comments and boundary stomping. If she had met Anita today instead of fifteen years ago, would she really expect them to be friends? *No,* Remy realized, and she felt a little less guilty about taking Anita's rental car.

If Isabella is the one with Lino's location, then this will be the most roundabout wish-granting ever. Maybe dealing with Isabella would be the price for the wish. But Remy wasn't naive enough to think that the entire fallout from her wish would be dragging Isabella into her personal life. This was only the start, and it would only get worse from here.

"Are you going to invite me in?" Isabella asked. "Just a moment; you don't live here." Then, like a queen, Isabella sidestepped around Remy and let herself into the cottage.

The murmur of conversation ceased when Isabella appeared in the doorway. María's eyes were red as she looked up from the close circle she made with Bieito and Afonso, their heads bent close together.

"Oh, my lovely cousin!" Isabella said, sweeping her arms wide and running forward to embrace the shell-shocked woman. "I came as soon as I heard the terrible news. Lino is missing!"

"How did you—"

But Isabella had already let go of María and turned her attention to Bieito. She grasped him by the shoulders and kissed him on both cheeks. "Terrible, terrible!"

Bieito wiggled out from underneath her claw-like grip and turned to Remy, question and confusion written all over his face.

Isabella continued to babble. "Never in my life would I have thought one of our own would turn criminal!"

"Now just a minute—" Bieito's father tried to interrupt.

"None of this started until *she* got here." Isabella pointed a finger at Remy. "Bad luck or bad influence? We can never know with outsiders—"

"Isabella, be quiet!" María snapped, the force of her words greater than her small figure. Remy was willing to bet money that María had never used that tone on anyone in her life. "If you have something useful to say, then say it. Otherwise, get out."

"Strong words from a woman whose husband is committing *treason,*" Isabella said.

"You have no proof of that," Remy pointed out. They all knew the truth, but Isabella was just speculating, seeing if she could get a rise out of the family. However, much to Remy's surprise, Isabella *did* have useful information.

"Well, if he wasn't committing treason, then why did Juan see him riding his horse through Ortigueira, galloping as though the devil himself was chasing him?"

"Which way was he heading?" Bieito's gaze could have burned a hole right through Isabella as he stared at her, which Remy was gratified to see made the woman squirm.

"West," Isabella said.

"Toward Lugo?" Remy asked Bieito.

"Or the many other towns along the way."

"At least someone saw Lino alive this morning." Remy knew her words were cold comfort. Evidence of Lino's involvement was mounting.

"Fleeing the area and going toward the colonel," he pointed out.

"We can track him. Somebody else will have seen something." Remy laid a hand on Bieito's arm, noticing that Isabella couldn't take her eyes off their contact. Remy rubbed it with comforting strokes.

"Yes, Bieito," Isabella said, voice raised to an uncomfortable pitch. She looked desperate to get back into Bieito's good graces. "I will ask around. With everyone's tongues wagging, we will find what Lino knew, where he is heading, and who his accomplices are. But for the life of me, I cannot figure out why these rough men would desecrate the back of the main house before disappearing. What purpose could that have served?"

"Isabella, what are you speaking of?" María asked. "I found Remy behind the main house mere hours ago. There were no damages."

"The entirely inappropriate drawing on the back wall. Rather vulgar, in my opinion."

Remy's heart nearly stopped. "Was it a painting? A painting appeared?"

"If you could even dignify it by calling it anything other than vandalism," Isabella said. "At first, we thought it was a cruel joke. But now with talk of the coup movement, nobody is sure. That was what we were all discussing before I was needed in here to help you all."

Is it my painting? It was completely plausible. Nothing else *that* major had followed Remy through her time hops. The red door had been strange, the wine, her clothes...but the idea that her artwork, a piece of her soul, had traveled to this version of the village to be displayed to the public struck her as significant. There was a reason if her painting had appeared here, the most intimate part of her laid bare for all to see.

My wish.

Remy was out the door and onto the street before anyone inside could react. By the time they joined her behind the main house, Remy had recovered while they were all out of breath. Just as she had suspected, her spray paint mural stared back at her. *There is something...wrong about it though.* The essence of the painting was still the same, perhaps a bit more sensual looking now that she was looking at it in the context of a more conservative time period.

"It's beautiful," María murmured. "How can hands that insist on fighting create this?"

"That's because they didn't," Bieito said. He stood, transfixed, next to Remy. He grabbed onto her hand and squeezed it. *He knows.*

There was a message here, Remy was certain of it. Her subconscious had created it, and then her wish had sent it to her. The answer to Lino lay in the painting, but Remy was too emotionally connected to her own work to see it. "Where is it?" she whispered.

She tried looking at it like a map. Nothing. Remy felt like a foolish art critic, the very column writers she despised who would come to her shows and demand an explanation for each and every painting. "What was your inspiration? What are you trying to tell us? What is the greater message within the context of a post 9/11 world?" On and on. Then they would type up their own interpretation anyway, ignoring most of what Remy said, praising work they had no real understanding of. The reviews gave Remy the notoriety that she needed, all while she bit her lip so hard she drew blood, nodding and smiling and giving the people what they wanted. Critics wanted to feel superior and insightful. She never told them they were wrong, just got a gold star for keeping silent. To ease her frustration, she told herself it didn't matter, as long as she knew the true message.

The same was true with this mural. It was only for Remy, so only she could find the message within it. She took a deep breath and forced her eyes to relax. Remy let go of Bieito's hand and took a couple steps back, never taking her eyes off the wall. The contrast, light and dark, positive and negative, were in equal parts within the painting. In fact, had Remy tried to purposely create the painting with this exact ratio, she wouldn't have been able to do it. Exactly fifty percent of the artwork was black spray paint, the other fifty percent was negative space. Half and half.

Remy stared so hard her eyes started to water, the

figures swirling together until they no longer looked like two people entwined and instead looked like a jumbled mass. Colors appeared, but when Remy focused on them too hard, they turned back to black again. The painting was in constant movement, until Remy started to see a pattern emerge.

What she had mistaken earlier for a crescent moon now looked like a *C*. The space between the bodies pressed together was arrow shaped, or an *A*. The curve of their pointed feet formed two *R* shapes. The hands reaching in prayer formed another *A*. Remy's eyes jumped from point to point all over her painting, searching for more hidden letters. The final letter almost hit her in the face with its obviousness. The legs crossed to form the letter *L*, though it was upside down.

C. A. R. R. A. L.

Remy imagined Maggie's voice saying the word. Her friend had mentioned the revolution and how the coup had failed. *Yes, the Martyrs of Carral. That's what we are trying to avoid. Wait, what is Carral?* Remy had originally thought it was just a strange title they had assigned to the executed men. But what if it was more than that? What if it was a location?

"Bieito, what is Carral?"

He jumped at her voice, and Remy realized she must have spent several silent minutes in her trance. "Carral? The city?"

"It's a city?"

"A town, I guess. A bit bigger than Ortigueira, but not as populated as Santiago. Why?"

"That's where we will find Lino."

Chapter Twelve

"Carral?" Bieito asked, skeptical. The others—María, Isabella, and Afonso—turned to listen. "Lino has never been to Carral before. I doubt he even knows the way."

"I don't know if that's where he's heading right now, but I do know that that is where he will end up eventually. We just have to be there to meet him. Otherwise, things are going to go very, very badly for him."

"How would you know that?" Isabella challenged. "That's impossible."

"I don't know exactly what will happen," Remy conceded, "but you'll just have to trust me on this." Isabella rolled her eyes. "You know what?" Remy snapped. "I don't think this concerns you any longer—"

"None of this concerns *you*, you-you-American! Go back to where you came from."

"That's enough," Bieito said. His calm timbre rumbled through the group. "If Remy says this is where I need to go, then I am going there."

His father spoke up. "Bieito, I know you mean well, and I adore Remy as you do, but Isabella raises a good point. How do we know for sure this is where we will find Lino? The chances seem far too slim. Act rashly, and we could miss our true opportunity. There is no evidence that this is where Lino will end up…"

Remy spoke up. "This is my painting," she said, eliciting gasps of shock from everyone other than Bieito. "It's here because of me. And it's important. That's all I can tell you."

"How? You've been with me all day—" María started to protest but was silenced by a head shake from Bieito.

Giving her friend a reassuring smile, Remy continued. "Bieito and I need to go to Carral as soon as possible. I can't remember the exact time line, but I know that this coup won't last very long." Realizing her slip, Remy added, "I would assume."

"*I* will go to Carral," Bieito said. "Alone."

"Like hell," Remy argued.

"These are dangerous people, and a volatile situation. I know how to reach my brother. Too many people will draw attention. The last thing we need is the entire family accused of treason."

"I am coming." Bieito's father straightened up to his full height, which still put him about even with Remy. "My boys need me."

"Father, I appreciate—"

"I'm coming too," María said. "Lino is my husband."

"You are all mad!" Isabella said. "This is nonsense. I cannot be associated with this any longer." The gossip and speculation had been fun for her, but now that the family talked about serious action Isabella was ready to flee. *Good riddance. One less problem.*

Before the woman could go run and spread the new information she had acquired, Remy grabbed her arm. "Tell no one of this," she warned, voice too low for the others to overhear. "If you do, I'll make sure you never get married again. No one will want you." Isabella's face went white at Remy's unladylike threat, before flushing red with indignation.

"How dare you—" she sputtered, but Remy had already turned her back on the other woman. Isabella slunk away in a huff, and the family turned back to discussing the more important matter at hand.

"We should go back inside," Bieito's father urged. The other villagers had been watching their heated exchanged with curious faces. Remy could just imagine what they were saying to one another as they watched her analyze her painting—*That strange woman...She is a distant relative of María's, I heard...Last anyone saw of her was at the wedding...Isabella says she is of questionable morals, and American...*

Now with her obvious connection to the artwork, she wondered if they were adding "vandal" to her description. If they hadn't already, Remy was sure that Isabella would make that happen. *As long as she stays quiet about Lino, I don't care what she does or what she says about me.*

The family walked briskly back to the cottage; all the while María argued with Bieito about why she should be allowed to go. Bieito's father said nothing, but Remy noted the grim determination in his face. He was not going to be easily persuaded to stay behind, either. The old man was unable to withstand such a journey. They needed to move quickly and quietly, and though he was fairly fit for his age from a lifetime of working outdoors, Remy didn't want to risk his fatigue or injury. The hard part was going to be tactfully pointing this out without offending him. The key would be to convince María to stay behind, so Bieito's father would have the important job of looking out for her. Plus, it was a good idea to have them remain anyway, in case Lino should return unexpectedly.

And if Afonso and María still wouldn't listen to reason, then Remy wasn't above leaving with Bieito in the middle of the night. She just hoped it wouldn't come to that, especially after finally getting María to look past her disappearance at the wedding. However, if it got Lino back to his wife safe and sound, Remy figured that all would be forgiven.

Remy could not remain behind, even though she knew Bieito was going to try his damnedest to convince her otherwise. But Remy wasn't about to have anything happen to either Bieito or Lino, even if it meant another wish. The first wish got the ball rolling to find Lino, and it was easy to think about making another one, should the situation arise. That was the danger of wishes. Remy was determined to prevent Lino becoming a Martyr of Carral in any way possible.

She admired the cause, she really did, but history was written by the victors. Lino was on the losing side. Even being made into a martyr wouldn't be worth the cost, not for his family anyway. The only thing this coup would accomplish was bloody violence and unnecessary deaths. Maybe if Remy knew for sure that it would affect something in the future, she would have been more hesitant to get involved, but pulling Lino out and saving his life wouldn't cause too big of a ripple, would it? He was just one person. The rebellion would still fail, only there would be eleven men executed instead of twelve. *Just a minor change in the history books, right?*

And if Lino and María had children, their

descendants would live in the village until it was eventually abandoned. A couple extra people in Ortigueira wouldn't change the big picture. Remy would still come to buy the village a hundred years later. Saving Lino wouldn't dramatically change her own life path trajectory, would it?

It might not even matter anyway, if she was permanently stuck in this time instead of allowed to return to her own century. *What if I change it so much I can never go back to my old life?* Questions gnawed at Remy the longer she thought about the far-reaching implications of what she was about to do.

However, the only other option, the safest option, was to not act, and in Remy's opinion, that was not a choice. She was just going to have to go with her gut on this, and deal with the consequences later. The best-case scenario would be if they were able to extract Lino before the revolutionaries even went to trial. Worst case scenario…well, she didn't want to think about that, and what it would do to Bieito to witness his brother's execution.

By the time the family reentered the cottage, the only thing that had been decided was that nobody wanted to be left behind, and tempers were starting to flare.

Sweet María, red-faced and shouting, was laying out her case to Bieito and her father-in-law, who were apparently on the same side for the moment. Their alliance would be short-lived, though, once Bieito turned against his father with the same arguments.

"I think," Remy shouted above the din, "that we all need to sleep, and figure it out in the morning." Nobody wanted to see reason in that argument, but the truth was that everyone's nerves were too frayed to discuss things rationally anymore. *We are further along now to getting Lino than we were before,* Remy consoled herself. *At least we know where we will find him. Better than nothing.*

"Each moment we waste—" Bieito started to argue with her but was cut off by Remy's meaningful look. *We'll talk later,* it said. That shut him up, and he nodded. They needed to find a quiet place to meet, away from María and Afonso. Then the real planning could begin.

María sighed. "I think you're right, Remy. Nothing will be accomplished on an empty stomach. Here, let us finish making dinner." Her hands were already busy with the half-finished meal preparation from an hour before, prior to the interruption from Bieito. It was always easier to think rationally when one's hands were occupied. Remy couldn't help but notice that María's hands trembled.

Poor girl. She is so strong, trying to keep it together. She must be terrified. It made Remy feel all the guiltier for what they were going to put her through.

"Actually, María, I was hoping to have Remy's help out in the barn," Bieito said. "Father, will you gut the fish for your daughter-in-law?"

A hesitant truce was declared between father and daughter-in-law as they silently worked next to each other in the kitchen, while Bieito and Remy slipped outside. Instead of heading to the barn, Bieito steered them toward the orchard. Once among the rows of trees, Bieito grabbed her hand and pulled her behind the largest one.

"First," he said, and kissed her breathless. Remy

felt the anxiety, regret, and sadness pour out of him as he focused his attention on her. Kisses were easier than words, and way more effective.

He broke away. "I'm glad you are here," Bieito whispered. "That painting...you did it? Truly?"

Remy blinked, trying to clear her mind from the passion-induced fog that Bieito created. "What? Um, yeah. My first one in a long time, actually. And apparently it turned out to be pretty useful."

"It is the most beautiful piece of artwork I have ever seen. Your talents are indescribable. I won't pretend to know how or why you used it to guess the location of my brother, but if any painting held a divine message, that one would." Bieito stared at Remy, awed that her mind had created the image out of nothing.

Remy squirmed under the praise, suddenly feeling like she was on display. The speculation that her hand had produced a divine message made her uncomfortable. She needed Bieito to still see her as she was; just Remy, not Remy the world-renowned painter. The last thing she needed was Bieito to fear that they came from completely separate worlds. *Which, technically, we do, but that's not the point.* She leaned in to rest her cheek on his chest. "When this is all over, I want you to take me sailing again."

The tip of Bieito's chin dug into the crown of her head. "I promise, *mi amor*. Only if you promise to paint something just for me. It is selfish, I know, but I want something to keep by my side when you disappear again."

Remy pulled back and smacked him on the chest. "I already told you I don't like leaving you! It's not like I'm *trying* to do it—"

"Then marry me. Stay here with me." Bieito's liquid brown eyes stared at her with wild hope. He looked just as surprised saying the words as Remy was hearing them.

"What?"

"We can build a life together here," Bieito said. "Even if you are…elusive. Some of you is better than none of you."

Remy shook her head, still trying to find words. Just a few months ago she had been a recent divorcee, and now she was listening to someone propose. Bieito couldn't be serious, could he? *He's afraid to lose his brother, so he is trying to do everything in his power not to lose me, either.*

Fear wasn't enough of a reason to propose. In fact, Remy didn't know if there was *ever* a good enough reason to propose. Granted, Bieito was a much better partner for Remy than Jack ever was, and she was older and wiser now. But would marriage set her on the same doomed path as before?

Not to mention the fact that Bieito knew nothing of Remy's traumatic past. There were too many secrets between them. A promise to him wouldn't be fair until Remy unpacked all the baggage from her past.

Still, the hopeless romantic teenager inside wondered, *What if I said yes?* Did Remy dare allow herself to dream of a future with Bieito? To focus only on the good instead of what *might* happen? Remy waged an internal war for a long moment, so lost in her thoughts that she didn't see Bieito still staring at her expectantly. He cleared his throat, and Remy snapped back to the moment.

"No."

Bieito's face fell. "No?"

"It's not the right time to ask me that. So, no."

"But later?"

"You can try. I can't promise I'll say yes. But you can try."

"That hope is good enough for me."

How many times had Remy said that? Each time she and Jack had tried for another baby, there had always been hope. How many times could Bieito have his hopes crushed before he, too, ended up disillusioned like Remy? Did she want to be the person to teach him that lesson? This was too dangerous of a road to go down right now.

She changed the subject. "We can't allow María and your father to come with us to Carral."

"I agree. Though I think it would be safer if you stayed as well."

"Nice try. I knew you were going to suggest that. Remember how I said I know way more about this than you do? You'll need me if we are going to get Lino out of this alive."

Bieito sighed. "I wish it could be otherwise." Remy cringed at the word "wish," but Bieito didn't notice. "My father and sister-in-law will not stay willingly, however. Especially if they know you are accompanying me."

"Which is why we need to leave tonight, while they are asleep and unaware. I know Lino took the horse, but is there any way you can get another one? Or should we leave on foot and try to borrow one later on?"

"We will have to walk, I think. Part of the Camino de Santiago will take us to Carral. We can be pilgrims if we are questioned by any of the Crown's men."

The opportunity to walk the infamous Camino. It sent a little thrill up Remy's spine. The aura of mystery and reverence surrounding it still impacted people in her own time. Experiencing it in the past might be all the more potent. The experience would be rougher, more real and less commercialized. No guidebooks or hotels, no graduate students taking a semester off to "find themselves" with social media documenting every step of their journey. She would encounter true believers, drawn by promises of miracles they couldn't understand.

Would walking it give them the miracle they needed to rescue Lino? *Maybe it will nullify my wish,* Remy wondered. Walking it as penance could balance out the bad juju she had coming her way to pay for the knowledge of Lino's location. *If only.* Until then, step by step all the way on their pilgrimage, Remy would be on edge.

Bieito looked torn. "My poor father, when he awakes to find us gone…"

"But think how happy he will be to have both his sons home again," Remy pointed out.

"It will be a difficult journey," he warned. "And not entirely safe."

"Do I get to wear a shell?" Remy asked.

"Shell?"

"Like the one you were wearing the first day we met. You told me that all pilgrims get a shell to symbolize their trip. Even though we aren't really going to the end of the Camino, I still want one."

"That is your only concern about the trip? Your shell? Here I am, thinking about food and supplies—"

Remy gave him a tiny smile. "I want you to make it for me."

He gave a little chuckle, the first in a long while. "I would do anything for you, *mi amor.*"

"But before we get to that, I *need* to change out of this dress. Into some pants."

Bieito blushed at the mention of Remy taking off her clothes, and Remy could tell that for the moment at least, his thoughts were no longer on Lino. Part of her toyed with the idea of stripping down to her underwear right there in front of him, and sending him to go get her an outfit she could travel in. Considering how strung out he looked though, she decided that now probably wasn't a good time to throw in a heart attack on top of his stress.

Bieito cleared his throat. "I have a few items that might fit. It would be a good idea to disguise you as a boy on the Camino anyway," Bieito said. "Though right now María will insist on getting you something suitable of hers to wear instead."

"We just have to act like everything is normal and then sneak out tonight. Can you pack and hide enough supplies in the barn?"

"I will gather what I can. You will share a bed with María tonight. Father will insist." *So much for hoping we would be sharing a bed,* Remy thought. If they were back in New York, or even modern-day Spain, the idea that it was improper for two people in their thirties to share a bed was laughable. The earnest way Bieito had looked at her…There was no telling what she would have done to him if left alone with him in bed. *It's been so long—*

Bieito interrupted her daydream. "Wait until she

falls asleep and then meet me here. Take care that none of the other villagers see you either. I want to be a good distance away by morning."

Remy sighed. *It's a long walk to Carral, though. All sorts of things can happen along the way.* Bieito seemed pretty old school in the way of romance, but she bet it wouldn't take too much convincing to see the benefits of a more modern relationship. If his passion in the way he kissed her was any indication, more good things were sure to follow. *It might make it harder for him to let go of the proposal though.* Remy didn't know if that was good or bad, or something she should feel guilty about.

"I'll meet you back out here," Remy agreed. "Don't you dare leave without me." Then she laid such a kiss on him she made her own knees weak and felt Bieito tremble underneath her touch. "Got it?" she asked.

He uncrossed his eyes and swallowed, nodding.

****

The family was so drained from the day that they mostly ate dinner in silence, and then everyone headed straight to bed. Each was too lost in their own thoughts to resume arguing, collectively agreeing to continue the discussion about Lino and Carral in the morning.

The bags under María's eyes spoke of more than just one sleepless night. When the two women went to bed, the young bride's eyes closed the moment her head hit the pillow. It was almost as though her body was shutting down in self-defense. There was only so much worrying a person could do before their brain decided that enough was enough. Remy waited until she was sure that María was too deeply asleep to hear anything, then she boldly walked outside of the room, never having changed into María's borrowed pajamas.

There were no noises coming from the other room, so Remy assumed that Bieito had had as little trouble with his father. *Or Bieito already left.*

Under cover of darkness, Remy scurried to the orchard. There was nobody else there. *I can't believe he would do this to me!* Remy's anger flared at Bieito's lie. It was such a Jack thing to do—assume he knew what was best for her. Were all men programmed to do this?

"*Fuck.*" The curse echoed through the trees. *Can I find my own way to Carral? Which way do I go? I guess I can ask directions from people.* Remy's thoughts grew saltier as she stewed. *Well, maybe I'll just go home if he doesn't want me here. Problem is, I already tried to go back home, and it didn't work. I think I'm stuck here until I do whatever I was sent here to do.* "Shit!"

"That is the opposite of stealthy, *mi amor.*" Bieito's voice reached her from behind. He was walking from the direction of the barn. "You are here early."

"Weren't planning on ditching me, were you?"

"Not at all."

Remy still couldn't see Bieito's face in the darkness, but she knew by the sound of his voice that he wore a hurt look at her distrust. "I have clothes for you," he said, and then handed her a wad of fabric. "I wish they were nicer, like your dress, but I'm afraid that is all I have that might fit."

Remy shook out a pair of slacks and a loose, billowy shirt, but it was impossible to tell what color they were in the darkness. "These will be fine," she said, grateful to wear something that reminded her more of her own century. "Sorry for accusing you of leaving me."

"Father fell asleep rather quickly, but I needed to gather a few extra supplies from the barn. Nobody saw you come down here?"

"Nope. Looks like the whole village went to bed early. Too much excitement for today, maybe."

"I saw a few people by the main house, still discussing your painting."

"And what did the critics think?"

"They think it is blasphemous," he said. "But I can tell they are awed by it. They have never seen an image of its like before."

"Blasphemous? I'll show them blasphemous." She turned around and moved her hair to one side of her neck. "I need your help. Can you unhook me?"

Bieito made a strangled sound in his throat. After a moment's hesitation, Remy felt warm fingers stroke between her shoulder blades and move down to free her from her fabric prison. With a shrug, the sleeves dropped down to her elbows and left her back bare.

Remy sighed. "Ah. That's better." A wiggle and a shimmy later, the deep red dress was a pool of fabric at her feet. Slowly, she turned around to face Bieito, clad only in her underwear.

As she had hoped, his jaw had become unhinged and he was staring at her in what could only be described as utter disbelief. He reached out to touch the smooth skin on her collarbone, only connecting with his fingertips, as though he was afraid she would disappear at any moment. Part of Remy expected to disappear, to be yanked back to her own time just as things were starting to get good. She remained there as he touched her, and a jolt of electricity ran through both of them.

There was not a scrap of insecurity inside of Remy. *This is me.* A bold invitation for Bieito to gaze at her as long as he wished. She had earned every curve, every freckle, and every wrinkle in her path to him. The fact that Bieito remained clothed while she stood mostly naked did not seem unequal. His gaze worshiped her.

If either of them leaned in at this moment—even to gently kiss—all control would be lost. Remy had no doubt that it would involve both of them unraveling into a frenzy as they finally gave into all their urges. Once they started, Remy knew it would be impossible to stop.

Their own little world was waiting for them; waiting to seduce them into leaving responsibility and reality behind. Remy had her world, Bieito had his, but there was a third, even more secret and exclusive option. A hidden world that only belonged to them. It didn't force them to choose between either time period. It called to both of them under the cover of darkness, with an ever-increasing sense of urgency.

Just give in, a voice whispered in Remy's head. *You deserve this.*

As Bieito's dark eyes drank her in, Remy could hardly remember her own name. He didn't seem to remember anything either, outside of the bare woman in front of him.

In a trance, she stepped out of the fabric rose at her feet. Time moved in slow motion as she closed the distance between them, their breath and heartbeats increasing in sync. Remy reached out to mirror Bieito's touch on her collarbone, and her fingers connected with something familiar.

Bieito's necklace. The Camino shell.

Like a slap in the face, Lino's presence suddenly stood between them. A ghost forcing their bodies apart. Change came over Bieito, and he looked away from Remy in shame. Nothing ruined the mood like a little brother.

"I apologize, *mi amor*. Now is not the time for this. That you should think I dishonor my family—"

"No, I get it. It's probably a good thing that you stopped us. I don't know what I would have done." Remy knelt down to pick up the pants. Shoving her legs in as fast as she could, she promised, "We'll have time later." She pulled the shirt over her head while Bieito watched regretfully. He sighed when she stood before him, fully clothed.

"You looked lovely in the dress," he said. "But I think I prefer you in this. You look like you did on the day we first met, but now in my clothes. American, but Galician. A perfect blend."

"I have to admit, I'm feeling more Galician these days than ever." *Especially because I'm stuck here. Might as well embrace it.*

Like a gunshot, the sound of a stick snapping cracked through the night. Both Bieito and Remy froze, only their eyes darting back and forth, searching for the disturbance.

"What was that?" Remy mouthed.

Bieito simply put a finger to his mouth, motioning for her to stay quiet. Was there someone out there? Had they been there the whole time, even watching Remy undress? The thought of a voyeur witnessing what they almost did made Remy's stomach a little queasy. *What if our romantic moment had been unwittingly shared with some creep in the bushes?*

It was a sharp reminder that the outside world was currently in an upheaval, with no regard for the private and wonderful bond developing between Remy and Bieito. It was not a safe time to be caught cavorting in the shadows. This creep could have weapons, or even try to kill them to avoid being seen. By this point, Remy was also fairly certain that should anything happen to her in Bieito's time, she could say *adios* to her real life, too. She wondered if her body would be magically returned to her village, and who would be the person to find her. *Sebastian, probably.*

Her death would be a great mystery. Foul play involved, but no suspects or evidence. Nobody would dare try to restore the village after that. *They'd all think it was cursed or haunted or whatever. It probably is, considering everything that's happened since I bought it.*

This narrative flitted through Remy's head in the thirty seconds she and Bieito were assessing the situation. *The artist's imagination.* Was there anyone more prone to thoughts of the fantastical?

Pushing thoughts of death deep down, she analyzed the evidence so far and came up with the conclusion that the village would help keep her safe. *It doesn't want to be abandoned and left to rot again.* Remy was the link between the past and the present for the village, and she figured it gave her some immunity. Maybe. It needed her, right? Or maybe it wanted her to change enough in the past to change the future, then it would be done with her.

It was a gamble to assume anything, especially

with lives at stake. Her death might be off the table, but serious bodily harm might still be an option.

It would also really, really suck if they never even made it out of the village or got to walk the Camino de Santiago.

Bieito was up on the balls of his feet, ready to launch toward an attacker at any hint of a threat, but none came. After another minute of this standoff, Bieito motioned for Remy to get behind him. He picked up his bag of supplies, and together they crept the rest of the way through the orchard and toward the path down to Ortigueira.

As they exited the trees, Remy looked behind her. She thought she saw the familiar silhouette of Jack watching them, but the wind shifted the shadows and the image disappeared. *Just my conscience.* A shiver ran up her spine. It felt like he watched her through the veil of time, searching the village for clues as to where she disappeared. He could look all he wanted, but she knew she wouldn't be allowed back until she finished her business with Bieito in the past.

****

The pair walked at a brisk pace, without looking backward at the village behind them. They kept to the side of the road, ready to blend into the foliage should they run across anyone else out in the middle of the night. After the scare they just had in the orchard, Bieito had regained his hyper-focus on their mission, and they walked in silence.

Remy kept pace with him without issue for the first few miles. Ortigueira soon passed by them as they skirted the edges of the town's borders. Part of Remy wanted to walk boldly through the main streets, just to see how it was changed from the Ortigueira that she knew and loved. She was sad that she couldn't even see the vaguest of impressions about the town in the dark, especially because it was so far away. To stave off the boredom of putting one foot in front of the other, she kept herself occupied imagining what the inside of the city looked like.

Would the streets be familiar enough for her to navigate through without getting hopelessly lost? Some of the architecture was probably the same, especially the old churches. But her favorite restaurants, grocery store, and food carts would be absent, not scheduled to make their mark in Ortigueira for another hundred years at least. *Maybe we can stop by on the way back,* Remy consoled herself. It would still be the charming town she fell in love with, just in a different, more authentic way. *With no guarantee of running water. Well, win some, lose some.*

Running on adrenaline left no room for fatigue. However, once the sun started to come up and the excitement of escape wore off, the exhaustion started to creep into her bones. The warm rays hit, and she longed to lay down in the tall grass and sleep until the sun went down.

"How much farther today?" she asked.

"It is close to ten *leguas* to Ferrol from Ortigueira," Bieito said, speaking for the first time since the orchard. His voice rasped with disuse and worry.

Leguas? What the hell is a legua? If he had said kilometers, Remy would have at least had to do some rough math to estimate the distance in miles.

He sensed her confusion. "We will walk an hour or two more, then rest for a siesta. I would like to continue onward until nightfall. I don't believe anyone from the village followed us, but it is best to travel farther than anyone would expect."

"Then we will keep going tomorrow morning?" Remy asked.

"Yes, with the rest of the pilgrims. It would be more suspicious to travel at night, I believe. We can blend in with the other travelers once we are far enough away for anyone to recognize us."

"How many days until we get to Carral?"

"At this pace, we will be in Ferrol in three days. Carral is another three to four days away from Ferrol."

A week of walking. What would have taken Remy a scant few hours by car would take days traveling by foot. She hoped they would make it to Carral in time to intercept Lino from being captured and executed. But unless they magically happened upon a horse, it was impossible to get there sooner.

At least the walking gave them the impression that they were doing something and moving forward. Even though it felt like a snail's pace, Remy wondered if it was better than driving there for a "hurry up and wait" scenario. They had a buffer of a few weeks from when the colonel's rebellion started to when the revolutionaries were executed, but timing it perfectly was necessary for the least amount of damage, both for the people involved and the historical time line she was trying hard not to totally mess up.

****

Now south of Ortigueira, Bieito and Remy started to come across more and more travelers heading the opposite direction, mostly to trade.

"Good morning, pilgrims," the travelers would say,

nodding their approval at Bieito and Remy's religious journey, as though they were part of some grand noble cause. Remy tried to remain as quiet as possible, lest something like her accent or her clothes made her memorable enough to bring as a story back to Ortigueira. After the fifth person wished them safe travels and offered them what little extra food they carried with them, Remy began to feel like a fraud.

Though her growling stomach was grateful for the bread and sausage she wolfed down, she wondered if Karma was going to come back and bite them for deceiving people. Thanks to strangers' generosity, they hadn't needed to break into the supplies that Bieito brought just yet.

His pack wasn't as big as Remy would have assumed for a week-long journey. In fact, it looked worryingly small on his back. The path they took was through rural farmland, no other towns or villages in sight, save for the occasional farmhouse standing on its own.

We can travel unnoticed, but what are we supposed to do once Bieito runs out of food? Or had he counted on the fact that by being a pilgrim, they would get most of what they needed provided for them?

"Is the small pack in order to look the part, or is the major plan to actually rely on "God's will" and "providence" to feed us for the next few days?" Remy asked, as she polished off the last bite of her snack.

"Both," Bieito confessed. "Though with the coup happening and the Spanish forces mobilized into Galicia, I was not completely sure if it would be as effective as last time. The Camino still provides, though, through it all."

"Oh yeah. Your original Camino de Santiago journey. How long ago was that?"

"I decided to take my pilgrimage after my mother died. It also started out for selfish reasons, as a way to escape my father's grief and the responsibility of taking care of Lino. My actions were regrettable as a young man, and it is difficult for me to talk about my pilgrimage. I felt like an impostor."

"Much like what we're doing now."

"I gained some peace on my journey, and an insight to myself and the world surrounding us, but"—Bieito hung his head—"it had nothing to do with religion. I did not feel closer to God. In fact, I had almost reached the Compostela when I turned around."

"Why?" Remy couldn't imagine traveling all that way and not crossing the finish line.

"I realized that reaching the end and entering the church would not bring me purpose or closure, it did not hold the answers I sought. Other people returned from their pilgrimages more pious and holy than ever. I wondered if something was wrong with me."

Remy reached for his hand, and their steps stumbled for a moment, and then continued. "Does your family know?"

"By the time I returned home, my father had started to emerge from his grief, thanks in part to stubborn Lino, who refused to be ignored." Bieito gave a wry smile. "Leaving ended up being a good thing for my family, but I still regret abandoning them."

"You were in a bad place, too. You had just lost your mother. You can't take care of other people until you take care of yourself. Don't burn yourself to keep others warm."

"The village still judged our family for my mother's lack of Christian burial. But when I returned from the Camino, it was as though I had redeemed my family in their eyes. I wanted life to be good for my father and brother, so I lied about a great religious experience. I used the Camino to run from my family and lied about what I truly experienced on the journey to gain others' approval. In the end, I felt so much shame. I have wanted to try the journey again, with a more open mind and with fewer expectations, but now…"

"You feel like you are doing the same thing all over again," Remy said. "But did you ever think that maybe your original experience was still valid? You say you felt like a failure for not having the same experience as everyone else. But maybe you were on your own path, and you got what you needed out of the journey, even if it wasn't what you expected." A light bulb went off in Remy's head. "It was the path. The walk itself. The Camino holds the magic, not the church."

A crazy thought occurred, and her first instinct was to squash it. It made no rational sense. The Camino had a long history of the inexplicable. What if that magic had been there all along, and had merely been adopted into religious Christian doctrine? Saint James was credited with bringing Christianity to the Iberian Peninsula, or so Sebastian had told her. What if he had just tapped into what was already there, as a tool to convince others to convert?

It was convenient to use religion as a way to explain the paranormal that happened along this path, a vein of the fantastical running through the earth. This vein, however, had been there long before James ever walked it. He just came along and gave it explanation, and people who had previously shied away from the unknown were able to embrace it once it had "rules."

From then on, any strange happening on the Camino was seen as a religious miracle and as evidence for a Christian God, mounting evidence that His presence was here on earth. As word spread and more people walked in hopes of experiencing their own miracle, how many were made up and then used as propaganda to draw future believers? The rest had been hype, and now the real truth about the Camino had been lost and buried among the false claims and doctrine.

Maybe the miracles had been rarer in reality, only affecting a chosen few, possibly even messing with time and space. Maybe there were people who were more sensitive to it and could tap into the weirdness that was this part of the world. If that was true, then was Remy one of these special people?

The sweat on her skin turned ice cold at the thought. Just how long had she been influenced by it? Since landing in Spain? Since living at the village? Her whole life? Was this Camino shaping her path and her identity, manipulating her for its own gain?

The farther she walked along this path, the more familiar it seemed. Her sense of déjà vu was so overwhelming that Remy could picture what was around each bend before they reached it. Sebastian had said that she was the *Milagro de Santiago* her village had been waiting for. The miracle it needed to restore itself to its former glory and save itself from ruin.

This train of thought was beyond Remy's realm of understanding, as well as the ability to prove any of these conjectures. She doubted they would sound halfway reasonable if said out loud. However, there was something about this path that was more than meets the eye. *Maybe I'm just stretching to try to find an explanation that encompasses everything that has happened to me. Blaming it on the Camino is pretty convenient.*

The Camino granted miracles. What was a miracle, if not a wish? Could her wishes be considered "miracles?" Was it possible that only the good part of the Camino's miracles had been documented, while the karmic balance and negative effects had been ignored? Maybe nobody had ever linked the two together before, because the Church didn't want the bad publicity.

Whatever Remy's link with the Camino was, it was obvious that the closer she was to it, the stranger her life had become. Walking right on top of it now—well, Remy could feel a pulsing beneath her feet. It felt neither sinister nor good, it just *was*. And it was powerful. Here long before she arrived and would still be here long after she was gone. Eternal.

In her periphery, Remy caught impressions and glimpses of buildings and objects that disappeared once she turned to look at them closer. Movements startled her, just out of clear sight, like the intruder in the orchard. It happened so fast it felt like a car speeding past her. She clutched her head, unable to focus on what was there versus not there. Her legs felt like lead, her feet ached, and the sun was now right overhead. They had been walking for over ten hours.

"Remy?" Bieito's voice broke through the pain. "Are you all right? You were just fine a second ago...are you faint?"

"I think I need to sit down."

"Can you make it to the tree up ahead? We can rest there until you feel better. Here, drink some water." He handed her the flask and took her elbow, gently steering her off the main path and to an ancient tree waiting to embrace them in its shade.

Remy had never perfected the art of walking and drinking and spilled quite a bit down her front as she swallowed deep gulps.

"I pushed too hard this first day," Bieito said. "We should have stopped an hour ago. I just kept thinking, a little bit farther—"

"Don't worry about it." Remy waved him off, already feeling her head clear in the cool shade. "I felt that same push, too, like we were being urged forward. But now that we've stopped, I can't focus on anything other than my feet!"

"Sit, sit," Bieito urged, helping Remy lean back against the broad expanse of tree trunk. "Sleep if you need to. I will take the first watch."

Though her brain wanted to protest, her body had other ideas. She sighed gratefully and felt her eyelids droop. It had been the longest, weirdest twenty-four hours of her life. *But I guess this is my life now.* The goal of an art school seemed unreal, like a long-ago dream. So did the memories of Jack and Anita. Even Maggie and Sebastian seemed like pieces of a story she could no longer remember. Nothing else seemed as important as being here, in this time, with Bieito, on the Camino. The path hypnotized her. It pulled her forward, the singular point of focus in her world.

She felt Bieito's tense posture beside her as he guarded the camp, somehow immune to fatigue. *I'm slowing him down.* She bet that Bieito would walk for days and nights straight to get to his brother, and sitting down was driving him crazy. He needed to rest, though, because they would be no use to Lino if they arrived in Carral half-dead on their feet.

Remy hadn't even realized she'd fallen asleep until the warm crackle of a fire woke her up. Her butt was completely numb, legs splayed out in front of her at an odd angle. Bieito had covered her with his traveler's cloak, though, and was now crouched in front of the small fire he had started for their supper.

"I have a gift for you," he said, sensing that she had woken up before she even moved. Remy wiggled her toes, feeling pins and needles shoot down her legs as she tried to get the blood flowing again. Sleeping the afternoon away had done wonders for her mind and cleared her confusion, but now she felt every single mile they had traveled in all of her muscles, some of which she wasn't aware even existed until that moment.

"*Ow,*" she groaned, as she struggled to move. The promise of a present was the only thing that motivated her to get up. Her curiosity was just too great. The last time Bieito had given her a present, it had been the gorgeous dress that she'd subsequently destroyed beyond repair. *Hopefully this one is more durable.*

He dangled it on the edge of his fingertips toward her. It swung in the firelight, casting a pendulum shadow on the ground. A scallop necklace.

"I just finished boring the hole. It is a little rough, and I wish I had nicer leather for it—"

Remy had already closed the distance between them and snatched it out of his hand. "I *love* it!" Unlike Bieito's pure white shell that had been bleached by the sun, this one looked fresh out of the ocean. Each ridge of the shell held multiple shades of purple and pink that swirled together. The shell was so beautiful in and of itself that the necklace needed no other ornament. Bieito had strung a thong of the supplest brown leather through the hole at the base where the waves radiated outward.

"Will you please put it on for me?" Remy asked. She pushed her hair aside and Bieito walked behind her. He placed the necklace around her throat, and it fell perfectly into the hollow at the base of her throat.

"How does it look?" she asked. "As good as yours?"

"Much better than mine, *mi amor.* You make a simple piece of jewelry look beautiful."

"Now I'm official, right?"

"Yes, anyone we come across will assume we are pilgrims. We belong to the Way of Saint James now."

Chapter Thirteen

The next few days of walking were much like the first. Just hills, tiny farms, vast open space, and the occasional traveler. Remy and Bieito had settled into a rhythm. They mostly walked in silence, content to just be in each other's company and conserve their energy. By the time they stopped for the night, they were both too exhausted to consider anything romantic. Remy consoled herself with the reminder that it was just for a week, then the rest of their relationship could evolve.

If Remy had been walking the Camino in modern times, she would have had a map, a guidebook, and a handy list of trendy but authentic restaurants to stop at through the little towns along the way. There would be hotels with soft beds and welcoming hosts. A place to shower. Wine and conversation in languages around the world. Remy would have just been one of many post-divorce, middle-aged women looking for answers to undefinable questions.

But on this Camino, Remy had an end goal. Her journey and purpose were definable and critical. Bieito and Remy had to make do with what they were given, whatever they could find, and the rapidly decreasing supplies from Bieito's pack. For the most part, they had to keep to themselves.

"We are almost to Ferrol. I will get more food there," Bieito told her on the third morning.

Remy was hoping for more than food in Ferrol—they needed information. Sure enough, when they entered the city, the place was alive with excited whispers and gossip. Word of the coup had spread to the surrounding cities in Galicia, and as far as they could tell, most people were sympathizers of Colonel Solís and his cause.

Located on the banks of the Ría de Betanzos just off the Atlantic coast, Ferrol reminded Remy of a much larger and more militarized version of Ortigueira. Shipping and fishing were obviously important to the economy here just like in Ortigueira, but there was a military air about everything in this place. The grid of wide, straight streets was unsettling compared to the meandering, narrow roads that Remy had experienced in the rest of Spain. This industrial town meant business.

As Bieito bargained for some cured meats at the butchers, Remy eavesdropped on two older men outside who could hardly contain their enthusiasm.

"He is going to declare the *Reino de Galicia* once again," the man with the mustache promised.

"If anyone is going to do it, he can," his friend agreed. "The will of the people is behind him. For thirteen years we have been under the Kingdom of Castile. Did you hear what the colonel declared?" He looked around and dropped his voice. Though he was whispering to his friend, both of them were probably a little deaf, so Remy was still able to hear what he was saying. "Long live the free Queen! Long live the Constitution! Out with the foreigners! Down with the Dictator Narváez! Down with the system of tribute!" He then slapped his hand over his mouth and blushed, as if he couldn't believe he'd spoken the words out loud. Remy thought it was adorable, if it was technically treasonous talk.

The men stared at each other with wide eyes, then broke into two big grins. It was scary, yes, but also deliciously exciting. Changes were happening. The people were hopeful. Remy just wished she knew that there would be a better outcome for the Martyrs of Carral.

There had been no sightings of Spain's General Narváez or his forces anywhere near Ferrol, and no reports of a coming battle yet. Citizens of Ferrol were disappointed when Remy and Bieito revealed that they were coming from the north and traveling south, rather than the other way around. All of the action seemed to be happening farther southwest, and everyone was eager for news.

Still, they were treated with hospitality as travelers of the Camino and invited to stay the night at one of the local churches. Bieito waved off their generosity and insisted that he and Remy press on. They still had time to cover more ground before dark and would hopefully find the answers they were seeking closer to the action.

Remy was relieved not to spend any more time than necessary in the brutally bare city, and she breathed more freely once they were back on the road.

"You are still convinced that we will find my brother in Carral?" Bieito asked her as the miles disappeared beneath their feet. "It seems the colonel and his people are located much closer to Santiago de Compostela. We will never make it there in time. It is at the end of the Camino."

"No, Lino will end up in Carral. I promise. Though

not for a while longer." Remy debated with herself, wondering if she should tell Bieito the rest of the information, or if it would only worry him. *We will hear about a great defeat,* she wanted to say. *That's when we will meet Lino.* Bieito would only want to get there to prevent Lino from even being a part of the battle. *Knowing it was happening and being unable to stop it would be worse, right?* Remy convinced herself to keep her mouth shut. It was better to keep Bieito in the dark about the trial of the martyrs.

Even with a secret between them, nothing could stop the couple from growing closer every day. Remy felt in tune with Bieito the way she had never connected with anyone before. Some days she felt like she could walk the Camino forever as long as Bieito was by her side. The journey strengthened their bond until they could almost communicate without speaking. They took cues from each other's body language and could share the most intimate thoughts and feelings. Remy could tell Bieito knew that there was something she was holding back, and she could also sense his desire to completely connect with her in every way possible, as if he could forcefully tear down the last barrier between them.

A lifetime of Catholic guilt prevented Bieito from giving into Remy's more-than-obvious physical advances, and this unfortunate pattern held until their last night on the Camino.

"We will reach Carral by midday tomorrow," Bieito told her, as Remy leaned against his legs. The fire warmed her face, and Bieito's fingers tangled in her hair.

"That's great," Remy said, without much

enthusiasm. *It's good. We made it.* Still, she couldn't help but feel disappointed that this was the last night on the path. Bieito must have felt her sadness, because Remy felt a tug on her hair as Bieito tipped her head backward.

He leaned over her and gave her a heart-stopping kiss, filled with the desperate knowledge that tomorrow was a new chapter for them, a dangerous page of the unknown. Their private world of two was about to be invaded as they reentered society and all of its problems. Remy felt his need to savor these last moments together.

As her lips molded to his, she felt the instant Bieito decided to cast off the imaginary shackles that kept him from acting on his desires. His hands grabbed her shoulders and he pulled her into his lap. Remy wrapped her arms around him, leaving no room for doubt in their embrace. She felt his yearning to connect, and to keep her from being torn away from him.

Remy had one thought—*finally*. It had been a long time since she had been intimate, since that fateful time she had seduced Jack and her life imploded. Instead of feeling any fear and apprehension, Remy just felt the compulsion to keep going. It was as though she might die if they stopped.

It wasn't at all like she remembered. Or maybe it had just never been as good as she thought it was with Jack. Being with Bieito felt like he was healing parts of her she never realized were broken. Under the stars, she released her need for control and let the spirit of the moment take her away from any rational thought.

For a second, she felt her consciousness rise out of her body and look down at the figures entwined below.

There was an almost golden glow, an aura that surrounded them. Under the bright, twinkling stars, two people that should have never existed in the same time celebrated that fate brought them together. Time and space were inconsequential obstacles that could never prevent them from fulfilling their destinies to be as one. It was more than Remy could have ever wished for.

****

Once upon the streets of Carral, the word was that General Narváez was on the move, under orders to crush the uprising in Santiago de Compostela.

"We should be there," Bieito insisted. It was all Remy could do to maintain a calm and controlled façade. Each day that ticked by while they waited made her increasingly nervous, like the rug was about to be pulled out from under her feet.

So when the bells in Carral finally rang with Spanish victory a week later, the breath Remy had been holding for what seemed like an eternity whooshed out.

"It's over," she told Bieito. "The colonel was defeated."

The blood rushed out of his face as Remy's words sank in. His brother had been on the wrong side of history and would be punished.

"They have just been captured," she hastened to reassure him. "Lino isn't dead." *Yet.* No, that was way too morbid.

"You cannot know that," Bieito said. "Lino, what have you done?" he murmured to himself.

The people of Carral seemed just as shocked as Bieito that the uprising was put down so quickly. From start to finish in just a few weeks, it hardly counted as a rebellion. A few foolish men who believed they could take on the entire Spanish army. They'd had support from the Galician people, but words of support were nothing when what they needed was action.

The sentiment behind the coup was felt throughout the region, sparking a flash of national identity for just a moment, but not long enough. Flint striking steel. Enough for a bit of light, to catch a person's eye, but not enough to light a roaring fire without the proper conditions. Everyone would go back to their normal lives and routines now that it was over.

As for the Spanish General Narváez, he had casually swatted a fly that was buzzing obnoxiously around his face without a second thought. But Remy knew something that the rest of the people did not— that by executing the colonel and his followers, General Narváez would immortalize this rebellion that would have gone down as a footnote in history if they had all been imprisoned instead. *It wasn't all in vain.*

The trial of traitors would be held in Carral. Remy knew that they were all already on their way, heading for a more neutral zone than that of the city closest to the battlefield. Santiago de Compostela had not given the rebels the miracle that they had been counting on. El Camino de Santiago had betrayed them and their cause. Now they would be forced to travel back on the path to Carral to face their deaths.

Except for Lino. Remy and Bieito would be his *Milagro del Camino.* They just had to rescue him before the trial and give the general one less martyr to the cause. That plan included trusting Remy at her word when she swore up and down that Lino would be a prisoner.

"We need to intercept them outside of the city,"

Bieito said, once he had processed the news. He still looked like he was going to throw up but had enough control over his emotions to start to formulate a plan.

"Before the trial?" Remy asked.

"They will be too heavily guarded once they enter the city. The prisoners will be locked up inside of buildings. It will be best to catch the soldiers unaware while they are traveling."

"But the entire army will be with them!"

"Remy, we won't be able to get close to Lino while he is in the city. This is our best chance."

"It's stupid. It will be impossible to escape or blend in anywhere. They'll just shoot us as soon as we get close."

"The Camino will protect us better than Carral will."

Remy couldn't argue with that logic, as weird as that statement was. Plus, it was time she put her trust in Bieito's plan. He had put his brother's life in her hands for the past two weeks, trusting that Carral was the answer while his instincts had screamed at him to go to the battle where Lino fought.

It was a relief to have Bieito call the shots. While Remy knew her plan had been correct, being in charge of their decisions had been exhausting. And while she knew to go to Carral, to be honest her plan didn't extend much beyond that. She had spent the last few days while they were holed up in Carral trying to come up with a workable idea. None of her projections saw them all escaping in one piece, and she had started to panic.

Bieito's plan would eliminate the complications of the city. It was risky, yes, but striking quickly instead of waiting until after the trial results might have the best possible chances of them all making it out alive.

"With such a large army, the general will have to stop frequently to attend to the needs of the horses and his supplies. If they camp along the Camino, it will also be impossible to hide such a large presence."

"So what do we do? Stroll casually into camp and ask for the keys?" It was hard for Remy to keep the sarcasm out of her voice. Everything just felt too daunting, and like they were relying too much on chance.

Bieito looked hurt at her tone, and Remy immediately felt guilty. "The chance will present itself to us," he said.

Though Remy didn't want to examine their relationship too closely right now, she felt a growing distance between them the longer they were in Carral. They had started out their Camino journey on such a high, and she had felt more connected to him than anyone else in a long, long time. He had proposed, for God's sake. Now, they spoke to each other like strangers. How had this happened in just a week?

Their bond hadn't been the same since they made love that last night on the Camino. It had felt like the right thing to do at the time; a sweeping, romantic gesture as they gave into the moment. Throwing all caution to the wind as they were seemingly compelled by forces outside their control to come together as one. This high lasted until the moment they stepped off the Camino and into the city, when reality came crashing down on them.

Bieito could hardly look her in the eye as they searched for lodging. Remy felt his guilt at finding happiness with her while Lino was still in so much danger. She could also feel his frustration at the fact that the barrier he thought they could break down was still there between them. Sex hadn't fixed it. It didn't make the secret between them go away. She wondered if he regretted it. *Maybe we should have waited until after this was all done.*

Tragedy and hardship either drove couples apart or made them stronger than ever. If Remy had been asked what she thought would happen on their journey while they were just beginning in Ortigueira, she would have said without a doubt that the journey would bring them closer together. But every day that passed since they came together in the literal, physical sense, the wall between them became more impenetrable.

Remy knew it was her fault for hiding so much of her real story from Bieito, but he wasn't doing their relationship any favors either. Instead of opening up to Remy, he had withdrawn further into himself each day they waited for news in the city.

It wasn't until arriving in Carral that Remy realized by wishing to save Lino, she might have sacrificed her relationship in the process. The best thing in her life was unraveling, and she didn't know how to go about fixing it.

There was an awkwardness in how they addressed each other now, as if seeing each other with their blindfolds off for the first time. Bieito was no longer infatuated by the strong, independent American painter with a penchant for disappearing at inopportune times and turning down marriage proposals. She was who she was, sometimes irritating, complained while they were walking, and asked too many questions.

For Remy, Bieito was still the handsome Galician man she had fallen head over heels for, but his insistence on traditional beliefs and values had started to grate on her. What was wrong with embracing more modern ideals? Did he have to insist on treating her a certain way, just because she was a woman? Weren't they in this together? Logically she knew he was a product of his time and upbringing, but God damn wasn't it annoying sometimes.

As they argued about how to free Lino, it was clear that their honeymoon stage was over. This was the first real hurdle in their relationship, and dealing with life and death was not usually the first major obstacle that a couple had to overcome. It would either make them or break them. She did love Bieito, and she knew Bieito loved her, but this love had grown in their own private bubble. She was literally outside of time and space in all the time she had interacted with Bieito. They were now living in the nitty-gritty existence with no escape for Remy back to her own time. Her dream, or fantasy or whatever it was, had been replaced with reality, like her blinders had been pulled off. Now they had to test it to see if their relationship was real, or if it belonged in Remy's dream world.

In many ways, it would be simpler if it did. If Remy could somehow go back to living in her own world, single and happy, and if Bieito could fall in love with a girl from his own time. No explanations, no integration, no complications. Things that looked picture perfect on paper rarely were. Maybe it was better if she embraced the tangled mess that was her and Bieito's relationship, because at least it wasn't a false front, like she had with Jack. She couldn't fool herself with him anymore than he could fool her. They could fix it, because they could both acknowledge what was wrong with it.

And right now, what was wrong was that they both needed Lino to be okay before they could progress forward. The looming presence above their heads needed to be dealt with, then Bieito and Remy could build the *real* foundation of their relationship, not just one on magical encounters and mutual attraction.

I need to show him that I trust him, too. Even if the idea that the "chance will present itself" seemed a little too indecisive to ease Remy's anxiety about the whole thing.

It was with this attitude that Remy found herself hiding in the bushes by Bieito's side, watching as a seemingly endless parade of soldiers and horses streamed past them. The soldiers' postures were relaxed, jovial even, as they traveled the Camino. Their victory had been an easy one, and the trip had been short. They were on their way back to their families, having proved to the entire country that the Spanish government had things well at hand.

There was no sympathizing with their fellow countrymen, if Spaniards even considered Galicians to be countrymen. Galicians were not Spaniards. The Spanish army was bigger, stronger, and faster. End of story. There was a conflict, now there was peace. That didn't seem like a bad thing to the soldiers.

Remy and Bieito had walked west on the Camino, leaving a day's distance between them and Carral. They had to be sure that the army would stop for the night somewhere in their vicinity. Their access to the prisoners would be under cover of darkness, after much of the army had enjoyed their celebratory wine and sat around the fires talking about the battle.

Much to Remy's relief, the revolutionaries were near the front of the parade, and she and Bieito spotted them quickly. General Narváez rode at the front, sitting tall in his saddle. A grim slash marked where his mouth was, and he stared straight ahead. While his soldiers were celebrating, this was a man who took his role seriously at all times.

The men surrounding the general all wore similar expressions, and none of them spoke. The forward march was bringing these traitors to their deaths. It was not a time to celebrate. Whatever trial awaited the colonel in Carral, General Narváez knew it would only have one outcome.

The colonel and his supporters sat interspersed among several uncovered supply wagons, while soldiers rode around them, almost blocking Remy's ability to see.

"Do you see Lino?" Remy whispered.

"No," Bieito said, voice tight. "Wait, there!" He pointed to the last wagon, where a dirty and disheveled man sat slumped against the back wall. The wagon went over a bump, and the carriage jostled. Another revolutionary reached out with rope-bound hands to steady Lino's head and keep it from hitting the side.

"He doesn't look well," Bieito said. Remy had been thinking he looked like shit but was grateful not to have to be the one to say it. *He doesn't look like he is in any shape to run away.*

"He might have gotten injured. Or he could just be sick. As long has he can walk, we should be okay." If only Remy believed half of what she was saying. These were armed soldiers on horses. They were two people on foot, three if they even managed to break Lino out.

Bieito had been right, though. They had a hell of a lot better chance out in the open than trying to get to Lino while he was behind bars. It would all come down to timing, but ropes were infinitely easier than shackles to break.

Remy wished she could call out to Lino, to give him hope that not all was lost yet. Desperate to hold her tongue, she grabbed onto Bieito's arm instead. He jumped, but then relaxed a fraction under her touch. "I'm here with you, no matter what," she told him. *I told you nothing would happen to him on the battlefield. Carral was where we were supposed to find him.*

The sky darkened with a threatening thunderstorm. The air was heavy and wet on Remy's skin, and still not a drop of rain fell. With the sun so heavily concealed, it was impossible to tell what time it really was. It felt like dusk, even though Remy knew it was only around three o'clock in the afternoon. This confusion led to the illusion that Remy was outside of space and time once again, the same feeling she had experienced more than once within the village. Her brain and body struggled to make sense of the where and when.

The dreamlike unreality persisted as Bieito and Remy kept pace with the soldiers' march, staying far enough away so as to remain undetected, but close enough so they wouldn't lose which wagon Lino rode in.

They have to stop soon. The storm was imminent, yet the general kept his troops marching for as long as he could. The jovial troops grew quieter, and eventually their celebration stopped all together, and the men rode in silence. That, more than anything, sent a chill up Remy's spine. Hundreds of men, facing forward and riding in complete quiet while lightning cracked in the distance. They looked like a ghost army from long past, unable to make a sound. Which is, really, what they were—an army that a twenty-first century woman was never supposed to see in the flesh.

Finally, Remy saw General Narváez put up his hand and halt the procession just as her feet started to ache. Shuffling around off-road was definitely harder than the obstacle-free path of the Camino. She kicked a tree root and almost tripped, but Bieito caught her shoulders. The couple froze where they stood and waited to see what the next order would be. The army was too far outside of Carral to make it to shelter within the buildings, and the tumultuous clouds above made it too dangerous to be out in the open, especially surrounded by so much metal and gear.

The general motioned for his troops to make camp near the trees and off the Camino, toward where Remy and Bieito lay in wait. It was at that moment that the heavens opened up and unleashed a torrential downpour, making it impossible for anyone to see past their own hand in front of their face.

The men started cursing and shouting as they scrambled to set up makeshift shelters, the lightning illuminating their slow progress every few minutes. Remy and Bieito shivered together as their clothes were soaked to the bone. Bieito wrapped his arms around her and they tried to conserve body heat, but it was useless. She trembled violently and tried to stop her teeth from chattering, clenching them together so tightly her jaw ached and a headache throbbed in her temples.

"A-a-are the p-p-prisoners s-still in the w-w-wagons?" she asked Bieito.

Remy felt him tense, and then pull his body back from hers. "Yes," he said. "Stay here. I'll be right back."

"Bieito!" Remy said, as loud as she dared. Her heart leaped into her throat as she watched him boldly walk into the military camp, his presence disguised by the mud and chaos and rain. He didn't have a uniform on, but nobody could see clearly enough for it to matter or to raise an alarm. All around him, soldiers slipped and struggled as they carted supplies and their horses from the road to the tree line, their heads bent down against the wind.

Please don't let anyone see him. Bieito strode purposefully to one of the wagons, taking his traveler's cloak off along the way. He leaned up against the back of the wagon, and Remy thought she saw the tail of the wagon fall open. Another lightning flash blinded her for a few crucial seconds, and by the time she located Bieito again, she saw he was not alone.

A figure stood next to him, covered in Bieito's cloak. Bieito's arm was firmly around him, and still the figure swayed on his feet. Remy was doubtful that Lino could even make it a single step, much less run away from the Spanish army. As Bieito helped his brother stumble forward, Lino suddenly started thrashing against Bieito's hold.

What is he doing? Lino pulled away and was trying to turn back to the wagons. Remy couldn't hear what he was saying, but it was obvious that Lino was starting to cause a scene. *Stop! You'll both be killed!*

It looked like Lino was trying to go back for the

other prisoners. Whether he was fevered and hallucinating, or more of a zealot than they'd guessed, Lino was apparently not going to go along quietly with their rescue plan. Bieito had only moments before the struggle was going to attract attention. Remy watched as Bieito grabbed Lino's head, leaning down and speaking directly into his face. Lino's shoulders slumped as the fight drained out of him.

Remy exhaled with relief and watched as the brothers headed toward the tree line. If they could keep a low profile, it could be hours before the general realized one of his prisoners was missing. He assumed he had squashed the rebellion. There were no other followers that would risk their lives by attacking him out in the open. The colonel was still imprisoned, and no one was expecting a lowly follower to just randomly disappear. Remy gave thanks for the bystander effect; all of the other soldiers were expecting the rest to keep an eye on the prisoners while they tried to escape the storm, and by doing so, no one was paying attention. It was so easy it was almost stupid.

Until it wasn't easy anymore. Lino lurched again and turned around to run back to the wagons, only to slip and fall face-first into the mud. Bieito hauled him up to his feet, but the damage was done. A soldier had spotted them and was making his way over.

Bieito froze with one hand on Lino's collar, holding him up. The soldier barked a question at them, and Bieito answered, trying to look confident. Remy couldn't hear what was being said, but the soldier walked closer to examine the brothers. Bieito shook his head, then shook Lino by his collar. For a moment, Remy thought the soldier believed the performance. He nodded once, but then abruptly pulled out his weapon.

Time stood still as three pairs of eyes fixated on the end of the rifle. Bieito, Lino, and Remy all froze at the sight of the drawn weapon. Keeping it pointed at the prisoners, the soldier took a deep breath and prepared to sound the alarm.

Before he could get a shout out to alert the rest of the company, Bieito reached out, grabbed the barrel, and slammed the butt of the rifle straight backward into the soldier's nose. The soldier collapsed into the mud.

Through the waterfall of rain, Remy watched Bieito and Lino return to their original course. Their violent incident, however, had already been spotted. Someone was running over to help the fallen soldier and cried out.

At that sound, Bieito broke into a run, dragging his brother behind him. Remy could only stay hidden in horror while the brothers sprinted in the direction opposite from where she lay waiting, as their way was blocked by more soldiers joining the chase. Everywhere the brothers turned, they were almost surrounded. Their only advantage was the fact that nobody could see very well in the weather, much less shoot their weapon accurately in such a populated area. If anyone had the opportunity for a clear shot, both brothers would have been dead in a blink.

The soldiers weren't going to risk a friendly-fire incident though, and their numbers were great enough to easily surround two men on foot. Lino, at least, seemed to wake up from his fog enough to grasp the seriousness of their problem, and had started moving better without having to lean on Bieito for support. Remy imagined Lino's horror at realizing he wasn't experiencing a fever dream, but was, in fact, being chased by the enemy through the mud in real life. No matter what, real or imagined, it was still a nightmare.

Bieito and Lino were almost back at the wagons, dodging around camp supplies as they ran. The brothers ducked behind a docile cart-horse, still attached to her wagon and waiting patiently in the rain for her dinner. She was a dappled brown color and blended into the muddy scenery. A plain little thing among all the magnificent war horses.

Still, she was the brothers' only option. What she lacked in speed and agility, Remy hoped she made up for in sturdiness. A few cut reins and a drop of the harness later, Bieito and Lino sat astride the confused horse.

Don't come back for me, Remy begged. *Both of you, run. I'll be fine.*

But Bieito didn't hear her mental pleas. The area that separated them was now swarming with shouting soldiers, an impossible obstacle course to risk. Bieito sat tall in front, with Lino's arms locked around his waist. *We can't take the horse with three of us. Please, Bieito, take Lino and go!*

But if Bieito had really left with Lino and ditched Remy, then he wouldn't be the man she fell in love with. His sense of pride and duty obligated him to return on his promise, and he was not going to leave his lady behind. Squinting against the downpour, he turned his head side to side, calculating the best path back to where he knew Remy stood waiting.

With a kick of his left foot, Bieito spun the horse around, and another fierce kick with both heels got her moving. With a surprisingly agile leap, the horse made a beeline through the mess of soldiers, who scrambled to get out of her way. The smarter soldiers were already running over to their own mounts, ready for the chase. Bieito only had a few minutes head start on everyone before they could get organized enough to pursue.

Remy feverishly thanked the rain for giving them a few precious moments to disappear and hide their tracks, but it wouldn't buy them enough time to escape completely. Her eyes left the advancing horse for a few seconds, and she peered down at the other prisoners, who still remained in the wagons. They were yelling and encouraging Lino, who kept twisting around on the horse to look back at them.

He must feel so guilty leaving them all behind. Remy knew it would be impossible to make Lino understand why they could only save him and not the others and hoped that the guilt wouldn't eat at him every day. *Especially when he finds out the fate of everyone else later.* To be the sole survivor of a coup that resulted in everyone being executed and buried in an unmarked grave...Lino would never be the same again after this ordeal.

Remy even struggled with her own guilt, as she looked at the faces of those they had abandoned to die. They hadn't even attempted to rescue them, or at least cut their ropes and given them a chance on their own. *It would have changed too much.* Remy doubted she would have even been allowed to make such a drastic change to the timeline.

It was one thing to justify this decision, but it was quite another to stare at the hopeful faces of those who watched Lino flee and know that they were sentenced to die shortly. *Their fate has already been decided. It was decided over a hundred years ago,* Remy reminded herself. *These men went down in history. They are a part of Galician history. This has to happen.* But now that Lino was free, would the Twelve Martyrs of Carral be the Eleven Martyrs of Carral in the history books? Was a difference of one person just as bad as letting none of them become martyrs? Would they achieve the same notoriety as the original dozen?

Remy decided it really didn't matter at the moment. The only thing that mattered was getting Lino and Bieito out of the mess of soldiers in one piece. Her heart nearly stopped as she watched the carthorse squeal and slip in the mud as Bieito yanked the reins, circling for a way out. The horse regained her footing, and Bieito kicked her forward. The soldiers standing in front dove out of the way but were up on their feet a second later as the horse barreled past.

They're almost to the tree line. Remy started to breathe again. They were nowhere near clear, but at least they were no longer surrounded. Then she saw Lino's head slump over Bieito's shoulder, and his arms start to loosen their hold. Bieito must have felt his brother barely hanging on, because he turned around to grab Lino's waist before he slipped off their galloping mount.

Halfway turned in his seat, one hand on the reins and the other on his brother, who by this point was almost lying on the horse, Bieito was forced to slow their mount down.

It was just enough time for one of the soldiers to ready his weapon. Remy didn't see him aim, but she heard the crack of the gunshot. Bieito ducked at the sound but kept moving forward.

He's okay. It didn't hit him. Remy's attention turned from the riders to where the soldiers were regrouping. Through the rain, she watched as another took aim. *They're all going to start firing.* Now that Lino and Bieito were no longer surrounded, the Spanish soldiers risked nothing by blindly shooting in their general direction.

She wanted to cry out, to tell Bieito to go faster, to bring some attention to herself as a distraction, but the words died in her chest. They were almost to her. When she finally managed to take a deep breath and scream Bieito's name, her words were drowned out by another crack of gunfire. It was a blind shot through the downpour, a Hail Mary fire.

Remy saw Bieito's back straighten in shock and pain, before collapsing over the horse's neck. *"No!"* she screamed. The horse kept galloping, spurred on by the bullets that whizzed past her. Remy ran to try and intercept the mare, and something shot by her head uncomfortably close. *Fuck!* She doubled over to make herself a smaller target and continued to sprint after Bieito. The soldiers hadn't seen her yet, thankfully, or if they had, then she was too far away to hear them sound the alarm about her presence.

The brothers were still on the horse. *He can't be dead. If he was dead, they both would have fallen.* At this point she wondered if Lino had been hit as well, or if he had just passed out. Then she saw a body fall from the horse. Was it Lino or Bieito? The horse kept galloping onward with only one rider now, moving significantly faster. The sole rider lay across her back, staying on by some miracle, and soon disappeared out of sight.

Remy ran to where the body lay in the mud, facedown. There was no time for hesitation, especially since they were so exposed. Unwilling to be careful in her urgent need to know who it was, she flipped him over roughly. A wheezing groan escaped him. Remy's quick fingers wiped the mud off his face, and she let out a sob.

Bieito. His eyes found hers before they rolled up in agony. Warm blood mixed with the grime and rain, but it was impossible to see where it was flowing from. Moving him would only cause more damage, and he was too heavy for Remy to drag anyway. She could only cradle his head, helpless, as the rain poured down and the mud slowly drowned them.

The calls of the soldiers grew louder as they traveled closer, cursing and stumbling on the slick earth. They were still looking for the horse, and for a wild moment Remy thought that maybe they might pass by them unnoticed. Both she and Bieito were so covered in filth that they might as well have been part of the forest. It might have worked, had she been able to quiet the wailing that had risen up in her chest. The moans that filled her ears couldn't be coming from her own body, could they? It was a sound so full of despair and hopelessness that it frightened her, but she had no control over it.

How had it all failed so spectacularly? Was this her punishment for changing history? The cost of her wish that Lino would live, but Bieito would die. That she would lose everything. There would be Thirteen Martyrs of Carral instead of twelve now. The soldiers would come and take her and Bieito away. Bieito would die, not able to even make it to the trial, succumbing to

282

his gunshot wound while Remy wasted away, struck down by grief.

As she clutched him to her, Remy had a wild thought, one that had only occurred to her because they had nothing else to lose. It was risky, and there was a chance that she could be sent back by herself, leaving Bieito to die in the mud on his own, but it was a chance she had to take.

The soldiers closed in on them, and Remy closed her eyes. *I wish both of us were home in my time.* No cost was too great at this point. She made her wish freely and with her whole heart, feeling the want and desire overwhelm her fear and apprehension. It consumed her, pushing out any doubts that she was making the wrong choice.

Her fingers dug into Bieito's warm skin, leaving marks while she waited to pull him with her into her own time. "Everything will be okay," she whispered to him. "I've got you. I won't let you die." Modern medicine could save him.

One of the soldiers had spotted them, and he let out a shout to alert the others. He charged toward the couple on the ground. Remy and Bieito still lay there, half-sunk and trapped. Raindrops pounded Remy's head, cool rivulets streaming down to cover her body as she stared boldly back at her enemy. The soldier came closer, close enough for Remy to see the whites of his eyes as he screamed at them and leveled his weapon.

It was the last thing Remy saw before her vision tunneled and she blacked out, slumping protectively over Bieito's unnervingly still body. *Stay with me.*

Chapter Fourteen

Remy woke up trembling. She whipped her head around, trying to take in all of her surroundings at once. Her head and heart pounded in the same rhythm while she searched for danger. The familiar buildings of her village encircled her. *I'm back,* Remy realized in shock. *It actually worked.*

She still didn't trust it, though. Could she have brought back some of the army with her? Were they here, waiting and lurking around the corners for her to make a move? She froze and listened. There was no time for a slip up. Bieito was in serious trouble, and she needed to get him to a hospital as quickly as possible. With a gasp of horror, Remy groped for a body that wasn't there.

"Fuck!" The words echoed through the empty streets, promising Remy that she was as alone and isolated as she feared. The price of pushing everyone in her life away. "Help! Help, somebody, help me!" Even as her desperate cries echoed in her ears, Remy knew that there was nobody to hear her calls.

So far, the village had given her everything she desired. She didn't believe she could be kneeling in the middle of it, experiencing so much pain. To have everything and nothing, all at once. Her art, her village, and her normal life had all been returned to her, but in a perverse way. Her desires had been twisted and manipulated so much along the journey that she had no idea how she ended up back here, in a foreign country, holding onto only the memories of a dying man from another time.

Just as she was losing faith and cursing the village for bringing her only doom and destruction, she heard her name being called.

"Remy? Is that you?" A gentle, British accent tempered by disbelief called back to her.

"Maggie?"

Her friend appeared from around the bakery, dusting off her hands on the front of her well-worn jeans. Flyaway gray hair was tamed into submission by a handkerchief, and a pair of sturdy work boots were on her feet. "My dear, where on earth have you been?" Then she saw that Remy was covered in filth and blood.

Before Remy could ask how or why Maggie was at her village, her guardian angel whipped out her phone and dialed, speaking in rapid Spanish. *Huh, I can't understand it anymore,* Remy realized, just as she collapsed into Maggie's arms.

****

Beeping monitors. Bright lights. Sweat-soaked clothes. Goosebumps on her skin.

"Bieito!" Remy called, and she sat bolt upright. To her right, the person who had been holding her hand nearly fell off the ambulance bench.

"Breathe, child," Maggie instructed, once she had regained her composure. "You're in good hands."

Instead of sagging back against the pillows in relief, Remy was bombarded with memories from her last few moments with Bieito. "He might still be alive! Where is he?" She struggled to sit up, ignoring the spots that appeared in front of her eyes.

"Who?" Maggie asked. "Were you with Bieito? Did something happen? I was so afraid you had been injured, with all that blood...What happened?"

"No one else is here? You're sure he didn't come through?" Maggie shook her head, and Remy's eyes filled with tears. If he hadn't come through to her time, then his gunshot wound was certainly fatal. The last-ditch effort to save him didn't work. It was like losing him all over again. He'd been dead over a century, but Remy grieved for him now.

An EMT opened the back door of the ambulance, surprising Remy enough to keep from completely melting down. Straight ahead, the familiar sight of her village greeted her. The EMT spoke in Spanish to Maggie, and Remy tuned them out. She stared at the buildings, hating them, yet loving them at the same time. *Home.* How could she be here without thinking of Bieito? Every piece of it held a reminder of him now.

Maggie's voice interrupted her meditation. "They need to check some more vitals, Remy, but they don't need to bring you to the hospital. The blood on you was not your own, and is a story for another time, I think. They said you are very dehydrated and sleep deprived, but otherwise you are healthy. You just fainted. I know I overreacted by calling them, but seeing you in such a state...my heart could not handle it. We have all been incredibly worried."

Remy swallowed the lump in her throat, trying to figure out some way to tell Maggie her unbelievable tale. "First, can I ask—how long have I been gone?"

Maggie's eyebrows shot up. "Over a month. I was the last person to see you before you disappeared."

Maggie sniffed. "Quite a terrible position you put me in. Then there was no sign of you for weeks. I agonized over whether or not to list you as a missing person...I told myself you would be back. We had too many plans for the village, and I told Sebastian there was no way you would abandon it. He's been sick with worry as well. I decided to leave Madrid and come to Ortigueira and get to work on it while waiting for you to get back and explain to me just what in heaven's name you have been doing!"

Remy winced at the obvious anger in Maggie's tone. She felt terrible that she put her friend through such an ordeal. There must be some way to explain it to her without sounding delusional, and she tried to gather her thoughts. *Where do I even start? Start with the basics. At the beginning.* "Maggie, do you remember telling me that you felt something odd about the village when I bought it?"

Maggie still looked frustrated with Remy but nodded. "It is a property with a personality. One of the stranger pieces of realty I've sold over the years." She moved out of the way as an EMT checked Remy's pulse. He moved with quick efficiency and seemed uninterested in the developing conversation. "I wasn't prepared to sell a property like this. I think it fell into the right hands—your hands—but I would be lying if I said I hadn't had my doubts about whether it was in your best interest or the village's. Sometimes I wonder if I should have just shown you an apartment in downtown Madrid instead..."

"Oh, Maggie, sometimes I wish that too. It's been more complicated than I ever imagined."

"With the renovation?"

Remy hesitated.

"With your mental health?" Maggie prodded. She was being remarkably patient with Remy's roundabout answer, but the question cut to the core of the issue. Remy had vanished without a trace and was currently lying on a stretcher recovering from shock and exhaustion.

"In a way..." Remy began. "You have to promise not to ask any questions until I'm done explaining. I don't expect you to believe it, but you also have to promise not to have me committed or tell anyone else. If it helps, just pretend I'm just an eccentric artist telling you a crazy story." She took a deep breath. "I've been seeing things lately. Things that aren't, well, in this time."

"*Ella está bien,*" the EMT interrupted her. He turned to Maggie to explain the rest, knowing that Remy didn't speak Spanish. When he was done, he helped Remy sit up and assisted her off the ambulance bed. He escorted them both to solid ground and looked at Maggie with a stern expression.

"I'm supposed to tell you to follow up with your regular doctor this week," Maggie said.

"That won't fix what's wrong with me."

"You have to tell him that you will, otherwise he will take you to the hospital right now instead."

Remy sighed. "Fine. Okay."

He seemed to understand at least that much English and patted her shoulder. The team boarded the ambulance and headed down the driveway. The village's second visit from an ambulance in two months. *They are going to think this place is cursed with bad luck.* Once the sound of tires crunching on dirt disappeared, it was oddly calm. *Don't think about Bieito. Don't think about Bieito. Focus on finishing the story.* Remy felt that once she told her story, it would release all of her emotions in a flood, and she could say goodbye to Bieito properly. She couldn't do him justice here, in front of Maggie.

"So you think that your village is haunted." Maggie said it so matter-of-fact that it surprised Remy. The older woman caught on quickly.

"Sort of. More like…it has a mind of its own. And has been showing me stuff." *Is that less weird than telling her it took me back in time?*

"Why would the village show you things? What sort of things?"

"People that used to live here. Stuff that happened."

"Are you alone when these 'visions' take place?"

"Yes, usually when I'm by myself in the village."

"Don't get your knickers in a twist if I ask this, but have you been drinking or doing drugs?"

"No!" Then Remy remembered the copious amounts of that delicious wine she had been drinking during the first few instances. "Not always. Sometimes," Remy confessed.

"But this Bieito you've been frantic over…Is he real?"

Remy bit her lip, not knowing how to explain further. "Not anymore."

****

The pain in Bieito's eyes. The light fading out of his gaze. The strength of Remy's grip around his body. The roar of the storm.

Remy tossed and turned as she tried to sleep in her

tent. She couldn't bring herself to go near the cottage yet. It had been three days since she'd been back, and her thoughts refused to break out of a destructive cycle. *I should have stayed with him. I shouldn't have risked the wish. At least then I wouldn't have left him to die alone.*

Beside her, Maggie stirred in her sleeping bag. Even though Remy had begged her older friend to check into a hotel downtown, Maggie refused to leave Remy on her own. The Englishwoman had tried to talk Remy into going to the doctor, but every time Remy tried to leave the property, panic set in.

"Anxiety attacks," Sebastian had diagnosed. His exuberance at Remy's return could not be contained, and he took it upon himself to spread the good news throughout Ortigueira. He came to visit Maggie and Remy each day to check in but returned home in the evening. Remy was thankful for the supplies and food he brought with him, because Remy had yet to leave the village, even to grocery shop.

Whether it was trauma or guilt keeping her there, Remy didn't know. All she could feel was some unknown force that would not allow her to leave. She was tied to the village, an invisible tether keeping her within its borders.

The next morning, after another sleepless night, Remy decided to reach out to Jack and Anita, just to let them know she was okay. Maggie left to run an errand, and let Remy borrow her phone. *If Jack doesn't answer, then I'll leave a message.* Anything to keep her mind off Bieito and her loss.

It felt like forever since Jack's accident. An entire lifetime had passed since he showed up, unwanted, in her village. She assumed he had gone home. How long did it take for someone to recover enough from head trauma and some broken bones in order to fly to New York?

So much had happened between the last time she saw him and now. Most importantly, she had gone from being staunchly secure in her divorce to madly in love with another man. *Maybe it's me. Bad things happen to men who love me.*

She dialed Jack's number and couldn't believe who answered it.

Anita. Voice thick with sleep, she mumbled, "Who is it?"

Remy cleared her throat but couldn't find the words.

"Hello? Hello?" A pause and the rustle of fabric. "Babe, I think there's someone on the phone for you."

The thought should have sent her reeling. Her best friend and her ex-husband—it was the ultimate betrayal. Instead of feeling angry, though, Remy was just...numb. Picturing them together was like staring at two strangers. They existed in Remy's memories, but she already knew they would not have a presence in her future.

If they wanted to be together, then by all means they should be. Remy had been through enough the past few months so that no jealousy or envy remained in her heart. *Maybe they will be a better couple than Jack and I ever were.* There was no way to predict which way this scenario would go, and it wasn't important enough for Remy to need to know how it turned out. Hell, they could even get married and start a family together and live the life Remy always assumed she would. Even that wouldn't make her wish she was in Anita's shoes. Standing where she was now, Remy could see how that path would have been completely wrong for her.

Instead, she suddenly felt grateful for all the decisions that had led her to this moment in time. She wouldn't have traded her time with Bieito for anything. Loving him was a singular experience that had brought her back from the brink. Remy had been marked, or chosen, or driven by some unseen force to live a compelling life. She should have run away from New York long ago and listened to that inner voice that told her she wasn't home yet. Remy was nowhere near perfect. This entire journey she had questioned her sanity and her decisions and felt like a failure more often than not.

But this journey had brought her back to life. It had opened her mind to paint again. It had shown her that there was more to her than tragedy and curses, and that she could make a difference.

Jack's voice spoke in her ear. "Who is this?" he said. "Do you know what time it is?"

Remy didn't trust herself to answer. Anita and Jack wouldn't understand why she was so okay with everything. It was hard for Remy to understand it herself, just that she *was* perfectly fine with it. They'd think she was lying, masking her pain. It would require interacting with them more than she wanted to. Ideally, this was how she would leave things with them. Closing the door and closing the chapter in her life, for good. She hung up the phone with a tiny smile.

Remy had been so focused on losing Bieito that she hadn't thought much about Lino's fate. When she had woken up on the ground in the village, it had felt like the past spit her back out for the last time. After breaking God knew how many laws of the universe, to think that the village would just let her pass back and forth with Bieito in tow was too far-fetched. It had been getting harder and harder to move between time periods, and after being stuck in Bieito's time with no real way back for weeks, Remy was too scared to try it again now. Nothing was within her control anymore. She couldn't risk it.

Not knowing Lino's fate was agony, though. If she knew for sure he had survived, it might have eased her grief for Bieito. *No, Lino has to have survived. Otherwise, why bother sending me back?* Remy's entire existence had been nudging her to that moment in time in order to change it. Would she ever understand the long-term significance of everything though? Why bother changing such a small thing if it didn't have far-reaching consequences, further reaching than even she could imagine?

I wonder what María said to Lino when she saw him. Remy smiled at the thought of their reunion. She could just picture María landing quite the slap on Lino's face before launching herself into his arms. But slowly this joyous reunion began to unravel in Remy's imagination, for then she pictured Afonso emerging from the cottage, expecting to find both his sons. How Lino would look, dejected and thinking of himself as a coward for abandoning the brother who saved him. Regret at putting his family in this position in the first place. The confusion on his wife and his father's face when they didn't see Bieito or Remy beside him.

They would forever wonder what happened to Bieito and Remy. Remy's heart ached for them, and for the loss of a family that could have become her own if she stayed. She could only hope that they would somehow find peace and acceptance in the coming years. They had saved Lino so that he and María could start a life together, and Remy fervently hoped that they would embrace the second chance that Bieito had given them instead of squandering it away due to guilt.

Bieito would think it was all worth it, Remy told herself firmly. He had done his part to keep his little brother safe. There was no cost too high for that. She doubted he would choose to have done it any differently, as long as Lino made it out alive in the end.

There was something frighteningly isolating about the only one to possess knowledge of an event, to be the sole holder of the truth. The amount of time that Remy had spent doubting her own sanity the past few months only made her more afraid to trust her memory. The coup was such a small blip in history. But if she had inadvertently created a new future all together...*But everything else is the same,* Remy told herself. *That I know of so far. Time to focus on the future instead of the past.*

The scent of sun-ripened fruit hit her nose, and the phantom sound of rattling wagon wheels rolled in the distance, combined with the joyous nonsensical chatter of happy neighbors and the memory of sweet wine on her tongue...

It was all still there. Somewhere on a different plane, in another time, just beyond her grasp. It wouldn't be the village that Bieito left behind, but Remy believed she could build something just as wonderful. The essence of the place still yearned to be occupied and to serve a purpose. His was the glorious history of the village, while Remy represented a hopeful future.

Chapter Fifteen

Blood, sweat, and tears during the next three years transformed the property into the school of Remy's dreams. The main house was turned into a dormitory for the art students. The other houses were modified into classrooms and studio rooms. The bakery was now a sculptor's haven, the large stone oven re-purposed as a massive kiln. The mill was kept basically the same, preserved for history's sake, but Remy had dreams of eventually turning it into a gallery to display her students' work.

It took Remy nine months to move into the cottage. She worked for months in secret, not letting Maggie or Sebastian peek at her progress. In the beginning she could only see it as Bieito's house, but with loving care she designed her dream home, determined to do it justice and honor his memory.

When she finally escorted Maggie and Sebastian through the front door, the surprise left them breathless. A seamless mix of modern and vintage, with her own artwork adorning every wall. She had even added on a little alcove room, which was completed just in time for her own little surprise.

****

Now, pacing through the completely restored village, Remy bubbled over with anticipation while Maggie tried to calm her down. Sebastian was about to drop off the first of their students arriving for the summer art program. Remy had to pinch herself that this day was finally here, and that she had made her dream come true. The twelve students were from all over the world, handpicked by Remy for a life-changing experience. The students she had chosen to work with were scholarship students, mostly from poor or dysfunctional families. Most had never been away from their hometown and were about to embark on eight weeks in Spain with the famous artist Remington Day, and she was determined to live up to their expectations.

This was all financed by Remy's reemergence into the art world, more successful than ever. Now labeled a recluse artist, Remy was astounded to discover that the mystery of her life made her paintings even more in demand. Her style had changed, too, and critics praised her mix of modern style with historical aspects. Oversized canvases were her new trademark.

A van pulled into sight and stopped at the top of the drive. Sebastian hopped out of the driver's seat and opened the sliding passenger door with an exaggerated sweep. "*Bienvenidos!* Welcome!" he shouted, looking just as proud to introduce the students to the village as if he owned it. The long drive from the Madrid airport had done nothing to dampen his enthusiasm.

"Thank you, Sebastian," Remy said, striding forward in what she hoped was a confident way. *I hope I look like I know what I'm doing.* Maggie hung back while Remy approached the students.

"I hope you all had a good trip," she said. The eleven teenagers nodded, looking more than a little dazed and jetlagged. "I also hope you're ready to get some great work done this summer at this retreat! I'm Remy, you already know Sebastian, one of our helpers, and you'll meet Maggie later. Grab your bags, and we will show you around."

While the students busied themselves with their luggage, Remy pulled Sebastian aside. "Who are we missing?" she asked.

"The local boy. His mother is going to deliver him any moment."

"Oh, that's right." Remy was relieved not to have lost a student on their opening day. She had been astounded to discover the boy's talented portfolio in her stack of applications, and even more stunned to find out that his family lived in Ortigueira already.

"Here they come now," Sebastian said.

An old car rumbled its way down the long drive and parked behind the van. A woman with deep red hair got out from behind the wheel and grabbed a suitcase from the trunk. Remy couldn't see who still sat in the passenger's seat, but she assumed it was the woman's son. When a few minutes had passed and the boy hadn't gotten out of the car, Remy went to see what was wrong.

"He's just nervous," the woman explained in remarkable English, and gave Remy a smile that was so familiar it made her heart stop. When it started pounding again, Remy gathered up the courage to look in the car.

A boy with dark, curly hair stared down at his hands. His mother rapped on the window. "Afonso," she said. *"Tu profesora está aquí." Your teacher is here.*

His chest rose and fell with a sigh, and he gathered

himself enough to open the door. *"Hola,"* he mumbled, looking at the ground. Afonso was only thirteen, the youngest student in Remy's program by a good two years.

Remy fought hard not to let tears fill her eyes. She cleared her throat and said, "Welcome, Afonso. We are so happy you're here. I loved your portfolio, especially your ocean paintings. There's another boy here who makes sculptures inspired by water. I think you two will have a lot to talk about."

At the mention of his artwork, Afonso lifted his head, allowing Remy to confirm what she already knew in his distinct features. "Say goodbye to your mother," Remy instructed. "I'll bring you to the other kids."

Afonso threw his arms around his mother, dodged her kiss, and ran over to where Sebastian was giving an orientation. His mother waved at his back and turned to Remy. "Take care of my baby," she said.

"Like he was my own family," Remy promised. "He'll do great." Remy heard her name being called from the cottage. "Excuse me," she said, and hurried across the village to where Maggie summoned her.

"Look who woke up early from her nap!" Maggie said, her arms full of a squirming toddler.

"Catarina! You didn't want to miss the excitement today?"

"Mama!" The little girl squealed and reached for Remy. Curly bedhead hair flopped into dark brown eyes that were quick to take in her surroundings. "Beach? Beach?"

Her little water baby, so like the father she would never know. Remy and her daughter took nightly walks to the ocean to watch the sunset together. The path to the beach that had existed in Bieito's time had long since eroded, and they were forced to stay up on the cliff above the ocean. The sea air did wonders for their souls, but Remy could see that Catarina ached to be down on the water.

"We'll work out a way to carve a path down to the beach. Maybe we can try sailing," Remy had told her, grasping a tiny hand in hers. But that would involve leaving the boundaries of the village, something that neither of them seemed to be able to do. Their world scope had shrunk to just these few buildings and the grounds. The cliffs were the farthest they could reach, and even then, Remy and Catarina weren't able to stay very long before feeling compelled to return.

The ache in Remy's heart was physically painful if she thought about leaving the village. Remy wasn't sure if it was due to her own anxiety, but she suspected another force was at work, and suspected she had lost a piece of her free will. Coming back that last time had changed her. Wishing for them *both* to come back to the village tied them so securely to this place she wondered if she and Catarina could ever leave.

The village would never again be abandoned to time, and it had gone through great lengths to ensure this. It had pulled threads from the present and the past, breaking rules of the universe to bring two people together to create a miracle. Each step of the way had been a delicate balance of action and reaction, until Remy was desperate enough to make her wish. *Every wish has a cost.* But each night when the sun set, when mother and daughter turned around and walked side by side back to their cottage, Remy felt that the price for her happiness was worth it. A tiny part of her that she wasn't willing to admit existed asked, *Will Catarina think the price was worth it, too?* Remy wanted to avoid this question for as long as possible.

"Beach!" the toddler demanded. Right now, this was the sole focus of her daughter's happiness. A simple request had an answer. The real challenge would come a few years from now, along with a difficult conversation about wants and wishes.

"Not right now, sweetie. The students have just arrived. Would you like to go say hello?"

Child on her hip, Remy gathered the twelve students around her. "The goal of this intensive program is to force you to dig deep and unearth your hidden potential. I am simply here to guide you along this journey, and to teach you how to transfer your emotions onto your chosen artistic medium. Each piece you complete will bring you closer to understanding yourself, and the artist you are destined to become. These pieces will become your summer collection, with a common idea connecting them. The theme of our art projects this summer will be, 'What do you want most in the world?'"

A word about the author...

Taylor Hobbs writes fantasy romance novels while living aboard a sailboat with her family. Her debut novel *Cloaked* is also available through The Wild Rose Press.

To learn more about her books and adventures, please visit https://cannonstocruising.com/

Thank you for purchasing
this publication of The Wild Rose Press, Inc.

For questions or more information
contact us at
info@thewildrosepress.com.

The Wild Rose Press, Inc.
www.thewildrosepress.com

To visit with authors of
The Wild Rose Press, Inc.
join our yahoo loop at
http://groups.yahoo.com/group/thewildrosepress/